P9-DGZ-461

GIFTED

FEIWEL AND FRIENDS
NEW YORK

GIFTED

H. A. SWAIN

A Feiwel and Friends Book
An Imprint of Macmillan

Our books may be purchased in bulk for promotional, educational, or business use. Please contact your local bookseller or the Macmillan Corporate and Premium Sales Department at (800) 221-7945 ext. 5442 or by e-mail at MacmillanSpecialMarkets@macmillan.com.

Library of Congress Cataloging-in-Publication Data Available

ISBN: 978-1-250-02830-3 (hardcover) / 978-1-250-08685-3 (ebook)

Book design by Liz Dresner

Feiwel and Friends logo designed by Filomena Tuosto

First Edition: 2016

10 9 8 7 6 5 4 3 2 1

fiercereads.com

For my darling, Clementine

"... no hypocrisy is too great when economic and financial elites are obliged to defend their interest."

—CAPITAL IN THE TWENTY-FIRST CENTURY, Thomas Piketty, 2014

CHORUS

A dragonfly, perhaps one of the last, darts downriver, searching for another of its kind. Where have the others gone? Has anyone but this dragonfly noticed the species decline or have mechanical drones, the same size and shape with cameras for eyes, obscured their slow disappearance? Bigger drones, the size of birds, lift up from the roofs of warehouses built along the meandering river and fly a predetermined path from the Corp X Complex to the City where they deposit their packages in delivery chutes like babies from storybook storks.

Down on the ground, on the path by the river, people slip by, gravel crunching under feet, voices low. None of them will notice the dragonfly, though. The sound vibrations from its iridescent green wings are lost among the willow branches and low hum of delivery drones in the sky. Only a frozard hears it. Readies itself for the hunt. Head moving side to side, zeroing in on its prey. The dragonfly drafts higher on a breeze that sends ripples like fish scales across the water down below.

All around the dragonfly, electromagnetic waves oscillate

at the speed of light. With a transmitter and antenna anyone could ride these waves, although nowadays everything legit streams in zeros and ones across the digital divide. Analog broadcasts are all but dead as true radio began to fizzle a long time ago when FM and AM stations blinked out like dying stars. But there are holdouts. Old-school rabble-rousers. Like DJ HiJax, who snatches nighttime waves to play old songs, long forgotten, and reminisces in altered voices about the days when music belonged to the people.

Tonight, though, no such luck. HiJax is on the run, setting up another pirate radio station in yet another undisclosed location. And so, only the breeze disrupts the dragonfly's sound. Sound waves bend. The frozard misjudges, shooting out its tongue into nothingness. The dragonfly continues along the bend in the river, skirting around and over the people who search for a partially hidden path in the dim light of the moon.

Corp X workers come in twos and threes from the POD-Plexes and warehouses built along the river a half decade ago. They are quiet. No conversation yet through black masks on these class-war criminals. What goes on out here, a mere half mile from the Complex, is risky and must stay hidden. Quietly, they slip over a crest of matted grass and down a steep embankment, like squimonks scurrying into hidey-holes, hoping to be safe and undetected for the night. They find the door (built into the side of the earth with a "Welcome to Nowhere" sign) that leads into a dank room carved out from this riverbank.

Inside, anticipation crackles like heat lightning on a humid night. There's a wooden box at the end of the bar (two boards across old sawhorses). In the back, there's a makeshift stage (wooden pallets dragged from the dump) behind a large swath of discarded canvas with a faded, defunct logo—a swish turned upside down so it looks like a cresting wave. Everyone here knows what to do: drop cash into the box (no COYN accepted), pick up a cup of local Juse (distilled from wild potatoes and dandelion greens gathered by the river), and wait. When the curtain flicks, the crowd inhales and shifts, vying to get a better look, but it's not time yet so the canvas stays closed.

"How's it look out there?" Zimri asks.

"Full, I think," says Dorian.

Zimri's stomach tightens. She pats her pocket for the digital audio recorder and straightens the cord running to a tiny mic on her lapel. She'll capture the whole show and release it later on the waves. Then she palms a little sphere with a non-blinking eye that she uncovered in the mess of old and outdated gear her mother left behind when she took off five years ago.

"What's that?" Dorian asks.

"Might be a video camera," she says. "It connects to this." She points to an ancient laptop where she has preloaded all the backing tracks for tonight's show. She plays every instrument—the crappy old electric guitar and bass her mother left, a synthesizer with missing keys, and a ZimriDoo she made herself from scavenged PVC pipes and oil pans, funnels and air tubes, strings and stoppers—part drum, part fiddle, part accordion—a one-person band strapped over her shoulders. "Thought it might be fun to see what we look like up there."

"Just as long as you don't broadcast live," Dorian says with a nervous chuckle.

"Nah," says Zim. "Wouldn't know how if I tried."

Outside, a mere quarter-mile away, Nonda searches for Zimri. She knows the place is around here somewhere. Near the elbow in the river where the watercress is thick and raspberries sometimes still grow in summer. But the walk takes longer than she remembers. Her legs are tired and slow. Not like when she was young. She listens carefully for the music but her hearing has grown dim. Too many years in the warehouse, metal on metal on metal bouncing around the vast space under one roof where the whole town used to be. Cacophony, that's the word. Sounds like what it means.

Still, she hears music in her head. Symphonies and jazz. The old stuff. Way before her time, and she's seventy-five. She passed her love of old music down to Rainey, who liked to listen from the start. A tiny baby soothed by Haydn sonatas, Coltrane riffs, and Sarah Vaughn lullabies. Nonda filled her head with the stuff. Maybe that was the problem. Why Rainey couldn't stop. And now Nonda suspects Zimri is making music, too. Girl has it in her just like her mother, despite Nonda's best efforts to keep it tamped down. Shushed her when she hummed. Took her spoon away when she banged it in rhythm. Smacked her mouth when she matched notes on the tram. The dominant seventh chord of the horn. The dissonance of the squeaking brakes. The girl has it bad. Music is inside her and Nonda always knew it would eventually find a way out.

She'd recognize that girl's voice anywhere. It's pure and sweet like Rainey's was—a two-octave range with a little smoke around the edges. Nonda might be old, but she's not dumb. She built herself a receiver years before Tati started selling them in her Old Town shop, though she never expected to hear Zimri coming through it. Child's just like her mother, which is why Nonda must keep searching along the riverbank with her ears perked up like a frozard listening for a dragonfly to pass by.

For every Plebe worker out at Nowhere, there are twenty up on the Strip because what else is there to do after a twelve-hour warehouse shift? Personal Occupancy Domiciles are small, each POD only two hundred square feet with retractible furniture and one screen per family unit. But at the Strip, warehouse workers zap COYN from their HandHelds and step inside what used to be a grocery store, a bookshop, a bank, and a restaurant way back when Nonda was a kid. Individual shops have gone the way of critters that used to inhabit the riverbank. Who needs them all when you can squish them up together? A single super space for all your entertainment needs! Here the bar is large, expansive, taking up an entire wall. No cash, no masks needed. It's on the up and up. With frothy Near Beers and steaming bowls of grubworm-meal noodles in hand, Plebes flock to the three-story-tall, one-block-wide screen showing perfectly legal digital entertainment.

So far the Buzz on screen is filled with images of the richest and most beautiful Plutes posing for endless pix at tony events in the City Distract. Gallery openings. Movie premieres. Hottest ticket restaurant seatings. What more could Plebe viewers want? Those who've made it on the Buzz must be worth watching, right? Otherwise, you're a has-been or never-was and not worth anybody's time. Like Libellule, the last self-made superstar of pop, curled up beneath her duvet in a PONI apartment on the outskirts of the City, dreaming of the days when she ruled the waves.

Then the scene on the screen switches. There's a LiveStream tonight from Chanson Industries Arena. Cameras focus in on the crowd mingling at the Arena while waiting for celeb singer Geoff Joffrey to take the stage. He waits behind a curtain of finest blue silk. Melodies buzz like gnats inside his brain, so many he can't capture them all. Sometimes his head aches with so much music. He's a lucky one, though. Kept himself relevant for years. The Chanson PromoTeam gets half the credit. They've updated his look every three months, leaked preplotted stories of romantic ties to up-and-coming talent, pulled favors and made enemies to keep him in the Buzz. But he's getting tired. Wearing down. He's already twenty-two years old—five years past his Acquired Savant Ability surgery that rewired his brain for musical genius. No doubt, the ASA has paid off and set him up for life, but sometimes he dreams that he is running from a swarm of locusts, each one singing its own melody so the sound becomes overwhelming. He watches himself trip and fall and curl into a ball, knees to elbows, head covered in a feeble attempt to protect himself from ten thousand tiny sharp jaws.

"It's time," his handler tells him. He nods and moves moth-like toward the lights as the curtain swishes open. Plutes in the Arena get to their feet while Plebes at the Strip sway and lift their cups when Geoff Joffrey takes the stage.

On the riverbank, Nonda slips and falls against a tree, exhausted and confused about why she's out here—was she picking greens for Rainey? A dragonfly momentarily alights on her arm. She says hello and blows on it. It lifts up to join the breeze that carries the faint vibrations of drums that Nonda feels beneath her sternum but can no longer hear.

The dragonfly follows those vibrations out past Nowhere, where inside a masked drummer has jogged on stage, smacking his sticks overhead. Hearts surge as he crashes a beat on a rickety kit (bass drum, hi-hat, snare). The hypnotic rhythm hits the masked Plebes in their chests and deep down in their guts and they begin to move like the beat has overtaken them. They stomp their feet, yell, whistle through their teeth, and lift their arms overhead, clapping hands together in unison. Fish mouths in the river begging to be fed. Zimri takes one last look from behind the curtain, then she shouts, "Now!" and hits record on her devices.

Electromagnetic waves carrying ones and zeros crash together, like drones and dragonflies colliding. (It's the waves that killed the dragonflies. Disrupted their chemical signals. Messed with the frogs and lizards, too. Squirrels and chipmunks. Coyotes and wolves. Pushed and pressed together, competing for shrinking space. Unnatural unions are now the norm.)

From out here—puny Nowhere on no map—Zimri Robinson will not be denied her place, though. Without music her world is askew. She has to tilt herself to fit in. Melody and rhythm set things straight. When she's on stage, she's no longer that weird girl singing to herself. An oddball chirping to the birds and humming with the trees. The one with an uncanny talent for navigating warehouse shelves to the rhythm of a countdown nobody else can hear. When Zimri steps through the curtain at Nowhere, she is her one true self. She is the music and music is meant to be shared—with the people who've assumed the risk of coming to Nowhere tonight and later those who scan the waves on black market receivers for what Zimri will release like a dandelion spreading its seeds.

Just as Geoff Joffrey starts "Your Eyes," his newest song (and biggest hit yet, the PromoTeam has assured Mr. Chanson), the giant screen at the Strip flickers, then Geoff Joffrey disappears. The Plebes stop, stare, and wonder what's happening, when in his place a black-masked face fills the screen and a different crowd roars.

Back at Nowhere, Zimri leans into her camera and shouts, "We are Nobody from Nowhere and this is our song!"

VERSE ONE

ORPHEUS

When the pointed toe of Arabella's silver shoe trips the laser sensor, the MajorDoormo kicks into action. Sliders part, spotlights illuminate, and the scanner identifies us before we've fully stepped over the threshold of the Nahmad Gallery.

"Orpheus Chanson and Arabella Lovecraft," the automated voice announces, then sends the headline straight onto the Buzz. I know exactly what it will say since all my life I've been defined by the success of my parents.

> Orpheus Chanson, son of pop diva legend Libellule and ASA patent-holder Harold Chanson—one of the most powerful music patrons in the world—arrives at the Quinby Masterson premiere with stunning starlet-in-the-making, Arabella Lovecraft.

Heads turn and conversations lull. A cluster of dragonfly 'razzi drones swarm the entryway. Ara and I step into the spotlight and stop on the mark (a small gold star embedded in the floor).

"Just like we learned in SCEWL," I remind Ara through my smile.

She momentarily panics. "SCEWL?"

"Paparazzi Pix Posing 101, remember?" I say, trying to coax her synapses to fire.

She still looks blank so I take a half step back, keeping one shoulder behind her as I guide her with my hand on the small of her back. "Look right," I whisper. "Then left, and smile. Chin up, eyes wide. Top lip down to hide the gumline. Shake your head slightly. Look humble. Now a little laugh. Always having fun."

She follows my direction effortlessly as it all comes back to her. The Kardashian School for Cumulative Entertainment Wealth Living trained us well.

"You did good," I tell her when the photo-op is done. She sighs and looks relieved as we waltz into the crowd.

Quinby's opening is popping, just like Rajesh said. I lead Arabella through the throngs of people who've come to pay homage to our friend—the newly minted art-world It Girl of the moment, rocking the scene with her images of fractal decay. To me her paintings look like repeating patterns of dead trees and leaves, but for whatever reason Quinby's work has hit the *sosh* like a major earthquake, which has driven the prices sky high. Her patron, Hermela Nahmed, couldn't be more thrilled and it shows, given the money she must have pumped into this opening. For the past hour there's been near-constant chatter on my EarBug about which Celebs are here and what we're wearing, eating, drinking, and talking about.

"I've got to turn this thing off," I say and kill my EarBug. "I get immediate ADHD if I'm in a crowd while the Buzz is talking to me."

"Get some methylphen in your pump," Ara tells me, still preening for the few 'razzi buzzing around us. "That stuff will focus you right up." She pops a fist on her hip and smiles with her eyes for one persistent dragonfly drone.

"Is your pump back on already?"

"Not yet. Still too fragile up here." She taps the side of her head. "No benzos, no SSRI, no appetite suppressants, only a smidge of oxycodone to manage the headaches."

"God forbid your brain regulate itself," I joke.

"What am I, a three-year-old?" she says, then cringes. "Sorry, I forgot you're *au naturel*."

"That's what happens when your mother's a former addict," I say and nudge her to the left. The grit of her crushed iridescent body glitter grinds beneath my fingertips. Her dress, which is made of tiny shining scales, glints and changes colors as we pass beneath the lights.

We walk by a group of DespotRati. I recognize one of them, Ios, from summer camp. She nods and lifts her left hand so I can see the carapace of her ExoScreen glove, lavender to my deep purple—a good compatibility rating but nothing like my connection with Arabella, whose carapace still gleams deep dark purple like my own. I was worried the surgery might have changed our compatibility, but so far so good. I pretend not to recognize Ios and keep moving.

"Who was that?" Ara asks, nose wrinkled as she glances back. Ios's paint job, intricate swirls and curlicues, waves and striations in aquamarines, purples, and pinks, looks like some complicated bruise over her arms, legs, back, and chest. Her shimmery silver dress dangles from a loop of metal around her neck and hugs the barely covered curves between shoulders and thighs.

"Daughter of the former EU prime minister. You know how they still love government over there." Ara looks blank. "She has that new song." I hum a few bars of "(Quark) Charmed, I'm Sure." "Probably debuted while you were recovering. They're trying to push it as a new genre, Quantum Pop, but I think it sounds like Sparkle Jam. They needed something more atmospheric to create a truly original sound."

Ara laughs at me, which she often does when I talk about improving songs. How a key change would add depth to the bridge or adding strings for a harmonic overlay would bring out the emotion of a lyric. *Wasted energy,* people tell me. *A song is only as good as its Buzz.*

"Anyway," I say. "I heard she had a double ASA, physics and music, but I think that's just hype to sell her new line of gum. 'Now in all the quark flavors!'" I say in a falsely perky voice just like the ad.

"How do you know her anyway?"

"We both did a summer camp in Malta when we were fourteen. She knew all my mom's music and sang *Sugar Smack* to me."

"Oh my god," says Ara as we weave through a group of waning movie stars, all just past their prime, looking desperate for some Buzz. "She *sang* it to you?"

"And did the choreography."

"Ew!" Ara squeals.

"I know, right? I was like, no thanks. What guy wants to

think of his mother as a sexy teen pop star?" A tiny quake of revulsion goes through me.

From across the room, Elston and Farouk wave at us like they're flagging down a flying taxi. We make a beeline for them, whisking tangy drinks from a passing RoboWaiter along the way.

"First night out for Arabella!" I announce when we join our friends. We all lift our cups above our heads and laugh as if it's *freaking hilarious* that another friend had her brain zapped and woke up with a Chanson Industry trademarked and patented Acquired Savant Ability thanks to my father. Just a little brain surgery and POOF you wake up a genius. The hilarious part being, Plute parents pay for their kids to have the surgeries, then people like my father make a fortune off their talents, and we call this Art.

My friends and I clink glasses and down our drinks, everyone lifting hands up high and clicking pix with their Exo-Screen FingerCams. The images are sent into the data swarm and culled by some complicated algorithm that sorts sound-bites, 'razzi drone vids, and FingerCam images into what's Buzz-worthy for the night.

As soon as the group steps apart, they all check their palm screens, hoping that the moment we just experienced will get plucked from that deluge of data and fed into the Buzz for everyone else to see. Are you famous enough, are your parents, has your patron's PromoTeam pushed for more coverage this week? Fleeting disappointment passes over my friends' faces when our real-time moment doesn't reappear in the Buzz. None of us are worthy enough. Yet.

Farouk turns his attention back to Arabella. "You look

gorgeous! Amazing! Isn't she beautiful?" Elston and I nod and nod and nod. "So, what'd you have?"

She blinks at him for two seconds, like she can't quite remember. It takes a while for everything to come back online after an ASA so we all wait patiently, trying not to stare. "Music," she says after the delay.

"Nice," says Farouk.

"You?" she asks.

"Double in math and spatial reasoning. For architecture," he says, then adds, "My parents . . . immigrants, you know, wanted something practical." He lifts his shoulders almost as if in apology. "Anything happening for you yet?" he asks Ara.

Her vacant eyes settle on me. She is beautiful and empty— just the way Chanson Industry PromoTeams like their talent. It's a convenient side effect of the surgery. Sparking all that genius seems to short out other parts of the mind, at least long enough for a PromoTeam to fill you up with everything (besides ability) that will keep you rich and make you famous. If everything goes as planned, once Ara's auditory cortical pathways settle into their new wiring, her brain will be consumed with music. It'll be all she wants to do. In the meantime, while those circuits are getting settled, her PromoTeam will work their tails off to make her into pre-star material: the look, the walk, the talk, the network, the brand. Because as every one of us Persons Of Normal Intelligence knows, you can be the most amazing savant ever to walk the planet, but if you don't have a patron's corporate machine behind you, you might as well be singing to your reflection in the bathroom mirror.

"Don't worry." I rub Ara's shoulder. "It takes time, that's all."

Just then the crowd parts and Rajesh swaggers up. He's decked out. Vertical stripes on his jumpsuit, pulsating chartreuse polka dots on his bowtie, hair pomped up almost as high as the girls'. And he's trailing a cloud of 'razzi dragonfly drones because he's the current boy wonder of the literary world. His parents got his ASA in early. He was only fourteen when they did it, which can be tricky because as my parents found out the hard way with my sister, Alouette, the brain is so vulnerable at that age. Yet like everything Raj's family does, they hired the best in the world, which is an option when your father is a rare earth-mining magnate heir and your mother ruled Bollywood for two decades, so money is no question. And it paid off. In the two years since his literary ASA, Raj has gotten one of the largest publishing contracts in history. Now, his patron is about to release the final installment of Raj's Captain Happenstance trilogy called *Revenge of the Shadow Thieves,* sure to be another worldwide best seller.

"Friends, Romans, and countrymen!" Raj shouts and inserts himself into the center of our group, arms around shoulders, pulling everyone in for a round of photos taken by the drones. Girls lean in, boobs pressed forward, butts out, heads cocked to the side and huge smiles while the guys lay back, lift their chins and purse their lips, slouch to the side as if nothing is that important. Party pose, they called it at SCEWL where we all perfected it. I slip behind the line to give the others more prominent positions because (much to my father's chagrin) I'd rather stay behind the scenes. A few seconds later, something else catches the attention of the 'razzi and they move en masse across the gallery, casting shadows as they pass beneath the lights, except for Raj's stalkers, which stay close by.

"What's this?" Raj shouts as the others sneak peeks at their palms to make sure they were in proximity of his celebrity to make it in the Buzz. Yes, yes, they are worthy now. "The great Arabella is amongst us. Beautiful eagle heroine. Orabilis, I bow to thee in prayer!" He bows deeply as if waiting for applause.

"Easy there." Elston gives him a playful bump. "The drones are gone and we're not your adoring fans."

"Yeah, yeah," Raj says, beleaguered by our lack of fawning. "Speaking of adoring fans, anybody seen Quinby yet?" He cranes his neck.

Elston lifts her eyes to the ceiling and blows a puff of air into her tower of rainbow curls, which don't budge. "I'm sure she's in the middle of the hive, Queen Bee that she is now."

"Jealous?" Farouk asks.

Elston gives him a look of death. "Hardly," she snaps, but we all know better. Elston had an art ASA six months ago and while she's been mad prolific since she woke up, nothing has popped for her yet. She mostly works from photos, zooming in on details of fireworks in night skies or phosphorescence under the sea, then paints over the images in brightly colored squiggles. But what she really loves is distorting videos of the Plebes. Groups running, brawls for food, a protest gone terribly wrong. She takes the footage from security cameras or HandHelds, zooms in close, slows things down, and forces viewers to confront the faces of the masses. I think her work is brilliant, but it doesn't resonate with most Plute art collectors like Quinby's ever-repeating images of woodland decomposition does.

I step to Elston's side and touch her elbow. The bright yellow and orange stripes of her paint job twist around her upper arm and disappear beneath her steel-blue top. Unlike the other girls wrapped in skin-tight tubes, she favors billowy fabrics that dance around her when she moves. "You're gorgeous and talented, Elston, and it'll happen for you, too," I whisper close.

She sighs, weighty and sad.

Raj steps up. "Cover me," he says through gritted teeth.

On cue, the whole group huddles close, blocking the circling 'razzi dragonfly drones from view while pressing ExoScreen cams against our thighs so no pix get out.

"Lookie what Papa Raj brought you," he says and slips a slender silver bottle from his pocket. "My Plebe connection hooked me up with some fine black-market Juse."

Without hesitation, everyone shoves a glass close to the bottle. Raj tops us all off, then we toast once again. "Down the hatch!" Raj says. In unison we toss back our drinks, smack our lips, and wait for the night to get much more interesting.

ZIMRI

On stage at Nowhere, under one bright light, sweat pours into my eyes as the music pours out of me. My mother, Rainey, and Dorian's father, Marley, dug this place out of the riverbank before we were born. They made their own music here for years, then abandoned it to the frozards and squimonks when my mother disappeared. I rediscovered it a year ago and have been putting on concerts ever since, but tonight is the first time Dorian's played with me.

Although the space is small and cramped wall-to-wall with black-masked people, it feels like a cathedral to me. Dorian and I go from one song to the next, pushed forward by the backing tracks I prerecorded and his driving beats. When I sing, the crowd moves with me like beads of water drawn together to form a puddle. I tilt left. They tilt left. I bounce up and down and so do they. I lift my arms. Arms go up. They hang on my words, listening to me sing about working Plebes like us, perpetually treading water so we don't drown, a feat my father couldn't manage. The terror and thrill that we could all be caught at an illegal concert feeds the frenzy from first song to the last. And when the final note reverberates over the crowd, Dorian and I both yell, "Thank you!" then bolt offstage while everybody else streams out the door like floodwater spilling over the riverbank into the night, as black as the masks we all wear to protect our identities.

Dorian and I work quickly to dismantle any evidence of what went on here tonight. We haul the pallets out back. Take apart the lights. Carefully fold up the canvas curtain and put it, along with the ancient equipment, in an alcove my mother so cleverly constructed to hide all of her ramshackle instruments, mixing boards, turntables, laptops, and headphones back in the day. When we're done, the only things left of this evening are the audio and video recordings that I hold in my hands.

"What will you do with those?" Dorian asks. He slumps against the wall like he just worked a double at the warehouse, his dark skin sheened with sweat beneath bleached blond dreds. But in his shiny silver pants he's every ounce the rock star.

"I'll release the audio tomorrow," I tell him, and stick the little digital recorder in my pocket. "If that's okay with you."

"Far be it from me to stop a pirate," he says with a laugh.

I grin. After my mother left, I took one of her old transmitters to Tati who helped me get it up and running with a few spare parts scavenged from the electronics dump. Tati showed me how to hook up an antenna so I could start my own pirate radio broadcasts. For the first year, I used it only to search for my mother. "Rainey, this is your daughter Zim, come in Rainey. Please come in." Then I'd sing sad songs that she loved—Sarah

Vaughn, Mavis Staples, Mary J. Blige, Trinity, Libellule—like a siren trying to lure a sailor back to the rocky shore.

One day Marley pulled me aside. He squatted down with his hands on his knees so we were eye to eye. "I heard you on the air," he told me, which made my cheeks burn red. I hadn't thought about other people scanning the waves with the black-market receivers they bought from Tati and hid inside their PODs. "You have to stop. You don't have a license and you're broadcasting music you don't own the rights to."

"I'm just trying to find her," I told him.

"Honey." He put his hand on my shoulder, which made me feel small. "If your mother wanted to be found . . ."

I squirmed away. I didn't need him to finish that sentence but right then and there I knew that the music I'd make had to be for someone other than my mother.

"I just hope we pulled in enough," I say to Dorian. I never ask for money when I put on a show, but people leave it anyway and since I don't really need it, I give it to someone who does. "Levon's son, Luka, is coming home from the MediPlex tomorrow but Levon says the prosthetic leg is terrible. The kid can barely walk."

"Did they ever catch the person who ran him over?" Dorian asks.

I scoff. "Of course not. Just some Plute plowing down the road out by the river where Levon's son was riding his bike. At least the guy had the decency to drop the kid at the Medi-Plex, but then he took off like he'd dumped a half-dead dog."

Dorian shakes his head, disgusted by the same old story of Plute versus Plebe. "Do we take the money to Levon then?"

"It's already gone," I tell him and he frowns. "Hey," I say. "The less you know about it . . ."

"I get it," he says. "If we never touch the money, no one can say we profited, right?"

I nod. "But don't fool yourself. Even if we don't have cash in hand, what we're doing isn't exactly legal."

He shrugs as if he doesn't care, then points to the video cam in my hand. "What about that?"

I toss it up and down, catching the little orb in my palm where it fits so well. "It didn't work. I checked the laptop but there's nothing on it. I'll ask Tati to look at it the next time I see her."

I look over the empty room. What felt like a sacred space when we were on stage has returned to a small, cramped dugout with a low ceiling and musty dank air. "Want to get out of here?" I ask.

"Let's go," says Dorian.

Outside by the river, it's a good fifteen degrees cooler, which is nice after the stuffy air of Nowhere. And it smells good, too. Like moss on damp rocks. The moon has come up bright, making the path along the river glow soft yellow. I miss Brie then. She usually waits for me beneath the big willow tree after a show so we can walk home together, but she got demoted back to nights at the warehouse after missing three days of work with the flu last week. Now, I can't even ping her because they block our HandHeld signals while we're on the clock. That's the hardest part of being on opposite shifts. I've barely talked to my best friend all week!

Dorian picks up his bike, hidden in the reeds. "Want a ride?"

I climb on behind him and balance with my hands on his hips. He's gotten tall and solid, like a sturdy tree. And there's something about the way he holds his shoulders, back and down with his chin up, that hits me in the belly like a pebble in a puddle, sending ripples to the edges of my skin. I shake off that feeling because it's stupid. We've known each other since we were born.

As we ride along the river path, I listen to the squee and squonk of his bike chain, then make those the backbeat to a rhythm I tap on Dorian's hipbones. He keeps the pedals going, perfectly in time to the click of delivery drones taking off every other second from the mammoth Corp X warehouse roof. Squee and squonk and squee and squonk and zoom and zoom. Squee and squonk and squee and squonk and zoom and zoom. Dor adds his bike bell at the end, ting ting. I shoosh my feet in the gravel—shup shup—and he finds a bright screech on his brakes. I match the note, A#, sing a riff of nonsense as we ride along until he hits the brakes hard and I slam into his back.

"What the . . . !" I peel myself away from his sweaty shirt.

"Look at that!" He straddles the bike and points to the sky where a giant bird lifts off from the top of a tree. It glides out over the willows standing along the bank like tired women hanging their heads after a long day at work.

I slide off the back of the bike and hurry to the edge of the path. "Come on!" Dorian drops his bike and we scamper down a slope to see where the bird has landed. Halfway down, Dorian loses his footing and ends up on his rear, hollering, "Whoa, whoa, whoa," as he grasps for tree roots to slow himself down. I catch him by the back of the shirt. His arms windmill as he teeters on the edge of the bank.

"Whew, thanks, I almost took the plunge!" He stiffens. "Oh, god, sorry . . . I . . ."

"There!" I point, not interested in his apology for my family history. In the center of the river, the heron tiptoes through the water, silently hunting for its supper. "I haven't seen one of those in years," I whisper and plop down on a soft tuft of grass to take off my shoes. I slide my feet into the river. The cool water swirls around my legs and carries away the aches and pains of a full day running in the warehouse plus all that stomping on stage. Curious little frozards nibble on the ends of my wriggling toes, like tiny kisses from my father sending his love up from the depths. *Hi, Papa,* I say inside my head, but I don't cry anymore when I'm here. It's been five years since he took the plunge.

"Nonda told me that when she was a kid, there were creatures out here that we don't have anymore," I say to Dorian. "Things like foxes and beavers. Or separate species, like there were coyotes and wolves or squirrels and chipmunks. Those were all different things before Corp X came along and everything got squished together."

"I think your Nonda makes things up." Dorian squats beside me. In the dusky light, with a stick in his hands, he looks more like the kid I remember from when we were little and everybody played together in the Youth Activity & Recreation Domain, not the person he's become, tall and lanky, all arms and legs, his face rearranging itself into an adult version of himself. When he turned fifteen, he got a job on the warehouse box-packing line because he tested high for spatial reasoning skills.

I sing a song about an old man river and kick arcs of water in the air. I'm still jacked up from the show and can't quite settle my brain or stop the adrenaline pumping through my body. I feel like grabbing the heron and twirling around, singing at the top of my lungs, dancing across the riverbank, climbing trees, swinging on the moon. "I wish I could perform every night!" I say.

"Every night?" says Dorian. "Sounds exhausting."

"Not to me." I stare out at the swirling water below, always moving forward, and I imagine a life on the road like the old-time musicians on tour—going from town to town, a different venue every night. "Making music makes me happier than anything else in life," I say, my dreams clouding up my voice. "You can't touch it or live inside of it. Music can't protect you from the wind or rain. It's not like we can eat it or drink it. But if I suddenly had no music in my life, I think that I might die."

"You'd die?" Dorian teases.

"Shut up," I say and bump his shoulder with mine.

"Yeah, well, you better be careful, Zimri Robinson," Dorian warns. "If you get caught, you know what happens." He presses his fingers into my temples. "Bzzzt!" he says. "They'll zap your brain!"

I knock his hand away. "Nonda says I was born in the wrong era. Just like my mom."

"Or maybe we were born on the wrong side of the river."

Dorian tosses his stick. It makes a gentle splash that scares the heron into flight.

Bye bye birdie, I sing inside my head as we both look out across the wide, dark expanse of water to the road on the other side. The road that leads out. My father hated being a warehouse picker. Sucked his soul clean dry. It gets to some people—packing up boxes of things we'll never own to send off to the Plutes in the City who expect everything dropped into their delivery chutes at the push of a button. Geographically, we aren't far from the City, but the distance between here and there is enormous for Plebes like us, which is why my father only made it to the middle of the river. My mother, though, got out.

"I still can't believe you asked me to play tonight," Dorian says. "What if I'd been terrible?"

"Are you kidding?" I pull my legs out of the water and dry them with my socks. "You've been playing drums since you could walk." I reach up for his hand. "You're Marley's son, after all."

Our parents taught us a history of the world in music. From blues to jazz to rock to hip-hop and rap, from trance to dance and dub, from calypso to ska to reggae, through punk and emo and tech, from blather to echo and Sparkle Jam. They claimed music went bad after the 2065 pay-for-play technology went into effect. And who could blame them? I think people of their generation lost the most. One minute nearly all music was at their fingertips; the next, listeners couldn't own any recordings. Music lovers like them must have felt bereft.

Dorian pulls me to stand and leans in closer so our heads nearly touch. I can smell the river on his skin and see the moisture above his top lip. "Why'd you ask me to play tonight? Why now?"

I swallow hard because I don't have a good answer. I've been watching him at the warehouse lately, curious about who he's become. "I just thought it would be more fun with another person." I hear my voice go shaky, which seems odd—not to mention embarrassing. My palm is sweaty in his grip and my body tingles and feels warm at the same time.

Then his arm is around my shoulder. Resting there like it belongs, and I feel something shift inside of me. Like a switch gets flipped and suddenly I'm not standing here with somebody I grew up beside but with someone new and undiscovered.

The peepers and crickets and whippoorwills are in full chorus. A breeze kicks up, bringing along the smells of mucky water, green leaves, and sweet blossoms. "Have you ever heard anything so beautiful?" I whisper.

Dorian inhales deeply. I feel the heat coming off of his body, wrapping itself around my skin. "Yes," he says. I hear him swallow, lick his lips. Then he says, "You singing."

He scoops me in a half-circle toward him so we're facing one another. I can't look at his face so I stare at his arms. The vein on his bicep pulses. I press my hand against his chest. His heart pounds beneath my palm.

"Bm-bm, bm-bm," I say, echoing his rhythm. My hands creep up to his shoulders. They are safe and sturdy, like branches I could climb. His Adam's apple bobs. I lean in and inhale the scent of his neck. Then he pulls back and places one hand gently under my chin. Our eyes meet, our lips press together. For a moment, I'm fuzzy about where my body ends, the same way I feel when I get sucked into a song. But Dorian drops his arm and steps back quickly.

"Oh!" I press two fingers against my tingling lips.

"Someone's coming," he says and wipes the back of his hand across his mouth.

I hear the squeak of another bike on the river path behind us.

"Dorian?" someone calls. "That you?"

"Is that your dad?" I ask, my stomach in a knot.

Dorian grimaces when Marley pulls up beside us. His long braids are tucked up under a knit cap he's worn ever since I've known him.

"Were you out looking for me?" Dorian asks his dad. "I told you I'd be late."

"You forgot to mention where you'd be." Marley's voice is hard. "I overhead some kids at the warehouse say there was a show out at Nowhere tonight. You wouldn't know anything about that, now would you?"

My heart leaps into my throat. "I should get home." I tiptoe backward away from them. "I haven't seen Nonda since this morning. She might be worried. Sometimes she forgets . . ."

"We'll walk you," Marley says.

"That's okay," I tell him. "I'll be fine."

"No," says Marley. "I want to talk to you. Both of you. And this concerns Nonda, too."

I grip the recordings in my pocket and consider tossing them into the river like stones, but I don't. Instead, I walk far apart from Dorian, with Marley in between, calculating the hours until I can release the songs.

ORPHEUS

"You don't have to stay with me," Arabella says after the others go in search of the obligatory mingle to up their Buzz ratings and make their PromoTeams happy. But I stick with her in an out-of-the way corner of the gallery beneath Quinby's painting of giant pill bugs on moldering orange and brown oak leaves.

"Good for my cred to be seen with you," I say, but we both knew it's a lie—she's not established in the Buzz quite yet. Truthfully, I feel protective of Ara. She seems addled and easily confused, especially with the Juse now in her system, so I want to stay close.

Everybody says we make the perfect pair but our timing's always been off. She liked me last year when I was dating Europa Al-Asad. By the time Europa and I broke up, Ara was with Eleven Beckham. They broke up when he was recruited to play midfield for PetroChina. We got together for a minute right before her surgery a month ago and since then she's been recovering. Maybe now that things are getting back to normal we'll finally figure out what's between us.

"So . . ." she says, her words a little slurry from the Juse. "Does your father own my brain now?" She laughs and taps the side of her head.

"Does he own your brain?" I snort. Her hair is newly gold with tiny braids woven into intricate paths. I have an urge to follow one with my finger. "Your whole entire brain?"

"Don't make fun of me!" she whines. "I don't really understand the whole patenting and copyright thing."

"Don't freak out," I say and give her a quick hug, drawing in her smell—herbal and fresh like a newly planted garden. "Here's how it works. Chanson Industries bought the rights to any music your brain creates, just like Quinby's patron owns her paintings, and Rajesh's patron owns his books. You get a cut of the profits from all your songs that Chanson streams or the concerts they set up, or any LiveStreams that you do. Plus your PromoTeams will keep you in the Buzz. It's all a big machine," I tell her.

"Speaking of which," she says, "I'm supposed to get vid or pix into the Buzz of me with Quinby. You know, the phantom chatterbox. Pre-launch stuff. Blah ditty blah blah."

"Is that going to be your first hit single, 'Blah Ditty Blah Blah'?" I ask and laugh way too hard at my own dumb joke. Raj's Juse has definitely hit.

She tries to smile, but I see tears brim on her blinged-out eyes. "Hey," I say and reach out to comfort her, but then the shiny baubles embedded on the end of each lash mesmerize my fuzzy brain. "Must be hard to blink with all that weight."

I stare at her for another second, cocking my head from left to right. "Wait a sec. You look different."

"Different good or different bad?" She self-consciously pats the swirling structure on her head.

I get up closer to her face to study her. "It's your eyes, isn't it? They're bigger or something?"

"Double eyelid surgery." Ara bats her lashes, which makes the tears roll down her cheeks. She carefully wipes them away. "Makes them bigger. Less Asian-y."

"I thought Asian-y was good for marketing."

"Except in the eyes," says Ara. "Or so my PromoTeam says."

"They said that? Ugh. Who'd you get assigned to?"

Again, the hesitation. Like she knows but can't quite pull the info from the folds of her mind. "Piper," she says finally. "Piper McLeo."

"Actually, she's good. Knows what she's talking about," I tell her with a sigh. "She's an old family friend, you know."

Ara smirks. "Who in the music industry is not a friend of your family?"

"All of my dad's enemies," I say and we both dissolve into Juse-infused giggles even though it's definitely not funny. Ara nearly doubles over in hysterics. She grips my arm for support but then she starts to slump. I grab her beneath the armpits and shuffle her toward the wall to prop her up. She slings her hands onto my shoulders.

"Am I still beautiful?" she asks with her face close to mine.

"Of course," I tell her. Then we're nose to nose, lips quivering as we start to kiss, but Ara pulls away.

"Sorry, sorry, sorry," she mutters and looks around, hoping

none of that was caught by a 'razzi drone, since her contract specifically states that all public romantic ties must be pre-approved by the PromoTeam.

"No, I'm sorry," I tell her. "I should know better." I step back and take a breath to regroup. "Okay, look. Here's what we're going to do. I'll help you get your photo op with Quinby and then you leave with me, deal?"

"Orpheus," she says, straightening her dress. "If you can work that miracle, I'll go anywhere with you." She gives me a teasing smile—a glimmer of the old Arabella showing through. Both our carapaces glow.

I lead her through the crowd by the wrist. She hangs back, loose-limbed and lithe, waving to people and flashing smiles as we pass. SCEWL does a good job preparing Plute kids so that when we wake up from our ASAs we already have some skills, and everything's coming back to Ara. Her walk fools the 'razzi into thinking she's someone special. They send her image into the algorithm again and again, upping her chances of getting in the Buzz tonight.

I spot Quinby, literally on a pedestal, at the front of the gallery. She's posing for pix, dolled up beyond belief. Her hair is Marie Antoinette–worthy, piled high in dark brown twists fashioned to look like twigs with fake hummingbirds and butterflies woven in. The whole tree motif is carried through-out her look. Rather than paint her, her stylists have polished her nut-brown skin to a high sheen, and draped her body in silky shades of green to match her nearly neon eyes.

"Brilliant branding," Ara mutters with an eyebrow cocked.

"Quin!" I call up to her. "Quinbo!" When she doesn't

answer I take a deep breath and yell, "Hey, Q-Bert!" That gets her attention.

She squats with knees together at the edge of the pedestal and breaks into a smile. "Orphie! Don't call me that here," she says, but she's laughing along with me. I wonder if Raj has slipped her something, too.

"Oh, sorry, Q-Bert! You're stunning, by the way." I slouch against the pedestal base. "Q's mom and mine used to be best buds," I tell Arabella and ignore the flash of pity across Quinby's face when I say *used to be*.

"I've known this maggot since we were born," she says.

"Hey, do a favor?" I tug Ara closer. "My lovely friend needs a byte on the Buzz."

"Arabella! Oh my god! Is that you? I heard you were back!" Quinby squeals in that way girls have of being terribly over-excited to see one another, especially when they don't really care that much. But Q is a good sport and she knows the game. "Your look is so *snazbags*!" She reaches out and leads Ara around the back of the pedestal to the steps. "Come on up here, girl."

As soon as they're together, arms entwined like they're the best of friends, FingerCams up high to generate their own stream of pix, the platform rotates and the 'razzi drones zoom over. The buzzing cloud of dragonflies hover near the Girl-of-the-Moment and the One-in-Waiting taking a spin on the pedestal of fleeting fame. Piper will send Ara on hundreds of these ops before she drops a single song so by the time she debuts, she'll have made her way into the public psyche like a termite boring into wood. The Plutes will want her on their ticket dockets at my father's arenas and Plebes will pay for playing her songs whether they're good or not.

While I'm watching them, a girl walks up. She doesn't look like anybody else at the gallery. No over-the-top hair, no paint job, no makeup. Just plain, in baggy pants and a fading blond ponytail. When I look at her more carefully though, I see that she's older than me but still quite pretty, with a broad forehead, gray-green eyes, and a slightly upturned nose. I glance down for a peek at her carapace, but oddly, both of her hands are bare.

"Orpheus?" she asks and eyes me cautiously.

"Yes," I say. "Do we know each other?"

"My name is Calliope. I was in your sister's class at SCEWL, before . . ." She stops and stands awkwardly. "And your father used to be my patron."

"Oh." I step back, wondering if she's a nutjob. "He's patron for a lot of people."

Her eyes flash dark and broody like the sky before a storm. "I'm the one suing him."

"You'll have to be more specific," I tell her with a snort. Definitely a nutjob. Who else would show up at a gallery opening dressed like a Plebe? "There are at least fifty people suing my father on any given day."

Calliope's jaw drops. She steps forward, pinning me between her body and the wall. "Do you know what it's like to have music take over your brain? It never stops. It's like there's a band inside your mind and the band keeps playing on and on and on." She grabs the sides of her head.

"Congratulations," I say sarcastically. "Sounds like your ASA was a success!"

"I was the first," she says. "Did you know that? And your father paraded me around as proof for Plutes of what was possible for their kids. He has it all worked out, doesn't he?" She keeps herself positioned between the pedestal and me so I can't get past. "Who needs years of expensive private schools, backroom deals, and corporate ladders to climb when you can buy your kid an Acquired Savant Ability surgery and voilà— she's a genius."

I laugh at her. "And what's so bad about that?" I ask, even though I suspect it's horrifying. I see the way my friends change. How obsessed they become with their vocation, unable to enjoy most of life.

"Nothing," she says. "Except that your father is a liar. He never intended to let me have a career. He sold my contract out from under me along with hundreds of others who'd signed with him. Then he used that money to put the other patrons out of business so he could claw his way to the top and we were left with nothing."

"Hey," I say, hands up as if in surrender. "That's business."

"No!" She stamps her foot in my direction. "It was my LIFE! The only job I could get after that was as a warehouse picker. It took me years to save enough money so I could have the reversal surgery and not be haunted by music all the time."

"Look," I say, softer now. "I'm sorry that happened to you, but it's got nothing to do with me."

"Oh, it's got everything to do with you, Orpheus," she hisses. "You haven't gotten an ASA yet and who could blame you after what happened to your sister?"

The hair on the back of my neck bristles. I step toe to

toe with this crazy woman. "Don't bring my sister into this," I warn and think of beautiful Alouette, brain wasted, perpetually lying in the MediPlex since her botched surgery ten years ago.

"Why haven't you done it yet?" she asks. "You're nearly seventeen. You know he won't hand over the company to you unless you get the surgery. But I know you have your doubts."

I press my back against the wall, wondering how she knows so much about me.

She moves closer. In the bright lights of the gallery she appears otherworldly, as if she's stepped out of the past to warn me about the future. "You're just a pawn in your father's game. He'll use you like he used your mother and your sister. He'll claim everything he does is for his family's sake, but really that's just a smoke screen to hide his greed."

"Leave my family out of this!" I push past her but she latches on to me.

"Consider this fair warning," she says into my ear. "I'm only the first person in a long line who'll sue him over sold contracts and botched reversal ASAs. Think of me as the floodgate opening. Once we expose what's really going on, the system will begin to crumble."

I turn and look at her but I can't find any words.

"Join us!" she says. "Imagine the message it would send if Harold Chanson's own son questioned the system. Do it for your sister. You owe her that!"

Just then, the pedestal stops and the 'razzi drones fly off. As Ara comes down the steps, I grab her arm. "Come on. I need to get out of here. Now."

Ara and I make our escape through a side door of the

gallery to avoid the MajorDoormo announcing our departure. Outside, in the loading zone, cars zip in and out. Since it's after nine o'clock, the Distract is lit up like midday with LED displays on every building surface, but without my EarBug, none of the ads can talk to me directly. Above us, a twenty-foot tall Raj, arm-in-arm with Quinby, flashes across the side of the gallery building. Overhead, a hologram of Geoff Joffrey dances across the rooftops. He does a trademark spin, one arm up, then points at all the little people, teeming like ants following chemical trails from hot spot to hot spot, down below.

"Are you okay?" Ara asks, still flushed from her brush with the Buzz.

"Yeah, fine," I tell her, but it's not true.

"What'd that girl want?"

My Cicada pulls up in front of us. The topside doors open like wings. I glance over my shoulder, making sure Calliope isn't following us. "For me to convince my father to restart her career," I lie as we climb inside. "Happens all the time."

"What a pain," Ara says with an indifferent shrug. "So, what should we do now? Where should we be seen?"

She points at the WindScreen lit up with all the hottest destinations for us to hit tonight.

"The end of the Geoff Joffrey concert at your dad's arena? The first movie from Rajesh's Captain Happenstance trilogy is still playing. Have you seen it yet? Oh, look!"

She touches a pix of a cat in a tux to pull up info on a retrospective called *U Must B Kitten Me.*

"Do you remember that girl Lynna Orkowski from SCEWL? I heard her ASA didn't fully take and now she's totally obsessed with cats. She draws cats, paints cats, makes tiny outfits just for cats." Suddenly Ara looks horrified. "Oh, god!" she says. "What if that happens to me?"

"Can we just get the hell out of here?" I ask, then tell my car's V2V NaviSystem to take us home. "I can't handle any more *sosh* tonight." I reach across Ara and open the glove box for my own silver flask.

"Is that a receiver?" She points at a black device tucked behind the flask.

I nod. "I got it from the Plebe Rajesh knows who sells the Juse." I take a swig. I need another hit after that conversation with Calliope. I know it's dumb to let her spook me. She's just a brain activist with a vendetta against my father. But none of them have ever targeted me. Plus she knew so much about the situation—my parents' divorce that's lingered in the courts for years and my doubts about having an ASA. I can't help but wonder where she's getting her information and it's freaking me out.

"Wouldn't your dad kill you if he finds out you listen to pirate radio?" Ara asks and takes the flask from me.

"Market research," I joke and feel myself begin to relax as the Juse seeps into my bloodstream.

Since the traffic is slow on the ground, the Cicada prepares to lift off and bypass the congestion. "Windows," I command. The screens become transparent so we can see outside. I don't like the SkyPath, yet. It's still too new. Of course, my father insisted he be one of the first to have access to that space when it opened six months earlier, but the whole thing feels clunky to me. The car rumbles as the wings unfold, the air pressure in the vehicle changes too abruptly when we rise up, and there's a screechy sound as the wheels retract. I look out at the four other new-model Cicadas that form our self-navigating platoon.

"What do you listen to on it?" Ara asks, still poking at the receiver.

"You can find all kinds of interesting stuff on the waves." I take it out and turn it on. "Sometimes it's religious fanatics from their bunkers in the wastelands predicting the end of the world as we know it. Or oddballs spouting anticorporate philosophy and saying they want a revolution."

"Why?" she asks.

I shrug. "Well, you know, they all want to change the world, I guess."

"As if," she says, then she leans in close and whispers, "Do you ever hear illegal music?"

"Sometimes you can find a station," I say, not mentioning that most nights I spend hours surfing the waves, listening to tunes, imagining how I would rearrange the melodies and instruments to give songs a whole different feel. "But my dad's people catch on pretty quick and jam the signal. Not that it matters. The pirates are smart. They move around and find other waves."

Tonight the stations are crackly and hollow-sounding with all the interference from the Distract, but we catch a few snippets here and there from the handful of audio news streams that cover everything substantive the Buzz would never run.

Factory workers riot over unsanitary conditions.

A warehouse fire in India kills four pickers and destroys three million dollars worth of merchandise.

Corporation Xian Jai says it's considering automating all facilities by 2093.

The Kardashian SCEWL for Future CelebuTantes posted record-high earnings today.

"That's where we went, right?" Ara asks, smiling at the memories coming back.

" 'Give 'em to us and they'll be smart enough to know better when they graduate,' " I quote the SCEWL's motto, and we both laugh until the next headline hits.

Bad day for Chanson Industries. Calliope Bontempi filed suit against Harold Chanson for personal and property damages following the sale of her music contract and a reversal ASA. . . .

"That's the crazy girl who cornered me in the gallery," I tell Ara.

. . . And an unidentified group momentarily hijacked the LiveStream of the Geoff Joffrey concert. . . .

"Oh god," I groan. "My dad's going to be in a foul mood tonight!" I reach to change the channel, but Ara stops me.

"No wait, I want to hear this," she says.

I take another long drink from the flask.

Harold Chanson is widely credited with changing the music industry by patenting the first Acquired Savant

Ability surgery, known as an ASA, that rewires the auditory cortical region of the brain to induce musical genius. Since then, other companies have patented similar procedures for savant abilities in different regions of the brain.

Chanson went on to become one of the most successful music patrons in the world by introducing pay-for-play streaming technology in 2065 that prohibits consumers from downloading and owning individual songs.

In her complaint, Ms. Bontempi claims she underwent a reversal ASA (a procedure for which Chanson Industries also holds the patent) that left her with acquired amusia. "I can no longer sing, hum, or whistle. I cannot read or write music, recognize songs I once knew, or play any of the instruments I so dearly loved. My ability to make a living as a musician was stolen by Harold Chanson when he did not honor my contract, and now my ability to derive any pleasure from music has been erased from my mind by him as well."

"Enough!" I turn off the receiver. "I can't stand to hear about another person whose life was ruined by my father."

"That's cold." Ara leans away.

"Oh, come on! You know how this goes," I grumble at her. "Art is a cutthroat business and not everybody makes it. Calliope's career failed and now she's bitter. Next she'll say my father is evil and that art should belong to everybody."

The Juse must have hit Ara hard because this makes her laugh and since she's laughing, I start laughing, too. We howl and slap our knees.

Finally, Ara calms down enough to say, "What a stupid idea. Everybody knows art belongs to the elite."

ZIMRI

When Marley, Dorian, and I get to my POD, the lights are off and the blinds are down.

"Nonda?" I call. "You here? We have visitors." When she doesn't answer, I tiptoe in. My shoulder brushes against one of my father's paintings of the river, knocking it askew.

"Could she be asleep?" Dorian asks, clearly hoping for a way out of the awkward situation.

"It's not that late," Marley assures us.

I command the lights on low and see two pots on the stove. No freeze-dried, premade dinners in our house. Nonda always cooks. The smoky scent of beans and greens still hangs in the air. But the main living space is empty and her sleeping unit is retracted into the wall.

"Maybe she went out?" Dorian says. "We could come back another time."

Marley, Dorian, and I are all startled, then we laugh nervously when we hear the whoosh of the toilet before the bathroom door slides open and there's Nonda squinting into the bright light. "Rainey?" she calls. "That you?"

I glance over my shoulder at Marley. He knits his eyebrows, same as me. It's weird hearing Nonda call for my mom. "It's me, Nonda. It's Zim."

Nonda looks sleepy and confused. "Oh," she says and shuffles by. I notice her clothes are wrinkled and disheveled. Her pants are dirty at the knees.

"Sorry to barge in on you like this, Layla." Marley steps forward with his arms open for a hug. "It's late and—"

"You hungry, Linus?" she says and Marley visibly blanches. His eyes cut to the artwork hung all over our walls. It's been years since anyone mistook him for my father. "I went to the river today and picked some greens," she says.

"Is that why your pants are dirty?" I ask, following Nonda closely like a bloodhound sniffing for the trail of her day. "Because you were out picking? Or did you fall?"

Nonda looks down at herself. "Oh my," she says. "I am a mess!" She rubs at the smudges on her clothes. "Picking is messy business, but you know how your daddy loves them greens. Don't you? I got some watercress for your supper."

"I know it's been a while." Marley puts his hand on her shoulder and looks her squarely in the face. "But I'm not Linus. I'm Marley. Remember me?"

Nonda studies him then blinks as if she's concentrating. "Goodness me, so silly. I'm a tired old woman." She laughs and pats his arm then moves on. "Of course you're not Linus. He's long gone. You all hungry?" she says and opens one of the pots on the stove.

Marley starts to say no but Dorian and I jump in with a resounding, "Yes!"

"Good!" says Nonda and gets a spoon. "And who's this?" she asks, pointing at Dorian.

"That's my boy," Marley says.

"Nice to meet you . . . again, ma'am." Dorian offers his hand.

"I remember you and Zimri running around in diapers," says Nonda, which makes both of us blush.

"The reason I wanted to talk with you," Marley says, but Nonda isn't listening.

She ladles out great heaps of beans and greens into two bowls while talking nonstop. "Your parents were a heap of trouble when they were young," she tells us. I press my lips together so I won't laugh. "Always into mischief down by the river. That was before Corp X started that sham of a so-called education system. Zimri, set the table."

I push the button so the table unfolds from the wall. "You mean SQEWL?"

"Hmph," says Nonda, hands on hips. "Special Quality Education for Workforce Life, my butt! Brought in a bunch of RoboNannies to keep you kids on lockdown while we worked. Took the cost right out of our COYN. No art. No music. A travesty, if you ask me!"

Nonda's rant about SQEWL is a familiar one, so I'm glad when Dorian interrupts. "What kind of things did you do down by the river?" he asks his dad as we slide onto the benches across from one another, but Marley doesn't answer.

"Oh, I can tell you stories!" Nonda grins as she sets down

steaming bowls in front of us. "Once Marley and Rainey made a boat. Decided they were going to leave."

Dorian and I snicker. "Where were you going to go, Dad?"

"I don't remember," Marley mumbles.

"I do," Nonda says haughtily. "Going to the City to become famous."

"Famous doing what?" I ask between bites, even though I already know.

Nonda looks at Marley but he stares at the floor and mutters, "Music." Then he adds, "That was before those genius surgeries and pay-for-play laws and patrons owning musicians. . . ."

"I never did understand how one person could own all the music." Nonda settles on the bench beside me. "Seems like a bunch of crap to me."

Dorian and I giggle. Nonda's always a straight shooter.

"That's not how it works." Marley slides in next to Dorian. "Artists are like professional athletes and patrons are like team owners. They sign contracts with artists then own the copyright to all their work. In music they make money off of concerts, LiveStream vids, and audio streaming, which is why you can't own any music like you could back in the day. Just download a song and it was yours to keep and play anytime you wanted. Nowadays, the more money a song makes, the higher it moves up the Stream, the more you hear it. Ugh. Same thing over and over. Whatever the masses like best. You try to pull up an old song and they stick it to you big-time with a premium!" He shakes his head, disgusted.

"That didn't stop your mama, did it, Zimri?" says Nonda.

"No, sir. *Oh,* Rainey would say, *I don't believe in none of that copyright malarkey. Nobody can own ideas or art.* I told her, 'You better stop messing around with that music. Mixing it all up and saying that it's your own. Putting on shows and expecting people to pay you.'"

"Tati had a hand in that, too," Marley says and sniffs. "She figured out how to hack the HandHelds so folks could download Rainey's songs, which was dumb since she sampled lots of tunes for remixes."

"The fat cats in the City didn't like that, did they?" Nonda asks. Marley shakes his head. "And you know what happened to your mama when she got caught."

Beans stick in my throat. The audio and video recorders feel heavy in my pocket.

"They said she owed money for all the music she stole and if she couldn't pay it back, she'd go off to jail and earn them their money." Nonda shakes her head. "Mm-mm-mm. She always was a stubborn one. She said, 'I'd just be trading one prison life at the warehouse for another in the jail.'"

"Like the old song said," Marley adds, *"one chain makes a prison."*

Nonda laughs. "I think you got that wrong. It's the other way around—*one chain don't make no prison,*" Nonda sings. "And Rainey had more than one chain."

I swallow hard, forcing the mush down. We haven't heard from my mother in years. Truth is, we don't even know if she's still alive.

"But you." Nonda turns to Marley. "You had a good woman. She kept you on track, didn't she?"

"Yes, ma'am," Marley whispers. He keeps his eyes on his hands, which are folded tightly between his knees.

"After Rainey was arrested, you stopped."

I watch Marley carefully, but he won't meet my eyes.

"I promised my wife," he says.

"Whatever happened to her?" Nonda asks. "You two split up?"

"No, she passed a few years ago," Marley says. "Cancer."

Nonda sighs. "So many losses." She reaches across the table and pats his hand. "I'm sorry. She was a nice gal, your wife."

Marley nods while Dorian and I lock eyes. We've never talked about the fact that neither of us have mothers anymore. I suppose because his mom had no choice when it was her time to go, but mine chose to leave me behind, and those are two very different things.

"You raised up this fine boy." Nonda pokes Dorian's arm. "Good thing these young ones aren't so foolish nowadays." She looks straight at me. "You saw what problems your mother caused. That rat Medgers coming around, harassing me. So let me ask you this, Zimri Robinson." She folds her hands and leans in close to me. "You'd never do such a thing as make music, would you?"

Dorian and I stare at our bowls, not daring to make eye contact anymore.

"Would you?" she presses and leans in closer. "Because you know what happens if you do and you get caught?"

I'm silent, sweating, afraid she'll put her hand on my leg and ask me what's inside my pocket.

"They'll zap your brain," Nonda says. "Turn you into a blathering idiot. So I'll ask you one more time." She pauses, just long enough to really make us sweat. "You making music?"

Without looking at her I mumble, "No, ma'am."

"Good!" She slaps the table, which makes us jump. Slowly she rises from the bench, her knees creaking. "Now what did you want to discuss?" she asks Marley.

He's been kowtowed and it's no surprise. Nonda has that effect on people. "Your mother . . ." he starts to say to me and then trails off.

"What about her?" I stare at Marley, daring him to look at me but he won't.

Most of my memories of my mother are caught up in song. I remember singing together while she gave me a bath, her showing me how to play the ukulele, both of us humming while she made us breakfast. I have a few murky memories of playing with Dorian at Nowhere while Mom and Marley jammed. When I uncovered recordings of her old music, both what she listened to and the music that she made, I felt like I knew her better. Heavy, thumping beats that hit you in the gut and songs that sounded happy but with lyrics that were raw. Sometimes, I think my music sounds like hers—as if there could be a genetic link for music like the ones for the texture of my hair and the gap between my teeth that came directly from Nonda to my mother then to me. But there's a major difference between us. I make up my own songs and don't sell them. My mother appropriated other people's music to make a profit.

I continue staring at Marley. I don't see him very often anymore, but when I do, I'm always shocked at how old he's become. Something about how his face is shrinking in on itself and his hair is thinning and his eyes are losing some of their brightness. My mother would be pushing fifty now as well. "She wouldn't want you to . . ." Marley says and again he can't finish.

I shake my head. "She left," I tell him. "She doesn't get a say about what I do."

ORPHEUS

By the time Ara and I hit our Community, it's that in-between time of night when everyone who's anyone is still out trying to get in the Buzz and all the has-beens are holed up inside wondering why the public no longer cares. Even the RoboMestics have taken the kids and dogs in for the night, leaving our Community well-ordered and quiet with its smooth streets, wide sidewalks, and tall fences. Beyond big blank yards, every hulking house is a monument to success. And they just keep getting more elaborate: A replica of the Duoma, one of Mount Vernon. The woman who invented the HoverCam recently completed a scaled-down Versailles.

At neighborhood cocktail parties the adults talk about square footage, everyone complaining that they're growing out of their space and need yet another house on yet another coast somewhere else in the world. For a while salt therapy rooms were all the rage, then pet spas. I know at least ten families who expanded their foyers to accommodate walk-through microbe zappers. And hardly anyone uses their sensory deprivation chambers anymore. Quinby's family turned theirs into an antigravity tank. Good for the skin, her mother told mine.

At my father's house (a reconstructed Parthenon—modesty is not in his vocabulary), the MajorDoormo announces our arrival, but this time, instead of stepping confidently into a spotlight, Arabella and I stumble, hanging on to one another, and spill into the living room, laughing our butts off. We stop short when we see my father.

He spins around and barks, "Orpheus! What the hell!"

"Dad?" I say. "What are you doing here?"

"I should ask you the same thing," he grumbles.

"Hello, Orphie!" I look past my dad to see Esther Crawley, Chanson Industries second-in-command, sitting on our couch.

I hop past my dad to plant a sloppy kiss on Esther's cheek. Although over the past ten years she's moved up the ranks to become my father's most trusted confidante, I still think of her as blond-hair, blue-eyed Aunty Esther who used to babysit me when she was just a junior justice broker in the firm.

"Why aren't you at the Geoff Joffrey show getting some Buzz?" Dad asks me.

"We were tired," I tell him with a shrug.

He shakes his head and grumbles, "No work ethic," but Esther winks at me and I snicker, which makes my father's face turn red. "Get out!" he yells.

Ara turns back toward the door, but I grab her arm and point toward the kitchen. "I'm starving," I whisper.

Ara clenches her jaw and stares at me hard. Like most people, she's terrified of my father. Not that I blame her. Especially as he stomps across the living room again, jabbing his finger at poor Esther while shouting, "How long did it last?"

"Not long," Esther says coolly. "Less than two minutes."

"Two minutes!" my father shouts. "Might as well have been the entire concert. Ten seconds is all it takes for everyone to tune out. Switch channels. Hit a sports event. Turn on a god-damn book! Two freaking minutes is the lifetime of a song!"

"Less than two," Esther explains evenly. "And the quality was terrible. Amateur stuff. Dark and fuzzy and the sound was distorted. Nobody will even remember by tomorrow."

"That's where you're wrong," Dad says. "This kind of breach makes me look weak! Wounded. Limping to my death. And right when Calliope Bontempi and her little brain activist group filed suit against us! You think that was a coincidence?"

"Calliope may have nothing to do with the hijacking," Esther reasons.

This stops me in my tracks. Ara squeezes my hand tight. "Tell them," she whispers but I shake my head. The last thing I want to do is add to my father's bad mood, so I keep moving toward the kitchen door, which feels miles away with the room tilting and whirling in my Jused-up state.

"Of course she has something to do with it!" Dad bellows. "It's all a part of her group's plan to ruin me. They're vultures. Circling. Waiting for me to die. But, if they take me down, we go back to a decade when genius was a genetic crapshoot and copyright protection was a joke and any schmuck could throw music on the Web and call it art."

I pretend to shoot myself in the head because I can't listen to him yammer on about *the dark ages of modern humanity* (total overstatement) before he *single-handedly revolutionized brilliance* (in his dreams) and *saved the cultural elite from being subsumed into the mediocrity of the lowest common denominator* (snore).

Another jolt from the Juse hits me just then and I collide with the corner of the curio cabinet that Mom left behind when she walked out years ago. The bump sends a tremor through her collection of songbird figurines. They skitter and skate across the glass shelves on their tiny breakable legs. The fragility of the birds mocks me and I double over, clutching at the wall, laughing too much, too hard, even though nothing's really funny.

"Goddamnit, Orpheus!" my father rages. "I told you to get the hell out of here!"

"Sorry!" I call, then drag Ara into the kitchen where we eagerly raid the fridge and cabinets.

Ara pulls out a carton of leftover Mexi-Chinese nacho noodles from the fridge. "This is it? This is all you have?" she says, but she digs in with her fingers anyway.

"Something's wrong with the sensors that are supposed to reorder the groceries and my father would never do something so gauche and beneath his social standing as reprogram an appliance," I tell her. As I'm complaining, a box zips down our delivery chute. Overhead, we hear the drone zoom off.

I run over, grab the box and rip into the contents like a coyolf disemboweling a rabbit. Socks and tea and toothpaste. "Oh, weird," I say, pointing to *Nobody from Nowhere* scrawled in black marker across a six-pack of disposable umbrellas. I toss everything aside when I spot a bag of Crickers, our favorite crunchy rice and cricket cracker. "Yahoo!" I yell. "Krispy Krab and Bakon!" And stuff a handful in my mouth.

Ara sprinkles a whole pack into her carton of leftovers, then slurps a Cricker-covered nacho noodle so hard it smacks her forehead, leaving a smudge of ChinCheez like a yellow-orange bindi jewel between her brows. I start to guffaw, but something lodges beneath my epiglottis and I choke. Ara rushes over and slaps me hard on the back.

"Breathe, man, breathe!" She laughs while smacking me, as if she's enjoying the whole thing a bit too much.

A projectile of Cricker sludge flies out of my mouth. Immediately, five tiny SpiderBots skitter over the countertop to take care of the mess as I giggle uncontrollably. "When is this stuff going to wear off?" I whine. "Damn Juse."

"I know, right?" Ara slumps beside me in hysterics. I lean torward her, ready for another kiss, but she pops upright, dancing foot to foot. "Oh my god, I think I'm going to pee myself."

"Bathroom's that-a-way," I say and point. Ara makes a run for it. I sigh as I watch her go. Will our timing ever be right?

When she's gone, Esther comes in the kitchen. "You two are wound up tonight," she says with a smirk, then places her gold-rimmed cup in the BevvyBot, pushes a button, and waits for it to refill.

I pull myself together and hunch close to her. "Hey listen, I didn't want to tell my dad but I had a very strange encounter with Calliope Bontempi tonight."

Esther chokes on her frothing, smoking cocktail. Liquid dribbles down her chin, which she dabs at with her sleeve. "Calliope Bontempi! What did she want?"

"As best as I can tell, she wants to bankrupt Chanson Industries, dismantle the music industry, get rid of all ASAs, and give music back to the people."

"Oh, is that all?" Esther says with a chuckle, which puts me more at ease.

I hop up to sit on the counter next to her and ask, "Does this kind of thing happen in other industries or do people come after Dad more often because he's such a jerk?"

Esther chuckles then says quietly, "His personality doesn't help matters, but the music industry has its own unique set of problems."

"I doubt that," I say.

"It's true," she says. "It all comes down to profit margins in the end."

"What's that supposed to mean?"

Esther leans back against the counter and crosses her arms. "Think of it this way: When your friend Quinby sells a piece of art, someone pays a big premium to have the original. The artwork itself becomes a collector's item and a status symbol for the owner. Even after the original sells, lots of digital copies will also sell, over and over and over to make more money, but it's the actual artifact that is rarefied and valuable. So art patrons make money off the original work and the digital reproductions and downloads, plus the shows and tie-in deals for movies and products that use the image—posters, coffee mugs, t-shirts, umbrellas." She points to the delivery items imprinted with copyrighted artwork scattered on the floor. "But with music, there is no original, big-ticket item. One song is not inherently more valuable than the next. It's always two minutes and thirty seconds of sound that gets played over and over, which has to butter our bread. That's why your dad came up with pay-for-play and put everything on the Stream. Before that, music had lost most of its economic value. People were used to music being nearly free and at their fingertips anytime they wanted it. Even though we have more control over the profits, music is still easier to steal than other kinds of art. People do it all the time."

I look away, flushed with guilt over the receiver in my Cicada.

Esther bites the side of her mouth. "Song pirates are like little mosquitoes buzzing around Chanson Industries's head. A few don't matter, but too many will drain us."

"Calliope's not a song pirate, though," I say.

"True," says Esther. "She's another kind of parasite looking for a payoff."

I shake my head. "She wants more than blood," I tell her, then quickly hush when Dad stomps into the kitchen for a refill on his drink, too.

Ara comes in the opposite door and Dad bellows, "Didn't you just have an ASA?" which makes Ara jump. She nods, looking terrified. "Which one?" he demands as the BevvyBot mixes him up another bourbon and lime.

"Music, of course," she says.

"Am I your patron?" he asks as if there is any other option in the western hemisphere.

She nods again.

"Good." He takes his drink and narrows his eyes at her, no doubt calculating profits. "Then our PromoTeam's doing an excellent job. She looks great, don't you think so, Esther?"

"Jeez, Dad!" I complain. "She's my friend. Not your commodity."

"Now she's both," he says with a dismissive little shrug.

I can't hide my disdain.

"Don't give me any crap, Orpheus." Dad slams his glass down on the counter. "ASAs cost a lot of money and my job is to make sure they pay off for people like Arabella here."

"But not for Calliope Bontempi?" I snap and immediately regret it. There's no reason to bait my father except the Juse hasn't quite worn off, so everything that pops into my mind falls out of my mouth.

He scowls at me. "That girl will be sorry she ever crawled out from whatever Plebe rock she's been living under." He points at Esther. "Hire private detectives. Turn over every stone. Do whatever you have to because I'm going to destroy that little con artist and whoever broke into my LiveStream."

"I'm already on it," Esther says.

"Good." My father turns back to me. "And you. What are we waiting for? All your classmates, including Ms. Lovecraft here, have gotten their ASAs and started their careers. So chop chop. I don't want a lazy moocher for a son much longer. It's time we schedule yours."

I shake my head, tired of the same old argument. "Tell that to Mom," I say, expecting him to blow a gasket.

Instead he cuts his eyes to Esther then says, "Don't you worry. We'll take care of your mother."

I cross my arms and stare at him. "With you, Dad, there's always a reason for me to worry."

VERSE TWO

ZIMRI

Every day in the warehouse is a Picker Symphony. Ticka. Ticka. Ticka. Ticka. Boom ba boom ba boom. With my Hand-Held strapped to my palm and an earbud in place, laying down the backing tracks of bings and bonks like the hi-hat and the bass, hitting me between my shoulder blades and down deep below my belly button. It might not be a secret concert on a hidden stage, but when I find the music in this job, I can dance ten miles of aisles under one giant warehouse roof without losing my mind.

I slide across the concrete floor, then stomp stomp stomp. Clap my hands above my head when the first item pops up on my HandHeld screen.

Girls panties, three pack, size 6x
Aisle 14Q
Unit 24
Bin AA

The earbud chirps numbers in my ear. "Nineteen, eighteen, seventeen . . ." I improvise a line over the melody. "Countdown," I sing. "Counting down now here we go!" And I'm off, basket in hand, running through the wide center aisle of sector Q. When I hit Row 14 a BING signals for me to turn—odd numbers on the right, evens on the left. I dash down for Unit 24 (25 units per row, so second to the last). Another BING, different tone, C natural? Right on time. Ten seconds to go. I find column A of Unit 25 (columns are in alphabetical order so I move far left) and reach up among the grid of bins (AA top left, AZ bottom right). And there they are. Girls panties, three pack, size 6X.

I scan them with my HandHeld. Wait for the PING! A high F#. The sound of happiness. Forever the note of success. "I got you, babe," I croon as I toss the panty pack in my basket along with the other items I've already gathered for some nameless, faceless Plute. *Da blomp* goes my HandHeld and I know the order is complete. I have a few seconds before the basket's due to hit the conveyor belt so, since nobody's around and I'm out of the sight line of the security cams, I press against the shelving unit and slip out the permanent market I keep in my pocket. I take one more quick peek over each shoulder to ensure that I'm alone, then I scrawl *Nobody from Nowhere* across the panty package, the tissue box, and the bag of six disposable umbrellas. With marker stowed, I skip to the end of the aisle and attach the basket to the conveyor and watch it travel up and up, where it will be carried overhead to the packing line and boxed up by human hands (Dorian's perhaps? Will he see my secret message? Or will it go unnoticed as usual?). Then finally, within an hour of the order being placed, it will be plucked from the rooftop by a drone and flown off to a delivery chute somewhere in the City.

Levon passes by. He presses his hand over his heart and mouths, *Thank you.* I nod then I high-five Merle—one of the few human forklift drivers left. He knew my dad. It's a small miracle we haven't been replaced by A.N.T.s yet, but we all know it's only a matter of time before automated nanotechnology takes over and all ten thousand of us navigating these aisles will become obsolete. The others grumble about the inevitability of that day but I know it will set me free, which is probably why I'm the only one here dancing.

And so . . . Ticka. Ticka. Ticka. Ticka. Boom ba boom ba boom. Countdown, here we go! Another order up.

At 10:25 a.m. we get our first tenner. Before Brie got demoted, we'd always grab a bevvie from the bot or head outside to the river for ten minutes of fresh air. Without her here, though, I don't bother. Instead, I hit the bathroom and drink straight from the faucet. The water bites with chemicals, but it's wet, as Nonda says, so it'll do. I sing as I slurp.

Veronica, Rhiannon, and Jolene come shuffling through the door, chattering and nattering away like squabbling squimonks. They've been this way since we were small. Veronica, forever the nicest of the three, is the only one to say hello.

I shoot water through the little gap in my front teeth. Jolene harrumphs at my misbehavior then clump clump clumps across the floor to ratchet down a paper towel and rip it from the dispenser. I like that sound, ratchet ratchet bzzzzt. Scratchy paper against tiny metal teeth. Jolene takes no notice of me repeating it. She's like a little bulldog, all head and chest with spindly legs. No wonder her times are so bad. She isn't built to be a picker. You have to be nimble and lithe—a rubber band ready to spring. I get my own paper towels. Two of them. Ratchet ratchet bzzzzt. Ratchet ratchet bzzzzt. Then I rub them together to get the shup-shup-shup of an old soft shoe beneath a melody I improvise.

"Can it, Zimri," Jolene chufs, tired of my noise.

Spoilsport! Always has been. I crumple up the towels and toss them in the trash.

"What's that song?" Veronica asks me.

"I don't know," I say. "Just something I was singing."

"Probably made it up like all her weird stuff." Jolene pushes past me to a toilet stall.

I see *Nobody from Nowhere* written in block letters on the outside of the door, but it's not my handwriting and that makes me grin.

"Can you believe what happened during Geoff Joffrey's LiveStream last night?" Rhiannon asks as she tucks a spiral of hair beneath her cap.

"That was insane," Jolene calls.

"What?" I ask. "Did he fall on his face?"

"Where were you? You didn't watch it?" Veronica asks.

"I had better things to do," I tell her with a smirk.

"Oh, girl, you missed it!" Rhiannon says. Then she and Veronica hem me in on either side, both nearly quaking with excitement. "Just as he was launching into his new song—"

" 'Your Eyes,' " Veronica says, looking dreamy, then they

break into a pitchy rendition of the chorus, "Your eyes shoot right through me like a laser beam! A laser beam!" and I clap my hands over my ears. It's bad enough that that song is in the Stream all day. I have to hear it here?

"Some crazy person in a black mask broke into the feed!" Rhiannon squeals.

"What?" The floor falls out from under me and I back up against the sink.

"Some girl was on a stage screaming like a lunatic," says Jolene as she busts out of the stall.

I straighten up, offended. "What do you mean, screaming?"

"She was singing," Veronica says, "but the sound was all messed up so you couldn't make out the song."

"None of it?" I ask.

"Nope," they say.

"How long did it last?" My legs are weak and shaky with excitement.

Rhiannon shrugs. "Not long. Like a minute or so."

I swallow hard as sweat pools under my arms. "Who was it? Does anyone know?" I can barely speak above a whisper.

"Brain activists probably," Rhiannon says.

"Or just some random nutjob," says Veronica.

"Whoever it was, they almost ruined the LiveStream," Jolene says. "Everybody was like, Wha . . . ? And then all of the sudden, poof! The screaming girl was gone and there was Geoff again." She sighs. "He's so cute!"

"We missed almost all of the song," Veronica complains.

"Yeah, but . . ." I look from face to face. "Was she any good?"

"Was who any good?" says Rhiannon.

"The girl who broke in?" I bite my lip.

"Who knows? The whole thing was dark and fuzzy and distorted, which is lucky for her because if she ever gets caught . . ." Veronica shakes her head.

"Bzzzzt!" Jolene says and pretends to zap her own brain. "She'll wind up a drooling idiot in a MediPlex." Then she laughs maniacally.

I turn away, shaky from the news. My mind reels through the possibilities of how my video feed made it onto the LiveStream at the Strip and whether anyone could have traced the signal. I have no idea how the whole thing works. I have to talk to Tati and I should warn Dorian. I hurry out of the bathroom. If I run, I'll make it to the break room by the packing line and grab him before the tenner's done, but as soon as I'm on the floor, Jude shouts my name like I've been hiding from him.

"Dammit," I whisper and slow myself down. "Hey, Jude. What's up?" I do my best to look normal even though my stomach's in my throat.

Jude scowls at me from the driver seat of his little electric car idling in the aisle. "Someone's here to see you."

"Who?" I ask, hand pressed against my chest to keep my heart from leaping out because no one comes to the warehouse unless there's bad news or you're in trouble.

"How should I know?" he grouches at me. "Two women from the city. I got a ping to send you up to the main office, that's all I know." He scrunches his face like the whole ordeal is giving him indigestion.

My heart pounds and my head spins. Could they have tracked my signal or used voice recognition even though Veronica says the audio was messed up? Did someone recognize me from the video? Or did someone at the concert squeal? Can I deny it? After all, my face was always hidden. At the very least, can I protect Dorian if they can finger me?

"Get in," Jude demands. "The quicker you get to the office, the quicker you're back on the floor and the less our times suck today. I don't have to tell you that corporate's been breathing down my neck for better times, do I?"

"No," I say, resigned. It's his favorite threat. We don't make our times and A.N.T.s will replace us all. "Guess I have to face the music," I say, then laugh at my own dumb pun as I climb in beside him.

We speed off through the aisles as everyone floods back onto the floor, eyes wide as we pass by, no doubt wondering why I'm being hauled off by our boss. Jude takes a sharp left, sending me sliding across the seat. I stop myself from crashing into him. Then he stops short next to the office. I brace myself against the dash.

He turns to me and waits. I know the procedure for unsanctioned breaks. I take out my earbud then unstrap my Hand-Held. He overrides the system to program in an additional tenner. "Make this snappy, would you?"

"Like this?" I try to snap my fingers but they're too shaky at the thought of who's behind the office door.

"No," Jude says because he's devoid of humor. "I mean take care of it in a hurry. I need your times to up the average. With Brie off the shift, we're sucking bad."

"Bring her back," I tell him.

64

He shrugs. "You know the rules," he says and takes off.

"Well, well, well, if it isn't Zimri Robinson!"

I turn to see Medgers in her security guard uniform step out from the shadow by Jude's office door and I know things must be bad. She's had it in for my family ever since my mom skipped bail and never returned. Over the years, she's hit Nonda with every PODPlex infraction she can muster. Her favorite accusation is "improper use of company property." Hang your wash out the POD window to dry—improper use of company property. Plant a patch of mint and basil in the dirt behind your building—improper use of company property. Paint your walls yellow to bring a little sunshine into your life—improper use of company property. And yes, those are all infractions Nonda has received. Not that she cares. We still sip fresh mint tea in our yellow POD while the laundry flaps in the breeze.

"What's going on?" I ask.

"Don't play dumb," Medgers says then grabs my elbow and yanks me into the office.

Inside, two women in fancy suits sit at the table. They motion for me to take a seat across from them. "I'm Private Detective Smythe," the one with dark brown hair says and holds out her hand, which I cautiously shake. "And this is my associate, Detective Beauregarde." The blonde nods then looks down at her screen, exposing black roots at her skull.

Smythe smiles, not really all that friendly. "We're here to investigate Project Calliope."

I blink. Then blink again. They wait. "Project Calliope?" I say slowly. They nod. My heart slows down and I ask, "What's that?"

Medgers snorts from her post slouched against the wall and gives me a nasty look.

Beauregarde says, "Are you currently involved with Project Calliope?"

"Not that I know of. Is that a Corp X thing?"

"Do you recognize this person?" Smythe shows me a picture of a pretty woman in her early twenties with blond hair, gray-green eyes, and a funny turned-up nose. "She used to work here, seven or eight years ago maybe."

"I'm only sixteen," I say. "I don't know what was going on here that long ago."

"What do you know about Harold Chanson and Chanson Industries?" Smythe asks.

"The music guy?" I say.

They nod.

"He's married to Libellule and has a big arena in the City and he owns all music." *And will zap your brain if you cross him,* I think to myself.

Smythe and Beauregarde both chuckle. Then Smythe looks over her shoulder at Medgers. "Why is she here?" she asks, pointing to me.

"Ask her about making music," Medgers says. A trickle of cold sweat drips down under my arm but I keep my face placid.

Smythe rolls her eyes as she turns back to me. "Do you make a lot of music?"

"Do I?" I ask with as much innocence as I can muster. "Does singing to myself count?"

Beauregarde sighs, miffed. "Do you have a band?"

"No."

"Does anybody that you know?" she asks.

"Nobody that I know," I say with complete honesty and a suppressed grin.

"Have you ever played copyrighted music for which you were paid?" Smythe asks.

"Honestly, ma'am . . ." I scoot way back in the chair so my feet don't touch the floor. I might be sixteen, but I can look twelve if I try. "I wouldn't know how to do something like that."

"Has Calliope Bontempi ever helped you put on a concert?"

"I don't know who that is," I tell them.

"This is Calliope Bontempi," Smythe says and shows me the pix of the green-eyed girl again.

I shake my head. "Never met her."

"You little liar," Medgers hisses. "She was friends with your mother. They played music together!"

"That's not true," I say.

"Yes, it is," she insists. "And after your mother got arrested, Calliope skipped town."

Every time my life intersects with Medgers, she kicks up my mom's past trangressions like radioactive dust.

"That was years ago. I was a little kid. Then my father died," I tell Smythe and Beauregarde. "I was only eleven."

Smythe cringes.

"And she put on a show and people paid her," Medgers adds.

"Is that true?" Beauregarde asks.

"Not exactly," I explain. "My mother was already gone when my father died." I bow my head, hoping to play to their sympathy or disgust. "So my grandmother was working double shifts to pay for his funeral and SQEWL for me until I could work at the factory when I turned fifteen. I sang after his funeral because I was sad. Then, separately, people helped my grandmother financially. Is that illegal?"

Beauregard puts hands on her hips and stares at me like she isn't sure whether I'm a little bit dense or smarter than I look.

"Oh, for crap's sake," says Medgers. I shoot her a dirty look. "Her mother ran out after she got caught doing the same damn thing."

"Not true," I say. "She was a DJ not a singer. She got nabbed for sampling and distributing over HandHelds."

Smythe and Beauregard look at each other, clearly horrified by the dregs of society on the other side of the river. "This is ridiculous," Smythe says and turns on Medgers. "It sounds to me like you have a personal vendetta against this girl's family for something that happened years ago. And frankly, this isn't worth our time. We've got bigger fish to fry with Project Calliope."

"What if she's part of Project Calliope?" Medgers snaps and points at me.

"There's no way a warehouse worker could hijack a Live-Stream with an illegal concert," Smythe says. She shakes her head at the mere thought of a Plebe like me doing such a thing.

"She could if she had help!" Medgers insists. "Check the feed from her HandHeld. That's how her mother and that lesbo hacker Tati from Old Town distributed their illegal music."

I unstrap my HandHeld and shove it at the detectives. "Go right ahead. Check it." I turn to Medgers. "I'm flattered you think me so capable."

Beauregarde waves my HandHeld away. "We're done here."

Relieved, I flash my best fake smile at Medgers, but in the back of my mind I'm hoping no one has thought to search my

POD because the digital recorders are still there, tucked away in one of my mother's neatly hidden cubbies.

As I follow the detectives to the door, Medgers grabs my arm and pulls me close to hiss in my ear, "I'm not as dumb as you think I am. I hear things. I put the pieces together. I know who you are."

"Me?" I yank my arm away. "I'm just a Nobody from Nowhere doing my job." Then I stomp out of the room, twice as determined to do it again.

ORPHEUS

Every Wednesday afternoon, my mother and I meet at the MediPlex to visit Alouette. The halls are quiet, only a few RoboNurses making rounds but no other human visitors. As usual, I'm on time but my mom is late, so I go inside Al's private room to wait.

The minute I walk in and see my sister lying in her bed, EarBug firmly in place, eyes trained on the ceiling, I relax. For some reason, I find the wheesh, whirl, and click of machines recording Alouette's vitals strangely hypnotic. Blood pressure, check. Respiratory rate, check. Cognitive brain function, nope. Still, as always, I'm glad to see her. I touch her hand then sing, *"Alouette, gentille Alouette,"* but she doesn't join in.

Al's eyes stay forward, never acknowledging, only occasionally blinking. She is a shriveled version of herself, young but terribly old, although I can still see her as a smaller version of my mother with my father's intense eyes. Lest anyone forget the promise of her beauty there are framed photos all around the room of Alouette in her prime. Birthday parties. SCEWL trips.

Goofing with her friends. Both of us sitting on a horse during a rare family vacation out west. It's as if my mom holds out hope that one day Al will wake up and need a refresher course on who she was ten years ago. Or maybe my mother wants to make sure the rest of us never forget.

When I was a little kid, I believed that Alouette could hear me. I was sure my words were seeping in and the songs she sang back had meaning if only I could decode them, but I never could. Instead, I developed all kinds of rituals to trigger her miraculous recovery. If I did everything in the right order, if I didn't make Dad mad (an impossible task), if I could get Mom to laugh (equally difficult at the time), if I brought all the exact right things—a bird's feather, a smooth piece of sea glass, a perfect snail shell—and if I touched the doorframe, but not the wall and only stepped on the green tiles and if I saw three birds on the way over and at least two of them were singing, then maybe, just maybe she'd emerge out of her dream state.

But no. Of course not. That was the magical thinking of a doofus six-year-old. Now, nearly a decade later, I'm clear. This is it for Alouette—a bed in a long-term MediPlex surrounded by Mom's songbird fetish. Songbird sheets. Songbird pillows. A songbird clock that plays different calls every fifteen minutes. And scattered on every surface, more flightless figurines. Like my father, the woman knows no subtlety. Yes, Mother, yes, your prized songbird is forever caged.

The clock strikes the hour with the persistent name-chanting song of the whippoorwill which Alouette repeats, "Whip-poor-will! Whip-poor-will!" Although her hearing wasn't affected, the doctors say her brain can no longer process meaning, only echo back what she hears as songs. Over the years, she's become an expert at reproducing the birdcalls— the slurry song of a summer tanager, the metallic trills of the veery, the lazy whistles of a meadowlark. I sing the three whip-poorwill notes back to her so it feels as if I'm part of her conversation, until she changes the subject and hums the chorus to the new Geoff Joffrey tune called "Your Eyes." It's been near constant on the Stream this week, which Al gets through her EarBug, an amenity my father happily pays for since the least he can do is make sure she's well cared for now and in the future.

Mom arrives a few minutes later in a long, flowing Japanese kimono embroidered with tiny dragonflies that she used to wear as a robe but has reworked into some kind of wrap dress. And of course, she looks stunning. My mother is still beautiful—tall and lanky with big eyes, a sharp nose, and a long elegant neck. She looks like a large wading bird as she walks through the door with open arms, her ornate sleeves fluttering out behind her.

"Orphie, baby," she croons and pulls me into a long, perfumed hug. "How lovely to see you!" She lets go of me and plants a firm kiss on my sister's forehead, then fusses with Al's hair before dropping down in a new easy chair that wasn't here last week. "Can you believe someone would get rid of this?" She runs her hand over the soft brown fabric and pats a bright blue speckled pillow.

"Where'd you find it?" I eye the thing, wondering if she and her behemoth boy toy Chester dragged it off some street corner, which is how she furnishes her apartment since she left my dad.

"Rajesh's mother gave it to me," she says lightly.

"Seriously?" I ask, not sure which is worse, my friend's mom feeling sorry for my mother for walking away from our life or my mother dumpster diving like a Plebe.

"I re-covered it and made the pillows from fabric I got for a song at a thrift shop." She smiles, very proud. "I thought I'd forgotten how to sew, but it came right back to me. Made me think of all the crazy outfits I created when I first started out."

"You could be a stylist." I sit at the end of Al's bed.

She props her stocking feet up beside me and says, "No thank you," with exaggerated zeal. "Any proximity to the music industry is too close for me. I'm thinking of opening an upholstery business called Re-covering Recovery." She laughs. "Because I'm in recovery and I'd be re-covering furniture. Get it?"

I roll my eyes. "Mom, if you have to explain the joke . . ."

"Well, I think it's funny anyway." She shrugs off my dig, then settles me with a serious look. "Is your father still pressuring you?"

"Record time." I pretend to check the clock. "Less than five minutes and here we go. How about if we talk about something other than my ASA for once?"

"Orphie, honey, just hear me out. Your father never would, but you owe me that, don't you?"

Part of me wants to tell her that I don't owe her squat. She might be the fun and kooky mother that all of my friends adore with her crazy stories of stardom, but when it comes to actual parenting skills, she doesn't score much better than my father.

As if she's reading my mind, she says, "I know I wasn't a good mom when you were little." She leans over and wraps her warm fingers around my ankle. "But I'm trying to be better now," she adds.

I settle back on my elbows because once my mom gets started, the only thing to do is sit back and listen.

"I was so self-absorbed back then. That's what years and years in the industry will get you. A big false sense of self-importance when really you're just a balloon with nothing inside but hot air. Thin-skinned and easy to deflate. If I had been stronger . . ."

She stops and scans Alouette's room as if she's seeking solace in the songbirds all around. "I was just so young when I started. I never had a chance to get myself grounded. To find my center." She presses her fist against her sternum. "I was only a little younger than you are now and the drug use didn't help."

"I know, Mom. You were self-made. You had to scramble and scrape for everything you could get. . . ."

"God, that's for sure!" She throws herself back in the chair and launches into a speech I've heard dozens of times. "There were no patrons then and most record deals had dried up except for the biggest, most established acts. When I started out you had to spend all your time creating your own media presence to get noticed but nobody wanted to *buy* your music back then. Everybody expected you to give away your music for free. Download this! Stream that for pennies! Yes, please take the rights to my song and play it in your tampon commercial! It's good exposure. I don't need to eat.

"The only real money a working musician could make was off of touring, but the big-name acts had the venues booked up tight and boy did they stick together! It was this circle-the-wagons, keep-the-riffraff-out, protect-your-own mentality that made it nearly impossible for anyone new to break in."

"But you did. You broke in," I remind her. "You got lucky."

"Luck's a funny thing," Mom says. "You only get it if you work hard enough to be ready when you're standing in the right place at the right time."

Despite her faults, I respect how my mother started from the bottom.

"Now I'm here!" She tosses her arms open wide and cracks up as if that's the funniest thing ever.

"You were in the Buzz the other day," I tell her. "Another mini biopic. This one was called *Libellule: The Last Self-Made Pop Star.*"

Mom rolls her eyes but I see a little grin. "Oh, let me guess! It started with footage of me dancing in the flatbed of a pickup truck parked in the wreckage of Times Square." She sings the opening lines of "Pickup Truck in the City," a country-infused pop song with a disco beat that first garnered her some attention. "Then they moved on to 'Sugar Smack' with DJ LazyEye slapping my bikini-clad ass as I strutted around him."

I shudder at the memory of Ios strutting past me during summer camp, singing the song that catapulted my mother to a level of stardom she never expected. But Mom has confided in me that that kind of fame came with a price. LazyEye didn't stop slapping her around when the video ended. It took her years to extract herself from a relationship with him and then she landed with my father, which was only a half-step up the self-respect ladder, if you ask me. He never laid a hand on her, as far as I know, but his words could be nearly as hurtful.

Next, Mom puts on her best Buzz-worthy announcer's voice. "And every spectacular moment after that—her breakdowns, her burnouts, her phoenix-like returns! Until at twenty-five, at the pinnacle of her career, she recorded the last duet ever with Taylor Swift, the grande dame of pop stardom." She looks at me. "Am I right?"

"Bravo," I say. "Spot on." But no matter how much Mom tries to persuade me the music industry is no place for me to land, I know she loved almost every moment of her career and probably still misses it. "But if you had to do it over again, would you?" I ask.

Mom thinks, then says, "There's only one thing I regret."

I lean forward, eager to hear.

She reaches out for my sister's hand. "Alouette." We stare at one another. Her lip quivers. "Which is why I don't want your father to force you to have an ASA. I couldn't stand it if . . ."

"Mom, it's different now," I assure her, but the truth is, I'm scared, too. Dad swears it was a fluke that Alouette's surgery left her like this. But what if he's wrong? What if the problem was genetic and I wind up staring at the ceiling doing birdcalls for the rest of my life, too?

"Your father is a bully. He's controlling and emotionally abusive and has the emotional IQ of a toddler," Mom says angrily.

"It doesn't help when you try to fight with him through me," I tell her.

"You're right!" She holds up her hands and sighs. "I just want to help you. I want you to know you're not required to have an ASA."

"Oh, really?" I say, sarcasm dripping. I hop off the bed and begin to pace. "Dad will disown me if I don't and I won't be able to get a job without being some kind of crazy genius."

"That can't be true," she says. "If you find something you like to do. For example . . ." She stops to think.

I stand across from her and laugh. "I'll give you five hundred bucks if you can tell me one thing I like to do."

"Well," she says, biding her time. "You used to like building cars with your Blox."

"When I was *seven*."

"You could be a car designer!"

"For me to be a mechanical engineer, I'd need to go to an academic school, not a Plute playground for the future famous. And I'd still need a spatial reasoning ASA to be more than a low-level worker."

"Okay, fine," she says, waving away that example. "But when you really think about your future, Orpheus, when you think about what you want to be, what is it that you imagine yourself doing?"

"I don't know," I mumble, but that's a lie. I do know. I peer up at her. She smiles gently as if she's truly interested in what I want in life.

"I want to make music," I tell her and she looks surprised. "But not as a performer. I'm not like you or Alouette." We both glance at my sister, remembering all her promise as a kid, jumping up on stage any chance she got. "I don't like to be front and center. But when I hear songs, I know how I could make them better. And I don't mean how to improve the singer's look or by planting stupid stories in the Buzz to get more attention. I mean I want to work on the actual song itself."

"Like an old-fashioned producer!" Mom laughs, delighted. "I could see you doing that, Orpheus. You'd be good at it."

I shake my head. "Dad won't let me. He has no intention of handing over the reins of the company to me unless I get an ASA. He says business is cutthroat. That you have to be dispassionate and decisive, fully focused on the music. 'In this world,'" I say in my best grumbling Dad voice, "'either you're a genius or a loser.'"

Mom scowls. "Despite what he might think, your father isn't the ruler of the world."

"No, but he is the ruler of the music industry."

Mom lifts an eyebrow. "That won't last forever."

"Sure," I snort, disbelieving.

"Listen, honey, I'm here to tell you, the PONI life isn't bad. You can find something you love to do and be very happy without all the crap that comes with being a Plute celeb. Big houses, flying cars, constantly being in the public eye. Personal fulfillment is better than public success."

"Easy for you to say," I mumble. "You've had both."

"No, not easy for me to say at all," she insists. "My life might not look like much to you, but it's hard-won, Orpheus. I'd like to save you the trouble of going through everything I had to endure just to get right here."

I sigh and slump back onto Al's bed as confused as ever. "I wish I could be happy without an ASA," I tell her. "I truly do. I see what all my friends go through and I think it might not

be worth it. Sometimes, I just want to walk away, but . . ."
I trail off.

"Just promise me this," Mom says and reaches for me again.
"Promise me you won't do anything rash or stupid before I have
a chance to take care of your father."

"Funny," I tell her. "He thinks he's taking care of you."

ZIMRI

After my "interview" with Smythe and Beauregarde, I stomp through the rest of my shift, half furious that Medgers is picking on me again, and half nervous that she'll drag the detectives to my POD and demand to look around before I get home. Clueless, yet defiant that she has nothing to hide, Nonda might let them in. So, as soon as the final buzzer sounds at the end of our shift, I bolt from the warehouse. I don't even wait to see Brie during the switch. Instead, I shoot her a quick ping saying something important came up, then I run home as fast as I can. Luckily, when I arrive everything is in order and Nonda's not there. I grab the digital recorders from the nook where they've been hiding beside my bed and jog along the riverpath toward Tati's in Old Town.

When I hit the bend in the river—where Nowhere hides—I turn east off the path, hop a fence, and climb through a bramble patch into the cracked and weedy parking lot of Black Friday, the Corp X cut-price megastore filled with factory rejects and overstock where most of the warehouse workers shop. In the vacant lot, beneath one working light, a group of guys loiter around a trashcan.

"Hey Zim! Zimri!" the one with an old sailor's cap calls as I jog past. He raises a glass bottle of Tati's finest Juse in salute.

"Hey there, Captain Jack," I yell back. Jack was my dad's best friend when they were boys, then they worked side by side in the warehouse until my dad died. A year ago, Jack's arm got crushed in a bailer at the warehouse and he lost his job. The money from my first concert went to him after the Corp X–assigned justice broker worked a crappy deal that said Jack had to pay Corp X back for the damage his arm did to the bailer.

"You don't stop to talk anymore?" he yells.

"In a hurry!" I tell him.

"Go on then," he waves. "Don't let us slow you down."

Lots of PODPlex folks tell their children never to go to Old Town. If you're not originally from here, it probably seems seedy with all its abandoned buildings turned into "dens of iniquity" as Tati likes to say with pride. Need some Juse? Go to Old Town. Want black market electronics? Old Town is your place. Anything you can't get from the warehouse or Black Friday, you can probably find in Old Town if you know where to look. It's cash-only down here, no COYN accepted because Corp X has nothing to do with this self-supporting economy. *By the people, for the people* is Tati's favorite joke, as if she's a socialist and not a pure anarcho-capitalist who'd sell anything at the right price.

But I see something different when I jog down the empty streets here. This is where Nonda grew up and went to a school with real books and classes in art and music. Not just a place that teaches you how to be a good future employee like Corp

X's Special Quality Education for Workforce Life facility where Brie, Dorian, and I went. This is where my mom and dad were raised. I grew up on their stories of the starry ceiling and velvet curtains in the Paramount movie theater, parties in the Oak Room with live bands or deejays, church suppers, and card games, when the community was built by the people and not by a faceless corporation.

Then Corp X came in and bought up all the land surrounding the town for their behemoth business. They plowed down everything except what's left in the center of the town to build their warehouses, PODPlexes, and the Strip. They try to pass off Complex life as the community of the future. Since they're the only employer within hundreds of miles, people don't have much choice. Either you work for Corp X (and your POD rent, plus health insurance, and justice brokerage fees come out of your monthly COYN) or you scrape by on your own in Old Town.

So when I jog past the abandoned Paramount theater (its blue sign faded to gray), the dilapidated school (where Brie and I used to play), and the church caving in from neglect, I see a dying tree that's compartmentalized itself—first the foliage went, then the birds fled, and entire branches withered and died. But I know that the roots are still here, deep underground, trying to sustain what little life is left.

At Tati's shop, I hop up on the porch and stop to catch my breath while smiling for the cameras—Tati's first line of defense against a raid. Whenever an electronics company gets wind of what Tati does, they send security agents to shut her down. They come in the front, she goes out the back. She claims she doesn't care when they haul her gadgets to the electronics dump a few miles outside of town. They've cleaned her out many times but she just waits a week or so then goes back to the dump, digs out everything, fixes it all up again, and reopens for business.

Inside the shop, the shelves are loaded with her illegally refurbished transmitters, receivers, speakers, remotes, Hand-Helds, and old-model tablets no self-respecting Plute would still carry around. Mom told me once that Tati was the smartest person she ever met and I don't doubt it. The woman knows how to break apart, put together, fix and mix anything with more than two parts.

"Zimri, Zimri, Zimri." Tati comes through the curtain, wiping her hands on a rag and shaking her head. I've out-stripped her by several inches in the past year but she still outweighs me by at least twenty pounds. She's short and com-pact. All curves. Men love her but she doesn't care. Her heart belongs to Brie's mom and vice versa. "Girlie, what am I going to do with you? Mm-mm-mm."

"What?" I ask. "What did I do now?"

"Don't play dumb with me." She leans against the counter and smiles. "How'd you hijack the Stream?"

I hop up onto the counter beside her. "I was hoping you could explain that to me, because I have no idea." I dig the video camera out of my pocket and hand it over.

"Well . . ." She scratches her head as she studies the little machine. "Your mom and I used to hack around a lot with a video setup. Did you use that old laptop?"

I nod.

"I'd have to take a look again but my guess is, we set a signal to bounce off some satellite that happened to line up perfectly with you last night. I just wish I'd known you were going to do it so I could have gotten the sound quality better."

"I'm glad you didn't," I tell her. "A couple of private detectives questioned me at the warehouse today. They weren't happy but they figured I couldn't be the culprit. They said, 'How could a little sixteen-year-old Plebe be smart enough to hijack a LiveStream?'"

Tati tosses her head back and laughs long and hard. "Wish I could have seen all those clueless Plute faces when you broke in." She drops her jaw and bugs out her eyes.

"You think they could trace it?" I ask her.

"Nah, the signal probably looked like it was coming from Europe or South Africa. We always made sure to hide our IP addresses and make them bounce around. I wouldn't worry about it. Unless you're planning to do it again."

"You know I will," I say.

"Just like your mama," she says with pride, and I blush.

"I want to release the audio," I tell her as I pull out the audio recorder. "I played with Dorian last night."

"Marley's son?" Tati asks, eyes wide, and I smile. "Mm-mm-mm." She shakes her head. "You got him around your little finger, huh?"

"No," I say, but my chest warms at the thought of kissing him by the river.

"Funny how history has a way of repeating," Tati mutters. Then she tosses her rag on the counter and grabs a heavy ring of keys. "Come on. I'll take you over to the house. I have to check on some things anyway."

"Hey, do you remember a friend of my mom's called Calliope Bontempi?" I ask as we head out the back door.

"Sure. I'd forgotten all about her until she popped up in the Buzz this week," Tati says as she locks up. "She was real young when she showed up at the warehouse. Sixteen, seventeen years old. Pretty little gal. Sad as could be. Seemed traumatized. Rainey took her under her wing. Sometimes Calliope would sing out at Nowhere with them. She was around for a while then disappeared after your mom left."

"The detectives were snooping around about her, too. They think Calliope was behind the hijacking."

"Good," Tati says, laughing. "Let them think that. Idiots."

For years, Tati's let me stash my transmitting gear in the old house where Nonda raised my mother. Inside, the first floor is empty except for some bottles scattered around and burn marks on the floor from where someone once tried to start a fire. Tati taught me that the key to a good hiding place is to make it look just suspicious enough to take it off the radar of anyone who might be snooping. Too messy and they'll make assumptions. Too clean and they'll look harder for what you're trying to hide. If someone came in here, they'd think it was just another vacant house where the underbelly gathers. What they wouldn't know is that Tati has a Juse distillery in the basement and upstairs, beneath the peaked roof, is an antenna we've built from scavenged parts.

Tati moves a bookshelf to get down into the basement while I run up the creaking steps to the attic where the air is thick enough to make me sneeze. I turn on the lights to illuminate my father's old paintings. Dark studies of the river, swirling clouds about to rain, and several portraits of my mother. She was gorgeous back then. Tall and strong, with the same nose as me and a gap between her teeth that was handed down from Nonda to my mother to me. But most of the resemblance is in our hair.

Like my mother, I keep mine short on the sides and let the top grow wild and free. Nonda would prefer I braid it, but I like my hair au naturel. Sturdy tendrils wind their way out from my skull like sweet-pea vines searching for something to climb. At night, I rub my hair with shea butter and tea tree oil just like my mother did, then twist it up to sleep. In the morning, I run my fingers through until it puffs out like a dandelion gone to fluff.

After paying my respects to my parents, I pull the tarp off my setup. I love the way it looks—tidy black boxes with little knobs and switches begging to be tweaked. Then I hop on the stationary bike Tati and I installed to crank up the generator and I pedal fast. When the battery is juiced up enough, I transfer my audio file to the box. It only takes a minute for the whole concert to upload. Then I set the timer. For a brief half hour starting at midnight tonight the transmission will reach anyone within a five-mile radius who's scanning the waves. Finally, I disconnect the recorder, erase the contents, cover everything up again, and slip out.

The minute I get back to our POD, I know something's not right. The apartment seems too still. Everything is just as I left it when I popped in an hour ago. There are no shoes in the foyer. No cooking smells. No gentle sounds of Nonda singing to herself or snoring from the couch. It's as if she hasn't been here all day.

My heart slams against my rib cage. Since I was little, there's been a part of my brain that fears the worst every time I get home and no one's here. It's not a stretch to figure out why. I had just turned ten when my mom took off, and was barely eleven when my father took the plunge. Not that it was a surprise. He'd been slipping away synapse by synapse for months, especially after my mother left. By the time he threw himself off the bridge into the river, he was barely present anymore. Even his body had shrunk down to almost nothing because he hardly ate.

I check everywhere in the POD, but unlike last night with Marley and Dorian, this time Nonda does not appear. "Where did you go?" I whisper as I look out the window into the night. Most likely she got confused again. Maybe she went out looking for me and lost track of time. She probably got turned around and is wandering again. I ping her with my HandHeld, knowing it's a long shot. The older she gets, the more she resents any device. Says they're an affront to her personal liberty. I jump when I hear a faint noise coming from the sofa. For a moment I wonder if Nonda could have fallen between the cushions. She's gotten so small in the past few years she just might fit. I shove my hand in that soft place and pull out her HandHeld, blinking and pinging with my message.

A voice deep inside my head starts screaming, *This is your fault. You're selfish. Hurting everyone around you so you can make your music.* I know that voice. It's my father, yelling at my mom before she left. Now I've gone and done the exact same thing.

I wasn't here for the person who needs me and loves me most because I wanted to play my stupid songs on the stupid radio for the one random stranger who might be listening. How could I be so selfish? Especially when it comes to Nonda—the only person who protected me when our family fell apart?

ORPHEUS

As much as I want to see my sister, I'm relieved to get out of the MediPlex and away from the endless back-and-forth between my parents. From inside my Cicada, I ping Arabella to let her know I'm free because we've been missing each other all day. First she was at a movie premiere, then a fashion show while I was visiting Al, and now she's at an after-party for the release of a horror novel called *The School for Broken Children* in an old college where everyone is dressed as scholars as a joke. We agreed to meet for dinner, just the two of us at The Deep End, the hottest CelebuChef restaurant in the City, then we'll hit another premiere or maybe a concert, depending on how we feel and how much Buzz Ara stills needs.

While I wait for her reply, I turn on my receiver and scan the waves for pirate radio on my way into the Distract. But then my dad calls. Not even a ping, but a real live video connection, which can't be good. Quickly I stash the receiver as he appears on my WindScreen.

"Orpheus! What the hell have you done?" he demands. "Who the hell have you been talking to?"

"Hello to you, too," I say.

"It's all over the Buzz!" he yells as he paces his office, drink in one hand and the lights of the Distract behind him.

"What is?" I ask.

"That you're refusing to have an ASA!" He gesticulates wildly, sloshing bourbon on his shoes.

"I never said that."

"It must have been your mother then."

"Couldn't be," I tell him. "I was just with her at Alouette's."

"Well someone said it," he snarls. "The media is having a field day." He points to his giant wall screen where the Buzz is chaotic with images of our family.

I scroll through the headlines on my ExoScreen. Sure enough, he's right. It's everywhere.

"How do you think this makes me look?" he rages. "My own son, a freeloader, never worked a day in his life, now refuses the very thing that's made our family fortune."

"For the fiftieth time, I'd gladly work if you'd let me! There are lots of jobs at Chanson I could do."

"Is that so?" Spit flies from his mouth, leaving droplets on the camera eye. "What can you do besides be charming and appeal to a broad range of people? You're no genius yet!"

My face stings like he slapped me. "If I don't know how to do anything, that's your fault. You're the one who sent me to SCEWL. Which was a joke! All they do is groom CelebuTantes for fame."

"Which is exactly what I need from you. The heir apparent to my empire. You're supposed to look good and not screw it up. Now all you need is an ASA and this family stays in business."

"No, *you* stay in business, Dad! But what about me? What if that's not what I want?"

"You selfish little . . ." Now Dad is so mad, he's muttering. "I worked for everything this family has. I found your mother in the gutter and resurrected her career. I saw the writing on the wall for the entire music industry before anybody else did and I saved it. I bought the dead copyrights to huge catalogs of music then solved the digital distribution problem. You play a song, you pay. End of story. Before that, music had become a useless commodity aimed at the lowest common denominator of society. Anybody could shake their ass, auto-tune their voice, and give away a song for free on the Internet until I fundamentally changed the industry. And I did it all for you. But you'd throw it all away!"

"That's exactly what Calliope said you'd say!"

For a moment, my father looks startled. Then he recovers and slowly walks toward his camera so he looms large on my screen. "What are you doing talking to Calliope Bontempi? Are you on her side?"

"No, of course not," I say. "She cornered me. I told Esther."

He marches away, screaming, "If you or your mother or Calliope Bontempi think you can take me down, you're all sadly mistaken! I'm smarter than all of you combined."

"Or just greedier," I call after him.

He spins around and opens his arms wide as if to absorb my insult. "That's right! I'm a greedy man! But I'm doing the best I can for this family. So just you remember this, Orpheus."

He skulks toward the screen, poking at the air. "You are nothing without me. Do you understand?" He shoves his finger in the camera lens. "Nothing but a piece of crap on the bottom of my shoe. And I'm tired of you mooching off of me. You come to my office right now. I don't want you seen in public until we fix this Buzz debacle."

"No way," I tell him. "I'm not coming there. I have plans with Arabella."

"Cancel them," he growls. "Cancel everything. I made you an appointment. You're going in for an ASA tomorrow."

For a moment, I'm speechless. I sit and stare at him, trying to process what he just said. Finally, I blurt out, "No. I won't do it. It's my body. My brain. I have a say in my future."

"As long as you're under my roof and I'm footing the bills, your body, your brain, and your future belong to me!" Dad declares.

"Fine," I tell him. "Then I won't be under your roof anymore!" I disconnect.

Since I can't go home and I don't dare show up in the Distract with this much Buzz going on, I tell the Cicada to land while I figure out what to do. The car leaves our flight platoon and swirls off the SkyPath, looking for an empty space among the blanket of lights sprawling from the Distract center all the way out here on the edges of the City. On the WindScreen map I see that we're approaching the Alibaba E-Gaming Arena parking lot, a vast expanse of blacktop surrounding a 100,000-person dome. When we touch down, I call Mom.

Her beautiful face fills my WindScreen. The camera is still kind to her. "Calm down, Orpheus," she says when I tell her what Dad did. "Just take a deep breath." She inhales long and loud then closes her eyes and lets the air go slowly like a leaking tire.

"Mom!" I yell so her eyes pop open. "Breathing is not going to help me right now. What am I going to do?"

"You're overreacting!" She smiles sweetly. "Your whole life is in front of you. What I would give to be your age again! So much to experience . . ."

"Mom! Are you even listening to me? He scheduled me for an ASA."

"Doesn't surprise me," she says with a snort that disrupts her calm composure.

"And who's talking to the media?" I ask, bewildered. "I never told anyone I didn't want an ASA. I hadn't even made up my mind yet."

"Yes, you had, darling," Mom says. "I could tell. You didn't want that life."

"You only hear what you want to hear," I tell her and look out the window while I sulk for a few seconds. Cars are beginning to enter the lot. I check my WindScreen feed and see the Dota 26 Playoffs start in an hour. Soon this place will be crawling with humanity like everyplace nearby. I sigh and turn back to my mom. "Anyway, I need a place to stay. If I show up at home, he'll drag me off to surgery tomorrow."

Just then, Chester struts past behind Mom's sofa. He's bare-chested, as usual. Sometimes I wonder if the man owns any shirts. When he sees me on Mom's screen, he stops and leans over her shoulder so his stupid face takes up half my Wind-Screen. "What's this, a Plute pity party?"

"Shush, Chester," says Mom. "Harold has upset Orpheus."

"Boo-hoo," he whines. "Daddy won't buy you the latest flying car?"

"Shove it, Chester," I say. "This doesn't concern you."

"I think it does concern me if you're looking to crash here," he says. "Didn't your mother tell you the news yet?" He backs up a bit so I can see a fresh tattoo of a dragonfly with my mother's name, *Libellule,* in script across his heart.

"Mom?" I say. She looks everywhere but at me.

"You want me to tell him?" Chester asks, smiling slowly.

"Oh, now . . ." Mom's flustered. She fluffs the pillows all around her and readjusts her dress. "It's not that big of a deal."

"Hey, whoa, that hurts!" Chester frowns.

She turns and pats his arm. "I didn't mean it that way. I meant it in terms of Orpheus. I mean it won't affect him much."

"It will if he wants to stay here!" says Chester.

Mom turns back to me. "You are always welcome in my home," she says.

"But it's not just your home now," Chester says.

I clench my jaw. "Mom?"

She crosses one arm over her stomach and puts her other hand to her mouth. "Well now, you see, the thing is . . . Chester has moved in with me."

"Great," I say. "I'll be sure to send a housewarming gift." Then I disconnect and refuse to answer when she tries to ping me back.

Furious and frustrated, I get out of my car to walk off some steam. More cars stream in from the SkyPath overhead and the terrestrial SwarmPath circling the Distract a few miles away. I can't believe my mother has allowed that cretin to move in. Now I have no place to go.

Desperate for advice, I call Arabella. Not a ping but an actual video call. I need to see her face on my ExoScreen. But she doesn't pick up. Instead, she pings me back.

Still at the party. Geoff Joffrey just walked in.
Piper says I MUST get pix with him. Do you
know him? Can you help?

>> Can't that wait? I need to talk to you.
>> Something big came up.

Bigger than Geoff Joffrey?

>> Yes! My father's forcing me to have an ASA.

Good for you! Exciting.

>> No! That's not what I want.

Come here. Intro me to Geoff then we can
talk.

>> I don't know him. Can't intro you.

Why not? You're a Chanson!

"Damnit!" I yell out loud.

>> Is that all I'm good for? My last name?

Forget it! I'll find someone else to help.
Gotta go. I'm supposed to be working!!!!

She disconnects, leaving me abandoned in the midst of gamers dressed in hero garb, flooding out of their vehicles into

AutoTrams that will carry them to the dome. As a last-ditch effort, I reach out to Rajesh who, by some miracle, answers. He's in his house, his stylists flitting around him, pomping up his hair.

"Orph, my man! What's up? Your girl is getting mad Buzz at the scholar party. Are you headed that way?"

"No, I've got a problem." I spill the whole story. My dad. My mom. Arabella.

"Orpheus, come on, man," Rajesh says, as if he's bored. He stands up from his salon chair and tries on different bowties as we talk. "Get in the game, would you? Just get the dumb surgery and start your life already. You're getting left in the dust. Another year as a PONI and the Buzz will abandon you altogether as the dilettante son of a patron."

"But what if I don't want a life in the limelight?"

Rajesh screws up his face and shakes his head. "What's that supposed to mean?"

"I don't know!" I throw my hands into the air and look up into the sky. Somewhere far away the stars shine, but you can never see them this close to the Distract. "Sometimes I just think I want something quieter, behind the scenes, you know?"

"No," says Rajesh with a snort. "If that's the way you feel, then I don't know what to tell you." He disconnects. I stand there speechless. My best friend hung up on me.

Overhead, a large platoon of tricked-out flying cars circles the center of the Dome as it opens like a flower for them to land. Must be the superstar gamers come to play. Trailing them is a comet tail of 'razzi drones, swooping down upon the parking lot, making a beeline for the entrance along with all the fans.

I pace around my car muttering to myself, "My father is a tyrant. My mother has moved in with a jerk. And my two best friends don't care."

Out of the corner of my eye, I see one of the 'razzi leave its swarm and swoop around toward me, then it hovers just behind my Cicada, green eyes blinking. No doubt it has built-in recognition software and now I've been found. Sure enough, within seconds, more drones peel off from the swarm and head in my direction. I need to get away. Away from the Distract, from the City, far away from my father and nowhere near my mom and Chester.

I climb back in the Cicada and take off, uncertain where I'm going, but sure that I can outrun the 'razzi that are trailing me. Inside, I turn off the WindScreen, rip off my glove so I don't have to talk to anyone. Then I grab my flask of Juse and chug as I turn on my receiver, scanning the waves for a friendly voice to carry me away as my car lifts up to the SkyPath leading away from the chaos of the City.

ZIMRI

"Sorry," I tell Dorian when he meets me outside the security office. "I didn't know who else to call with Brie working nights and Tati all the way in Old Town and . . ."

"Don't apologize!" Dorian says. He opens his arms and pulls me into a huge hug. I feel so safe that I don't want to let go.

"Maybe we should look for Nonda first." I eye the security office warily. I have no interest in tangling with Medgers again today.

"If she doesn't have her HandHeld . . ." Dorian says, and I know he's right. She could be wandering around anywhere and we'll never find her. "The best thing to do is file a report and let security do its job." Dorian takes my hand. "Come on," he says and pulls me toward the entrance.

I hate the Complex security office. Ever since my mother's cyber hearing, it's given me the heebie-jeebies. I remember holding my father's hand as we walked into the room where Mom sat at a table with some schlubby guy who'd been sent by the Justice Consortium that repped all the Corp X warehouse workers whenever they got into trouble. A screen, divided into two panels, took up half the wall, dwarfing the rest of us. In the first panel was the Arbiter, an older woman with dark skin and hair set off against the bright red of her robe. She was stern and imposing, like the giant head of God sitting in judgment. And in the other panel was a young woman with bright blue eyes, shiny blond hair, and skin so light it was nearly iridescent. She looked like a picture from an old book. I'd never seen someone so white.

My mother glanced over and motioned for me to join her at the table. I was no slouch. I got the picture right away and sidled up alongside her, leaning against her as cute as I could be.

Her justice broker glanced at me and frowned, but the Arbiter asked, "Is this your daughter?"

My mother nodded then put her arm around my waist to hug me tight against her body. The Arbiter twisted her face, like she was seeing my mother in a different light. I smiled sweetly and laid my head on Mom's shoulder. The blue-eyed woman on the other screen said, "Hi, honey," to me and I waved, thinking she might be on our side, too.

"Do you have a song for them?" my mother whispered.

I lifted my head and broke into "You Are My Sunshine" and the Arbiter's face relaxed into a smile. But the blue-eyed woman said, "As we own the copyright to that song, I'd like to request that she cease and desist with her performance."

"The child?" the Arbiter asked.

"Yes," the woman said. That's when I realized she was the justice broker for the other side—the people charging Mom with stealing music.

The Arbiter sighed and straightened her red robe. "Request granted," she said and the trial began.

Inside the security office I groan out loud and turn around to leave when I see Medgers at the desk, but she catches sight of me before I can get out the door. "Well, well, well," she says. "If it isn't Little Miss Above-the-Law."

I steel myself against her snide remark. "I'm here about Nonda, my grandmother."

Medgers stands up and pushes her Taser belt down around her hips. "And here I thought you had come to turn yourself in."

Dorian glances at me. "For what?"

Medgers leans over the counter and looks hard at me. "Maybe you could fool those two idiot investigators, Zimri Robinson, but I'm on to you."

Dorian takes a step back.

"Look, Medgers, my grandmother is missing . . ." I tell her.

She looks down her nose at me. "She been gone longer than twenty-four hours?"

"No, but—"

"Then we can't do anything."

"This isn't the first time she's been missing."

Dorian jerks his head toward me. "Really?"

I look at my shoes. "Yes, it's true. This has been happening more and more but she's never been gone this long or this late."

"Maybe she went looking for your concert and got lost," Medgers says with a snort.

Dorian's eyes go wide.

"Medgers!" barks someone from behind us. "Are you helping these young people?" I feel a hand on my shoulder and turn to see another officer at my side. She looks about Marley's age. Her hair is pulled back in a thousand tiny braids tucked neatly in a bun at the base of her neck.

"My grandmother's missing," I tell her and my eyes well up. Embarrassed, I brush away the tears.

"And the officer on duty refuses to help us," Dorian says.

The other officer narrows her eyes at Medgers. "Is this true?"

"Just following protocol," Medgers mumbles.

The officer shakes her head, disgusted. "I'll deal with you later," she says to Medgers, then motions for Dorian and me to follow her. "Come on. I'll help you."

When we get settled inside her cubicle, the officer smiles at me. "You're Zimri, right?"

I nod, not sure if it's good or bad that she knows my name.

"I'm Billingsley," she tells me. "I grew up with your parents. I knew your family well."

"Oh," I say, surprised. "I don't remember you."

"My family left when I was a teenager. I just got a promotion and transferred here." She shows me the stripes on the shoulder of her uniform. "Now, then . . ." She leans forward on her elbows. "Tell me what happened."

Once I start talking, everything spills out. I tell Billingsley more than I've even admitted to myself about how confused Nonda has seemed lately, how many times she's wandered off, how truly bad things have gotten with her. When I'm finished, I'm exhausted and embarrassed. "I should have taken better care of her," I say, fighting back tears.

Dorian lays his hand on my arm. "You can't blame yourself."

"He's right," Billingsley says. "You're sixteen and working full-time. You've got a lot on your plate."

I don't say it aloud but I know they're wrong. If I'd been home, not out making music, none of this would have happened.

"Since there are extenuating circumstances," Billingsley says, "her age, her mental state, et cetera, I can file a special missing persons report. And I'll make sure it goes out to the officers on rounds inside the Complex and to the MediPlex so they'll be on the lookout for her."

"And we'll make signs to post in Old Town," Dorian says.

"Good idea," Billingsley says. "Other than that . . ." She trails off, looking sad.

I nod and thank both of them effusively so none of us has to say aloud that there isn't much else we can do now but wait.

ORPHEUS

"Prepare for self-navigation." I awaken to the dinging
AutoNav. I must have passed out from the Juse flooding my
system. I have no idea how long I've been in the air or how far
I've gone, but we must be far beyond the bounds of the City
SkyPath. I had no plan, no destination in mind when I took off.
I thought about flying to my father's ranch, or going to the cha-
let up in the mountains. I could have headed south to his place
on the beach. Or gone to the airport and left the country. But
the truth is, if he wants to, he can track me down and bring
me back for the ASA at any moment.

The Cicada shudders as the wheels come down and the
wings retract. I take the steering wheel and hold on tight with
sweaty hands as we touch down on a bumpy, ill-kept road,
nothing like the smooth streets in the City, which are long gone.
My headlights shine on trees and a road and a river that winds
its way across the land like a stumbling drunk. My father once
told me Corporation Xian Jai, some outfit out of China, had

wanted to straighten the river to make construction of the warehouse and factory complexes out here easier.

"Why didn't they?" I asked.

"They gave up," he said. "If you want something big, you have to dream big to get it."

Lights from warehouses peek through the giant willows growing along the riverbank. Up above, I think I see twinkling stars, then realize those are the tiny flashing lights of delivery drones taking off from warehouse roofs. I've heard each Complex has its own high-rise PODPlexes where all the workers live like ants, filing back and forth twenty-four hours a day, every day of the week, every week of the year, plucking and packing up crap from shelves for Plutes like me.

On the receiver, I hear the low rumble of a deejay's altered voice. "Hello, my minions, how you doing on this misty moon-filled night? It's DJ HiJax here with you along for the ride." I've heard this guy before, but every time I come across him, his voice has been disguised at a different frequency. Sometimes he sounds slow and low like tonight, other times high and fast as if he's a young girl, but always with the same name.

"We're going way back when tonight," he says. "To a time when music was a rallying cry. When Mr. Bob Marley and the Wailers told the people to 'Get Up, Stand Up.' Stand up for your rights, Bob Marley said, just like our friends at Project Calliope who are taking a stand against Chanson Industries. This is for Calliope Bontempi, taking back music for the people!"

"Oh jeez," I say. Will I ever escape my father? Even out here, his lawsuits are all anyone can talk about.

I hit the scan button on the receiver to find another pirate station as I drive slowly with my windows down to let in the night air. It's cooler than in the City and I can smell the muck and mud from the river. I haven't been in nature, real nature, in months. I inhale deeply. The waves on my receiver crackle. I reach down to fine-tune it, hoping to locate another voice to keep me company on this lonely road.

The waves go fuzzy for a moment, then I catch the hint of another song. At first it's faint, but then it comes in clearer. I don't recognize the singer. I turn it up and listen carefully to the strange instrumentation. Sounds like an old-school electric guitar and bass and maybe even real drums, but it's the singer's voice that punches me in the gut. Except for the mixing, which makes her voice go muddy around the edges on the high notes, the sound is beautiful and raw. The kind of song that could steal my heart. I try to imagine what the singer must look like, how beautiful she must be to sound like this, but I can't get a clear vision in my head because what I hear doesn't match up with the pictures my mind supplies. She wouldn't be painted and polished or surgically altered. Her voice and music are wholly unique and I can only imagine she must be, too.

"*I am Nobody from Nowhere,*" she sings.

I inhale sharply, trying to remember where I've seen that phrase before. On a package, I think, but I can't remember exactly what or why it would have been there.

A speck upon your screen
A non-automated worker that you've never seen
I've packed your purchased footholds
I'll tie them with a bow
But I live a life that you'll never know

By the end of the song, I'm singing along, "Nobody from Nowhere, I'm here, I'm here, I'm here! Nobody from Nowhere, I'll scream until you hear."

I don't want the song to end. I want to hear it again. I want to delve back into the melody, listen to the lyrics again. I want to know the world she's singing about. Become a part of it. That busy hive she describes and somehow makes it sound enticing. A place I'd rather be. Go to work, do your job, go home, repeat. No fighting, clawing, scratching your way to the top because there is no top. It's flat. One level with everybody on it. No omnipresent drones tracking your every move. No constant pressure to do better, be better, beat your best friend who becomes your biggest competition overnight.

A good, clean, simple life as a Nobody sounds fine to me.

My reverie is interrupted by a shadow flickering on the road. I swerve. See a flash. My headlight catches something bright. Two eyes. A woman's face. With Juse powering my arms, I overcorrect. The Cicada spins. I see her again in the middle of the road, one arm thrown up to protect her eyes from my headlights. She's small and old. My foot is hard against the brake. I hear the tires screech as I yell, "No!" My car continues to spin. I see trees and moon and the old woman around and around outside of my window and then I start to slide, sideways and down. The traction of my wheels fail. The smell of the river overwhelms me. I feel the car slip, then hear my voice spill into the night. "I don't want to die!" I scream as my car careens off the road.

CHORUS

A lone 'razzi drone, attached magnetically to the back of Orpheus Chanson's car, lies broken into four pieces near a guardrail by the river. The thorax, with its tiny CPU and six articulated legs, has come loose and skittered across the road to land beneath a pile of dead leaves. Tomorrow, ants and pill bugs will march over its carcass, indistinguishable to them from an ordinary rock. The wings and tail have shattered on the road, leaving a shiny trail like mechanized snail slime glinting in the moon. Only the head has stayed intact, stuck to the fender since the Alibaba E-Gaming Arena back in the City.

The vibrations and noise from the crash have disturbed a real dragonfly that alights from its roost on a reed. It zips toward two glowing green lights like fireflies blinking in the night. They are not insects but the last blips of the drone's compound camera eyes, failing to send images into the Buzz. The dragonfly whizzes away in search of a quiet place to sleep.

A boy emerges from beneath the car's winglike door. He struggles to get out and assess the damage: to himself, to his vehicle, to the body on the road. He is shaken up, perhaps in shock. Still not sure how he's not dead and praying that the old woman was a Juse-fueled figment.

He stumbles on shaky legs up to the road. The car's headlamps, knocked askew, cast an eerie, cockeyed light onto the old woman, still in a crouch next to the fading yellow line. She shades her eyes with one bent arm and slowly gets to her feet, bewildered. She struggles to remember what brought her out here in the first place. Why is she so far from home? Where did she think she was going? Who is this young man emerging from the river?

"Linus?" she calls. "That you?"

"Are you okay?" the boy yells and runs toward her, relieved she's not a heap of flesh and broken bones because he was sure he must have hit her. Then his legs give out and he's sitting on the ground, head in hands, wondering the same things: Why is he here? Where did he think he was going? And who is this woman? Orpheus squints up at her and sees that she's scratched and bruised, her pants are torn, and she has a faraway look in her eyes that makes him think she might be not be okay.

"What's your name?" he asks.

"Well, now," she says and seems to think this over.

"Do you live near here?"

"Um . . ." She looks around but nothing is familiar. She draws in a breath and shakes her head, completely at a loss.

"I'm just going to get my car out of the ditch," he tells her and forces himself up on his feet. Then he laughs, the nervous twitter of a goldfinch. "Guess we're both lucky to be alive."

"Sure are," Nonda says, her breath still ragged.

It takes all of Orpheus's strength to budge his car. He grunts and groans, curses, and falls. His knee knocks the mechanized drone head onto the ground where it bounces down the embankment and plops with the smallest splash into the river, then sinks, down down down to a resting place on the murky riverbed with keys and coins and other things dropped among the weeds. Finally, slowly, the car emerges onto the road. Orpheus walks around it once as the dragonfly, still searching for a sleeping spot, circles him. The passenger-side door is smashed pretty good. The back tire looks a little wonky. He hears a buzzing in his ear. Feels a tiny whirl on his cheek. He swats at the air, sending the dragonfly away.

It zips to Nonda. Lands on her shoulder. "Oh, hello," she says and blows, but the dragonfly says put. When Zimri was little, Nonda told her dragonflies would sew up her mouth if they caught her singing, but Zimri was far too smart for such nonsense.

"I have a granddaughter!" Nonda says.

"Okay," says Orpheus, focused on his glowing palm. "Do you know her name or her number so we can reach her?"

Nonda thinks but can't pull the info from her murky mind. She sighs and shakes her head.

"Look," he says and shows her the screen on his hand. "There's a MediPlex nearby. They'll be able to help you, okay?"

She nods, so he leads her gently by the arm toward his strange winged car and loads her inside.

As they rattle off down the road, the dragonfly swoops out over the open water. Tomorrow, mating season begins.

VERSE THREE

ZIMRI

The next day at work, my times are terrible and I keep missing products because I'm so preoccupied with Nonda's disappearance. At every little noise last night, I startled awake, calling for her, sure she was finally coming through the door. Now muddling my way through work, I feel like I've fallen back inside the dream—endlessly searching the labyrinth of warehouse shelves for my grandmother—that swallowed me whenever I drifted off last night. I'd find her in a metal bin, curled up with some measuring spoons. I'd see her strapped to the overhead conveyor belt on her way to the packing area. I'd watch a delivery drone pluck her off the roof to carry her to another family in the City. Each time I woke up, I would promise to give up music in exchange for Nonda's safety, but whatever higher power I was trying to implore ignored my pleas, because Nonda never came home.

After two hours of mistakes, Jude finds me in sector K.

"Zimri!" he barks from his little electric car, idling in the aisle.

"I can explain . . ." I quickly say.

"Explain what?" He slumps over the steering wheel as if he's carrying the weight of the entire warehouse on his shoulders.

"Why I'm so bad today. It's just that—"

He frowns at me then shakes his head like I've hurt his feelings. "Give me a little credit, would you? I saw the screens this morning. I know about your grandmother."

I lunge toward him. "Is she okay?"

"Sorry," he says. "I don't know. Get in." He jerks his head toward the passenger seat.

I walk slowly around the side of the cart, keeping my eyes on him like he's a coyolf that's wandered into the warehouse— skittish and unpredictable. "Medgers again?" I ask.

"No, nothing like that. I need a favor from you."

I stop, relieved there isn't bad news about Nonda, and Medgers isn't harassing me today, but also dumbfounded. "A favor? Now? But . . ."

"Just get in, would you?"

As soon as I'm seated, Jude makes a sharp turn into the main corridor, past the forklift operators ferrying bins with fresh products to the shelves, then rolls to a stop in front of the main office. He turns toward me. His face softens a bit, which makes him look older and sad. He slings one arm over the back of the seat and puts the other on my thigh, just above my knee. I stiffen and stare down at the hand on my leg. His fingers are pudgy and short, thick like sausages. The nail beds are ragged.

"Zimri, we could make a really good team, you know that, right?"

I don't like his clammy touch. I don't like how close he is to me, but I know better than to pull away. "I don't follow," I tell him.

"A guy showed up today."

"A guy?"

Jude looks over each shoulder. All around us the warehouse continues to hum with people rushing in and out of aisles and baskets zipping overhead. "Sometimes Corp X sends in someone to see from the inside how warehouses are doing."

"You mean like a spy?"

"Shh," he hisses. "*Mole* is a better word. They try to keep it under the radar, so no one gets wise, but I've got a pretty good eye for this kind of a thing. There's something about this guy. He isn't from around here. He's . . ." Jude mulls this over and chooses his word carefully. "Different. Not like us."

"What's that have to do with me?" I ask and lean away.

But Jude grips my leg tighter. "This warehouse isn't efficient enough and unless we turn things around, Corp X might do something drastic."

"A.N.T.s?"

He nods. "Our warehouse is one of the last holdouts, you know. It was one of the first to be built but because it's so old, it would cost them a boatload of money to retrofit it for full automation with those creepy little robo insects they use. Then again, unless we turn things around, I'm afraid they'll think it's worth the cost." Jude scoots closer. I can smell his eggy breath and feel the sweat coming off his skin. "I want you to train the mole. Keep him on a short leash. Only let him see the good stuff. And report back to me on any funny business."

"Funny business?" I ask.

"You know. If he's poking his nose in where it doesn't belong or asking too many questions."

"Jude, this is not what I need right now," I start to say.

"Hey," he snaps. "I'm doing you a favor here!"

"How is this a favor to me?"

His eyes lock on mine. "I'm trying to help you and everybody else keep their jobs."

"But with my grandmother missing . . ."

"You still gotta work," he says, and I sigh because I know he's right. What good will I do my Nonda if I don't have a job? "So, you going to help me or what?"

"Yes," I say wearily. "I'll do it."

Reluctantly, I follow him through the office door, preoccupied with how I'm going to tell Brie every single detail of that weird conversation Jude and I just had. Mostly I'm furious that he's laying the future of the warehouse on my shoulders. So when he says, "Zimri, meet Aimery, your new trainee," I barely glance up.

The person on the beat-up sofa stands and sticks out his hand as if we're fancy people in a movie. "Very nice to meet you," he says in a voice as smooth as the river on a calm day. "Jude speaks so highly of you."

I almost laugh as we shake. Who talks like that? But then I look at him and color rides into my cheeks because I'm stupefied by the most beautiful boy I've ever seen. He can't be much older than I am but he looks nothing like the Plebes from the complex. His skin is buffed a beautiful warm brown, like a bronzed statue of a human. His face is flawless, no angry acne on his cheeks, no pockmarks on his chin or bad teeth crowding his mouth. His nose is prominent but straight, his eyes are bright, and his teeth are perfectly white and aligned like little soldiers behind his full lips. He's so beautiful that I can barely take my eyes off him, even though I'm mortified to stare.

I make myself look away and whisper, "Thank you," then I clear my throat and say, "Nice to meet you, too?" but it comes out like a question.

"What a beautiful name you have," he says. "And fitting, too."

"What?" Flustered, I drop his hand as if it scalded my palm. Did he call me beautiful? Either he's full of crap or a liar because no one who looks like that could ever think the same of me.

To my surprise, he blushes. "Oh, uh, sorry, I meant that to be way less creepy," he says, which makes me laugh. Then he shoves his hands inside his pockets. I notice that his pants are way too nice to be from Black Friday. The fabric is thick and soft, subtly striped, and I can see why Jude is jumping to conclusions that he could be from Corp X.

"It's just that your name, Zimri, it means 'song' in Hebrew, right?" he asks. "And you were humming when you came in, and . . ."

"No, I wasn't," I snap, more embarrassed than before.

Jude snorts. "Sure you were. You always hum or sing or make rhythms with your mouth."

"I do?" I shrink into myself, feeling exposed, as if my clothing has become see-through.

"You're like a walking receiver. It gets annoying!" Jude smirks at Aimery as if he'll surely agree, but Aimery leans away from him and frowns.

"It wasn't annoying at all," says Aimery. "It was . . . beautiful, like your name."

I guffaw, stupid and loud. It's such a ridiculous thing to say that I can only assume he's trying to get under Jude's skin. I eye him. He winks. I press my lips together so I don't encourage him. "So then, what's Aimery mean?" I ask.

"King of work," he says with a self-satisfied grin. "What else?"

ORPHEUS

I follow Zimri into the warehouse feeling like a Plebe in the Distract for the first time, spinning around and marveling at a place I never imagined could exist. The building is enormous, no walls or halls, just one gigantic space with forty-foot-tall metal shelving units moving up and down on tracks from floor to ceiling. Each shelf has dozens of metal bins and inside each bin is all the crap a Plute like me could order straight off my ExoScreen. Toothbrushes, laundry baskets, guns, and books; clothing, frying pans, shoes, and soap; doorknobs, toys, and prepackaged food. Water bottles, dog beds, cut-glass vases, wine racks, dish racks, tie racks, and ties. Picture frames, baking trays, wastebaskets, and paint. Anything that could be packed into a box is under this roof, waiting to be plucked by the thousands of workers scurrying around like bugs.

"So," I say, trying to make conversation with Zimri as we walk, dodging the other workers. "You're the best, huh?"

She quickly turns a corner and I hurry to keep up with her.

"That guy, what's his name, Rude . . ."

"Jude," she says.

"'Rude' fits him better." I wait for her to smile, but she keeps marching forward as if I'm not here. I zigzag around the people hurrying by and catch up with her again. "Okay, so Jude. Was he lying?"

She glances at me then looks away quickly. "About what?"

"About you being the best?" Again she doesn't answer. "So, you're not the best? Are you the worst?" She ignores me, which only makes me want her attention more. "You're mediocre then?" That also lands flat. "Jeez, what's a guy gotta do to get you to talk?" I stop in the center of an aisle, causing a forklift to swerve.

"Watch it, buddy!" the driver yells.

Zimri reaches over and grabs me by the shirt to yank me out of the way. "Sorry, Merle!" she yells, then turns to me. "Maybe you should figure out why you need so much attention in the first place."

I laugh, dumbstruck, because no one has ever talked to me like that before.

"And besides, this isn't the time to chat," Zimri says motioning me forward. We turn another corner. People crisscross in front of us, each equipped with a mesh basket full of stuff.

"Why?" I ask. "No socializing allowed?"

"You can do that on your tenner."

"My tenor?" I ask, then sing, "What if I'm a bass?" in a deep resounding voice, which makes Zimri chuckle, so I continue, in falsetto. "Or maybe I'm soprano."

She smiles and shakes her head like she thinks I might be crazy, then she explains, "Your tenner is your ten-minute break. Not the way you sing."

As we walk, side by side, I can't look away. She looks different than anyone I've ever seen before. Her hair grows up and out in soft spirals and her eyes are fierce green, but not a fake color like they've been altered, more like the green of a dragonfly. Her skin is darker than mine, and she has a long straight nose and boxy jaw, but when she smiles, I see a gap between her two front teeth.

"Why are you staring at me like that?" she asks.

"I . . . uh . . . um . . ." I stutter. "It's just your teeth. . . ."

She quickly presses her lips together and frowns.

"You rarely see an imperfection like that," I point to her face, "on a girl as beautiful as you."

She stops and puts a fist on her hip. "Are you really this full of crap? I *know* I have a gap between my teeth and I don't care, but saying that I'm beautiful? What are you trying to prove?"

"Has no one ever told you that before?" I ask, bewildered. "Where I'm from, we tell each other all the time. In fact, if I didn't tell my female friends they were beautiful five times a day, they'd be offended."

"They sound charming," Zimri says and takes off again.

I walk beside her, chattering away. "Everyone is so uniform these days. It's like beauty gets boring. All the spit-shine and polish from the minute everyone is born. Any imperfection has been routed out."

"Maybe where *you're from* it's like that."

"I meant it as a compliment!" I tell her but she's back to ignoring me. "You know, if you were a celebrity, some Promo-Team would try to give you a look. Your hair, eyes, skin tone, and clothes. They'd try to tame you. Straighten your hair. Fix that little gap in your teeth. But that would be a huge mistake. In the end we, I mean, those celebs all end up looking alike."

"Lucky for me I'm just a Plebe then."

"Ha!" I laugh, which only makes her scowl more and march ahead of me.

Her walk reminds me a little bit of Arabella's. Fluid and easy, leading with her wrists and knees like we learn at SCEWL, but for Zimri, it must come naturally.

She glances at me, staring again, and says, "What?"

"Nothing." I glance away, but there's something in the way she moves that makes me want to keep looking.

Zimri pulls me to the side at the end of an aisle, out of the way of the forklifts and people scurrying by. "Here," she says and holds out a clunky prehistoric screen thingie I've seen other workers carrying.

I stare at it. "What's this?"

"Your HandHeld."

"What am I supposed to do with it?"

"Put it on," she says slowly like I might be a little bit dense. And apparently she's right because I can't figure out how to attach it to my arm.

"Like this." She slips the harness over my hand. When her fingers brush against me, I feel electricity dance across my skin. Immediately, I glance at the back of her hand for a carapace, but of course she doesn't have one.

I straighten the contraption so the screen lies against my palm and inner wrist. "It's so heavy!" Then I notice that she's staring at my hand, which is pale from being constantly cov-ered by my ExoScreen glove. Quickly, I move it behind my back.

"Put in your earbud," she instructs me.

I struggle with the cord attached to the HandHeld but only manage to get it tangled around my arm.

"Clearly, you didn't go to SCEWL," she says, and motions for me to snake my arm in the opposite direction.

"Yes, I did!" I try to follow her instructions but I end up in a knot. "But the Kardashians didn't teach me how to do this."

"Kardashians?" She looks at me funny as she untangles the wires. "Is that what you called the RoboNannies?"

"Uh, yeah, joke, right?" I half laugh but she only frowns. "What's this for, anyway?" I hold up an old-fashioned earbud.

"How else would you hear the instructions?" She runs the cord up my forearm, clips it to my shirt collar, then loops the cord behind my ear and slips the bud in place.

"Ow!" I reach up and accidentally touch her hand when I adjust the bud. She quickly pulls away. "How can you stand to wear one of these?"

She sticks out her bottom lip and waggles her head. "Guess my widdle ears aren't as delicate as yours," she says in a baby voice.

"That's mature," I say, but she only laughs.

"Okay, push start on your screen," she instructs.

When I do, numbers fill my ear. "What's with the count-down?" I ask her.

"Keeps you on track."

"On track for what?"

"Good times," she says.

"As in fun?" I smile and wiggle my eyebrows because, to me, this whole thing is hilarious. A Plute inside a warehouse! I half wish I could send pix into the Buzz—if I weren't hiding from my father, that is. I figure as long as he's not sending someone after me, I'll stick around here for a few days, maybe a week, make him sweat, then show up again.

Zimri, though, doesn't find any of this amusing. She frowns, but in a way that makes me think she's holding back a smile. "Does it look like we're having fun?"

I glance at all the people scurrying from place to place, faces deep in concentration. Then I look back at her. "Zimri," I say. "I can confirm that it appears absolutely no one in this god-forsaken warehouse appears to be having a good time." Then I lean closer and whisper, "But we could change all that, you and I."

"Oh my god," she says, but this time she can't help it. She tosses her head back and laughs out loud. "Are you always like this?"

"No," I tell her honestly. "I have no idea what's gotten into me."

I run after Zimri for hours like a little lapdog at its owner's heels. From one end of the warehouse to the other, traversing what feels like every aisle, every shelf, gathering the stupidest bunch of crap I've ever seen. Baby pants, sun hats, spray paint, bug spray, plastic colanders, chewing gum, laxatives. None of it makes sense. Nothing is in order. We're just mindless drones, following the beeping in our ears and the numbers on our screens. I can't believe this whole place hasn't been automated yet. Zimri's amazing, though. She zips around the maze of aisles, always knowing exactly where she needs to be, but

I can't keep it straight. Every time we turn a corner I get turned around.

"Don't stop walking," she barks when I pause to get my bearings. "Can't you look at your screen and move your feet at the same time?"

"I don't know what I'm looking for," I admit, staring at the jumble of numbers flashing from my palm.

"Right here!" She jabs a finger at the HandHeld.

The top third is like a stopwatch; the numbers match the ones being pumped through the earbud telling me how many seconds I have left to find the product before the whole system implodes and a giant death ray zaps me into oblivion. Or something like that. The middle of the screen has a series of random numbers and letters that mean nothing to me.

"Can't you read?"

"Are you always this grouchy?" I ask, annoyed and tired.

"Are you always this much of a whiner?" she asks me back.

"I'm not whining," I insist, realizing I sound like a three-year-old.

"Then stop lollygagging!" she yells over her shoulder.

"You're just insanely fast!" I say, still dragging behind. "I'm the one moving like a normal human being."

"You've got to be better than normal if you want to do well here."

"Oh really?" I ask, running to catch up. "Is there competition for who's the fastest? Do you have to have an ASA here, too?"

She scowls at me. "An ASA? What's that?"

"You know. The surgery. On your brain. To make you a genius."

"Oh right. What Plute brats get so they don't have to work?"

"Plutes work!" I say. "They work very hard."

"Sure they do," she says.

"It's just a different kind of work than this." I motion to the commotion all around us and think for a moment maybe it's not that different after all. Plebes might be running after products to stick in baskets, but we're always chasing the Buzz.

"Anyway," I say, panting from jogging beside her. "Why's it matter how fast I go?"

For the first time she stops moving right in the center of an aisle. "Because," she says, hands on hips and chin held high. "If we're too slow then we'll all be replaced by A.N.T.s, won't we?"

"Ants?" I ask. "How could ants—" A loud buzzer blares in my ear, making me jump. "Now what did I do wrong?" I yell.

Zimri chuckles then she sings, "Time for the tenner," in a perfect tenor voice.

While all the other workers flood out of the aisles and head to the left, Zimri slips around a corner to the right. "Where are you going?" I ask, jogging after her.

"Most people go to the break rooms," she says without stopping.

"Is that what you'll do?"

She looks at me over her shoulder and says, "Do I look like most people?"

"No," I tell her and for some reason my heart speeds up. "You certainly do not."

Before we get too far, Rude Jude, the jerk who hired me this morning, zips up on his stupid little electric cart and screeches to a halt as if he's driving a top-model Cicada. "Zimri!" he shouts.

She jumps and spins around. "What? What's wrong now?"

"Someone's here to see you."

A security officer climbs out of the passenger side and Zimri visibly slumps. She grabs for a shelf to steady herself but she misses and stumbles. Quickly, I grab her arm and prop her up, just like I did for Arabella at the gallery the other night.

"You okay? What's wrong?" I whisper in her ear.

"Billingsley?" she says as all the color drains from her face. The officer reaches out to Zimri. I hold my breath, thinking I'm about to witness an arrest, and I have the urge to pull her away from the security officer and run.

But the woman smiles and pulls Zimri into an embrace as she says, "It's alright. We found her. Your grandmother is okay."

VERSE FOUR

ZIMRI

For the first two nights after Nonda was found, I headed straight for the MediPlex as soon as my shift ended. Tonight, I bolt for the massive warehouse doors that roll up when the seven o'clock buzzer sounds and the shift switch begins. It's fifteen minutes of controlled chaos as thousands of bodies spill from one end of the warehouse to make room for the thousands more coming in the other side so the drones never have to stop. I want to be among the first out the door to have as much time as possible with my grandmother before visiting hours are over. But as I hurry toward the exit, Jude pulls me away from the stream of workers.

"I need you to work a split," he says, waving his tablet in my face. "We need a better average productivity rate for today."

"You know I would if I could." I try to wriggle back into the crowd, but Jude sticks close to my side and everyone gives him a wide berth. "I need to visit my grandmother."

"Listen, Little Red Riding Hood." He wraps his hand

around my upper arm. "I said I need a split from you, so you're going back on the floor."

"And I said no!" I try to pry his sausage fingers off of me but he's square and stout, a good fifty pounds heavier than I am as if he is built of blocks, head, neck, and shoulders all stacked up on torso and pillar legs. He drags me back against the flow of workers who part around us, like we're trash floating in the river of no concern.

"Don't be a jerk," I tell him. "Let go!"

But he doesn't listen until someone behind us yells, "Hey, she said let go!"

Jude and I both spin around to see Aimery pushing toward us. Although I'm no longer training him we've been working near one another the past two days and he usually tags along with me during breaks. With Brie still gone, having Aimery around has made the days go quicker.

"This is none of your business," Jude tells him. "Your shift is over. Now get the hell out."

"Not unless she goes with me," Aimery says calmly.

The flow of bodies around us slows as people linger to listen.

"Aimery," I say quietly. "You don't have to . . . " He cuts his eyes toward me and I think I see the corner of his mouth twitch like he's trying not to grin, then he turns back to stare at Jude.

Jude lets go of my arm and gets in Aimery's face. "I said this is none of your business."

Instead of backing down like anybody else would, Aimery steps up. He's at least three inches taller than Jude. A crowd has formed around us as people stop to watch, creating a bottleneck in the flow of bodies trying to get out the door. "According to the Corp X contract," Aimery says, "employees are not required to work split shifts without twenty-four hours' notice, so get off her back."

The crowd begins to murmur.

"Contract?" Jude puts his hands on his hips. "What contract?"

"The employment contract you made me sign when I was hired three days ago," Aimery says. "Would you like me to pull up a copy on my HandHeld?" He lifts his arm and shows Jude his screen. Someone in the crowd snickers.

"I can ask any employee I want to work a split," says Jude.

"Yes and any employee is entitled to say no," explains Aimery calmly. "The problem is, you didn't ask her. I overheard the whole thing. You insisted she do it even after she turned you down."

Jude shakes his head then takes a deep breath, no doubt calculating his response in case Aimery is from corporate as he suspects. Although I agree with Jude that Aimery isn't from around here, I'm sure he's no mole. He's too clueless to be a spy.

"So ask her," Aimery says politely but firmly.

Jude swallows like he has a bad taste in his mouth, then he turns to me, eyes narrow with rage. "Zimri," he says, his voice tight and every word enunciated, "would you work a split shift tonight?"

"Say please," Aimery instructs him. I hear stifled laughter in the crowd.

Jude grits his teeth. "Please?"

I glance at Aimery who nods and I stand up straight,

bolstered by his confidence but still worried what the consequences will be if I say no. Then again, I always stay when Jude asks, and right now Nonda needs me.

"I'm sorry," I say. The whole crowd seems to hold their breath. "I can't work tonight, Jude. I have to go see my grandmother. But another time, I'd be happy to."

"Fine," says Jude. He meets my gaze for a moment, a mix of rage and disappointment in his eyes, then pushes through the wall of bodies and disappears into the crowd.

"Have a nice night!" Aimery calls after him, flashing his pretty-boy smile.

"You didn't have to . . ." I start to say to Aimery, but a swarm of people has subsumed him, slapping him on the back, punching his shoulder, and shaking his hand.

"I know!" he calls back to me as he's whisked toward the exit in the current of bodies. "But I wanted to."

By the time I get outside, Aimery is completely surrounded and he seems to be enjoying the attention. Something about him draws people—they want to be near him. Touch him. Talk to him. I try to push my way in, but someone catches hold of my arm. I gasp and spin around, expecting to see Jude ready to drag me back inside, but it's Dorian.

"Oh my god, you scared me," I say with my hand over my thumping heart. "What are you doing here? I thought you and Brie both had the day off." We're jostled from every side by all the people pushing past us, hurrying to the AutoTrams that will whisk them to the PODPlexes or up to the Strip.

"What happened in there?" he says, glancing at the knot of people around Aimery.

"Oh, that. Well . . . I'll tell you later," I say, not wanting to take the time to explain. "I have to catch a tram to the Medi-Plex before—"

"Wait." Dorian motions me aside. "I brought you something."

"Dorian, I'm sorry. I'm already late!" I step toward the trams that are beginning to fill up and pull away without me.

"The last time I talked to you," he says and tugs me aside, "you said the tram takes forever to get to the MediPlex. I realized that you could go the back way, along the river path, and get there in fifteen minutes and so I thought . . ." He points to a red bicycle parked by the building. He tosses up his hands and says, "Ta-da!"

"I . . . I . . . I don't understand," I say.

"I made it," he says, "for you." He looks at me expectantly. When I don't move he says, "I'm giving it to you. It's a present."

My jaw drops. I walk all the way around the bike, whispering, "You made it? For me?"

He shrugs like it's no big thing. "It was my day off, I had spare parts lying around, and . . ."

"Wow, that's the nicest thing . . ." I start to say then stop because it's actually the second-nicest thing that's happened to me today. I glance over my shoulder to see if Aimery is still here.

"You're always helping everybody else," says Dorian, pulling my attention back. "I thought it was time somebody helped you."

"It's amazing." I blush and smile. "I don't know what to say."

"Maybe 'thank you,'" he suggests.

"Yes, oh my gosh. Thank you. Thank you. Thank you!" I give him a quick kiss on the cheek. Now he's blushing. Ever since the night of the concert, we haven't had a chance to talk about what's going on between us. First his dad interrupted, made us talk to Nonda, and dragged him home. Then Nonda went missing and now every evening I rush off to see her.

Suddenly, he grabs me around the waist and pulls me in for a long hug. "I've missed you!" He puts his nose into my hair and inhales.

"Oh, wow!" I say and jump back, my stomach in a knot. I glance over my shoulder to look for Aimery again, but the crowd has dispersed and he's long gone. My heart sinks a little because I didn't get to thank him properly for standing up to Jude for me. Then I feel bad. Why am I thinking about Aimery when Dorian is right here in front of me? Giving me a bike! I turn back to him. "This is amazing, Dorian. Incredible. And I wish I had more time but right now I have to go."

"Of course." He steps away, brushes his fingers through blond dreads, embarrassed. "You should go. I don't want to keep you from your grandmother."

"You're sure?" I ask as I swing my leg over the bike, feeling shaky and uncertain. I haven't ridden one by myself since I was little.

"Of course!" he says and grabs the back of the seat to steady me. "Don't worry. Your body will remember what to do."

I start to pedal, swaying left and right, overcorrecting then finding my balance again as Dorian runs alongside me through the quickly emptying lot toward the river path behind the warehouse.

"I'm doing it!" I yell, excited to find the rhythm. I pump my legs and grip the handlebars. Dorian gives me one last push and sets me on my way.

"Be careful!" he calls after me. "Ping me later!"

"I will!" I yell over my shoulder. "And thank you again."

If the Security Office makes me paranoid because of what happened to my mother, the MediPlex breaks my heart into a thousand pieces each time I come here because this is the last place I saw my father. Nonda says children are wise. Mostly I think that's wishful thinking, but the day they fished my father out of the river, his pockets laden with heavy rocks, I felt old beyond my years. He was bloated and ashy gray, hair splayed like riverweeds across the gray sheet of the gurney, his mouth and eyes open in an eternal blank stare of a dead fish. In the plain white room, Nonda, Tati, and Brie's mother Elena huddled in the corner, gripping each other, trying to quiet their sobs while I climbed up next to my father's body.

He hadn't slept for weeks. I'd watch him through our POD window, pacing the Y.A.R.D. all hours of the night. I always imagined that he was waiting for my mom to return and I'd spin stories in my head that she'd finally come home, find Dad out in the damp night air, wrap her arms around his narrow waist, and lead him back inside. But, of course, she never came and Dad only got worse until he couldn't stand living any longer and he took the plunge like so many other workers had done before him and since. On that final night in the Medi-Plex, I leaned over and kissed his stone-cold forehead. "Sleep now," I told him like he told me each night before bed, then I climbed down with the understanding that I'd be taking care of myself from then on.

Inside, the MediPlex smells sour, as if all the doors and windows have been closed for decades. The halls are busy, though, with people scurrying from birth to death. Sometimes I think my mother got it right when she left the Complex life, even though I'm angry that she didn't take me with her. Then I remind myself, if I wasn't here, who'd look after Nonda? I realize that I should have brought her something from outside. Yellow flowers, willow leaves, a bowl of her favorite soup, raspberries from the bushes ripening by the river. Next time, I promise myself, I'll come with gifts.

I maneuver through the slow-moving people, ducking and weaving my way to Nonda's ward, where I scan my thumbprint. A buzzer sounds and I'm admitted into a dim interior hall. Two of the lights overhead are burned out and the other one flickers. The place is eerily quiet except for a constant low-level moaning of machines and human voices that sends goose bumps across my skin.

Nonda's room is large and round, subdivided like a clock. Twelve beds, twelve patients, each one surrounded by a flimsy curtain the color of grubworm meal. Everyone here is slack-jawed, wild-haired, and sleepy. They look up at me expectantly as I pass. I try to smile at them but my face falters. They all look terribly sad. When I step inside Nonda's area, she's asleep. I always thought of her as strong, but that's just her personality. Now, she seems tiny and frail. Part of me wishes I could take her home, but another part is terrified of what I'll do when

I have to. Who will look after her while I'm at work? What if she slips away again?

"Nonda," I whisper and stroke her wooly gray hair off her forehead.

She wakes immediately and blinks at me.

"Zimri?" she asks, and I smile because she recognizes me.

I lace my fingers with hers. Her hands have become tiny things, like bird skeletons we sometimes find near the river.

"Oh, good." She lays her head on my shoulder and sighs. "Have you come to take me home? Why am I here? They're not very nice. Mostly robots. I hardly ever see a person, except for that jerk next to me. He's constantly peeing himself. Not that I can blame him. Takes forever for those dumb Robos to help us to the bathroom."

I laugh, delighted to hear feisty old Nonda coming through.

For the next hour, I try to rub some warmth into Nonda's cold feet while listening to the same stories she's told me a thousand times, until a RoboNurse rolls in to check her vitals and dispense her medication.

"Hello," it says in a soothing, preprogrammed female voice, "Ms. Layla Robinson." There's a short pause as it scans my grandmother. "Your current vital signs are . . ." another short pause, "stable. Your last meal was at . . . 5:00 p.m. You are due for medication in . . . two hours. Your discharge date is . . ." The Robo checks its internal calendar then says, "Tomorrow at 1:00 p.m."

"Tomorrow!" I blurt out and nearly fall off the edge of her bed. "She can't go home then."

"Not soon enough, if you ask me," Nonda mutters.

With complete indifference the Robo says, "Do you wish to request a different discharge date?"

"Yes!" Nonda and I both say at the same time, then she beats me to the punch and adds, "I want to leave right now!"

"Expedited requests must be processed by 10:00 a.m. for same-day discharges. It is currently . . . 8:34 p.m." The Robo spins around and wheels itself away.

"Wait! Wait! Wait!" I run after it. "I need to speak to someone. A human being! Nobody told me this. I can't take her home tomorrow. I haven't made arrangements. I'll be at work!"

The Robo stops in the center of the room. Its head swivels toward me. "Do you wish to request a different discharge date?" it asks again in the same even tone that makes me want to short-circuit its CPU.

"Yes!"

"On what day would you like the patient to be discharged?"

Frantically, I pull up the calendar on my HandHeld and check for my next day off from work. "Friday," I say, then I add, "please!" as if that would matter to a Robo. I hold my breath while it processes my request. The other patients in the beds have all sat up to watch through their parted curtains.

"Your request for Layla Robinson to be discharged on Friday is . . ." The Robo's green-light eyes blink. "Denied." It swivels away.

"Wait, don't go!" I grab it by the cold metal shoulder but it's quicker than I am and wheels away from my grip. "Why was my request denied?" I call after it.

"Insufficient insurance coverage."

"No, no, no!" I follow it. "That's not possible. We have Corp X health insurance. I need to speak with a doctor!"

"The next doctor's visit will be . . . Saturday, 3:00 p.m."

"Not acceptable!" I tell it firmly, anger rising in me like rushing water. "I want to speak with a doctor, a human being. Right now."

The Robo goes quiet. Green lights blink at me. I have half a mind to shake it until its bolts come loose and roll across the floor, but then it says, "Please stand by. Video conference to discuss denial of request with Dr. Garcia will commence."

The doctor that appears on the Robo's face screen is younger than I expected. Her hair is pulled into a long black ponytail and there's a deep furrow between her eyebrows, surely etched there by exhaustion. She skips all niceties and doesn't look at me as she scans her screen. "The system shows me that Layla Robinson's coverage is good for only 60 hours in MediPlex care. Since she was admitted on Thursday at 1:00 a.m., her coverage will run out at 1:00 p.m. tomorrow."

"No wait, listen." I reach toward the Robo as if it's the human. It wheels back. The doctor glances up at me and I lay it on thick. No time to waste. I only have a few seconds before the Robo will disconnect us so I pull out all the stops. "She's my grandmother. She's all I've got. Both my parents are dead. I'm working at the warehouse to take care of her. And she's been so confused lately. Sometimes she thinks I'm my mother and she lives in the past half the time but can't remember to take her HandHeld when she leaves and then she gets lost. She was almost hit by a car in the middle of the night! I can't take her home yet. I don't even know what's wrong with her!" I force myself to get teary, shamelessly trying to evoke even a sliver of pity from the doctor who has no reason to do me any favors.

"Always the same story," Dr. Garcia says and shakes her head in disgust.

"Well, pardon us for being just another Plebe sob story!" I snap then spin on my heel to walk away.

"I'm not talking about you," Dr. Garcia says sharply. "This kind of crap happens all the time at automated facilities like the one she's in." I turn back. She's jabbing at the notes on her screen. "She hasn't seen a real doctor. She was admitted with dehydration, lacerations, and some confusion, so those are the only things the RoboNurses are treating for until your insurance runs out. Then you either have to take her home or pay up. It's despicable."

I stand there, speechless.

"From what you're telling me," the doctor says, "I think it's likely your grandmother has dementia. Do you know what that is?"

I step closer and say quietly, "You mean her memory is going?"

She nods. "Unfortunately, there's no cure but there are some good treatment options. If you can buy her another day or two here, I can order a gerontologist to visit her. If she gets a dementia diagnosis, then your insurance will cover the treatment."

"How much would I need to keep her here until the other doctor can see her?" I ask, hoping Nonda can't hear.

Dr. Garcia punches in some info and a dollar amount appears on the screen. I quickly do the calculations in my head. PODPlex rent has already come out of my COYN payment for the month, plus our usual grocery order, the justice and health insurance payments for both of us. "My next COYN payment isn't for two weeks. Can I pay you then?"

She shakes her head. "I'm sorry, MediPlexes are all automated. You have to pay up front to keep her here. Otherwise, I can make an appointment and you can bring her back next week."

"No," I plead. "I don't have a way to keep her safe if I take her home."

"Then you have to get the money before 1:00 tomorrow or she goes home. These privatized facilities are harsh."

My mind races as I try to formulate a plan. Who could I borrow from? Who could bring the cash here tomorrow afternoon while I'm at work? I pace around, racking my brain, trying to come up with something feasible, then Dr. Garcia says, "Hey, what's that song?"

I stop and listen, but don't hear anything. "What song?"

She laughs. "The one you were singing?"

"Oh, sorry," I mutter and blush. Now she probably thinks I'm half-insane, pacing and singing to myself. "I do that without realizing. It's a habit."

"Don't be sorry," she says and smiles. "I like it. I've heard it before. Sing it again."

"I don't know what I was singing," I admit with a cringe.

"Like this." She hums a line of melody, a half-step off-key. I can't believe what I'm hearing but I know exactly what she's trying to sing and I join in with the chorus, "We are Nobody from Nowhere and we have nowhere else to go. . . ."

"Yes! That's the one." She leans close to the screen and whispers, "You've heard it, too? On the waves? That song says it all, doesn't it?"

My heartbeat crashes in my ears and I can't formulate a sentence. I stare at her, not sure whether to be flattered or terrified. How many people have heard my song? Was it a mistake to put it out over the waves?

But Dr. Garcia smiles kindly. "How much time would you need to get the money?"

"A few days?"

She sighs. "I wish I could give you that long."

I don't want to lose this opportunity so without thinking it through, I blurt out, "How about tomorrow night by 9:00? I could bring it after work."

"Well . . ." Dr. Garcia lifts her eyebrows and scans her screen. "I have to find a way to keep her here until then. . . . Oh, lookie here!" She smiles, triumphant. "Your grandmother is due for a mammogram, which is covered by insurance. I'm going to schedule that for tomorrow at 7:00 p.m. That way we can keep her here past 1:00 and the test will take two hours." She looks up at me and winks. "But remember: tomorrow night at 9:00 she'll be released, unless . . ."

". . . I can come up with the money."

"Exactly," says Dr. Garcia. "If we buy her another day, I think I can convince the gerontologist to visit and get her a proper diagnosis."

"Visiting hours are now over," the Robo announces. "Your call will be disconnected. Please proceed to the exit."

"Thank you!" I call to Dr. Garcia. Her face fades from the Robo screen as it tries to direct me out of the room.

"Please proceed to the exit," the Robo repeats incessantly.

"I'm going, I'm going," I tell it. But first I hop around it to kiss Nonda good night. "I'll be back tomorrow," I tell her.

"To take me home?" she asks.

"I don't know yet," I tell her honestly as I stroke her hair, because the truth is I don't know how I'm going to come up with the money.

On my bike ride home, I get an idea so I swerve off the river path, cruise down the empty streets of Old Town, then burst through Tati's shop door, calling her name.

"Be right out," she yells from the back then comes through the curtain with a blowtorch in one hand, a hammer in the other, and a grin on her face. "Zimri! Just the gal I wanted to see. I rejiggered that old video cam you brought me." She sets down the tools and digs through a bin on a cluttered shelf behind her counter.

"I need a favor," I tell her. "It's Nonda—"

"I heard." She shakes her head sadly. "If I had known things were so bad . . ." She doesn't finish her sentence, probably because there's not much else to say.

"I need money," I blurt out. "By tomorrow night to keep her in the MediPlex."

Tati turns to me slowly. "How much?" she asks. When I tell her, she grimaces. "That's a lot of dough."

"Almost my entire COYN payment for two weeks." I slump against the counter. "But I'll pay you back. You know I will. I can reduce our grocery order, maybe sell some things. Or you can have some of Mom's old equipment in exchange."

"Zim." Tati puts her hand on my shoulder. "If I had it, I'd give you the money, but I don't."

"But . . ." I look around at the shelves full of equipment in her shop.

"I know, it looks impressive," she says with a sarcastic snort. "But people don't buy much out here. I make most of my nut when I go into the City to sell and I'm not going again until the end of the month. I just don't have it, baby. I wish I did."

"What am I going to do?" I slide down to the floor and wrap my arms around my knees.

"Child, you have a way to make that money." Tati looks down at me, hands on hips, shaking her head.

"No way," I say, peering up at her. "Putting on a concert is the reason Nonda went missing in the first place."

"No, it's not," says Tati. "That was bound to happen sooner or later. Maybe while you were at work or out with Brie. What Nonda needs now is to be in a doctor's care and putting on a concert will get her that."

"But Medgers has her eye on me and with those private investigators snooping around—"

"First off, Medgers is an idiot." Tati reaches down and pulls me to my feet. "And those investigators aren't interested in you. They're off trying to find Calliope Bontempi. Buncha dumb-asses."

My stomach churns. "But if I get caught . . ."

"You won't get caught. I got your back." She gives me a reassuring pat. "I'll make sure there's a distraction in the PODPlex to keep security busy during the show."

As I think it over, a swirl of excitement eddies through my body at the thought of being on stage again. Plus, Tati's right—making music didn't get me into this mess, but it can get me out of it.

"Okay," I say. "So, you'll get the word out, then? 7:45. Half-hour show. That gives me plenty of time to get to the MediPlex and pay."

"Got it," says Tati. She goes back to digging through the bin. "Aha!" she says and holds up a strange floppy glove with an unblinking eyeball in the center. "My latest invention: a camera glove. I see people wearing something like this in the City. I took apart that old video cam orb you brought me and attached it to the palm, then wired it up through the fingers and back of the hand so you can wear it instead of holding it."

"And it'll connect to the laptop?" I ask as I examine her clever invention.

"Only one way to find out," Tati says with a wink. "I hear there's a LiveStream tomorrow night."

"Oh, I shouldn't . . ." I say.

"Shoulds are for sissies," Tati tells me. "And besides, when has that ever stopped you before?"

I grin because I know she's right. There's a rebellious streak in me, surely inherited from my mother. Seeing *Nobody from Nowhere* scrawled on the bathroom stall door in the warehouse, then yesterday on the wall by the Y.A.R.D. fuels it. Hearing Veronica, Rhiannon, and Jolene describe the hijacking at the Strip or lying to Smythe and Beauregarde while Medgers stood by makes it burn brighter. Listening to Dr. Garcia try to find my melody makes me want to sing out loud and sing out strong for *everyone* else to hear.

I pull on the glove. "It's perfect," I say.

"And it's all right there," says Tati, touching the eye. "In the palm of your hand."

Back on my bike, with the camera glove safely inside my bag, I ride along the river path toward the PODPlex to meet Brie. Finally our schedules have collided. A day off for her, a free evening for me. Which is a mighty good thing because I have so much to tell her I'm about to burst.

As I come to the curve in the path where Nowhere hides, I see the silhouette of a person illuminated from behind by the sun cresting over the treetops. I squeeze the brakes to slow down but I'm going too fast and the curve is too sharp. "Watch out!" I yell and skid.

The person spins around. Goes right then left, but can't seem to decide. I lean hard to swerve but the wheels go out from under me. I fall with the bike, sliding through the gravel and dirt. My back tire swipes the person's leg. Pebbles grind into my calf. My elbow hits a rock. A cloud of dust kicks up all around us as our bodies tangle with the bike.

"Sorry! Sorry! Are you okay?" I yell.

"I'm fine," the guy says as he gets to his feet and brushes himself off.

His voice is familiar. I squint up and get a twinge in my belly when I see Aimery.

"Zimri?" he says, clearly confused, but then he smiles big and broad.

"A little help here?" I struggle to get my pant leg free from the bike chain. He squats and spins the pedals but only makes it worse. "Other way!" I swat at his hand and notice that he's wearing a strange glove. The fingers are a soft flesh-colored mesh with black tips at the ends but the back has a beautiful glowing dark purple shell. I reach out to touch it. "What the . . . ?"

He quickly hides his hand behind his back and uses his other hand to turn the pedals. "There!" he says when my pant leg comes loose. "You're free. But you're bleeding." He points to my elbow as he helps me to my feet.

I turn my arm this way and that, trying to get a good look at the scrape.

"Here." He slips off the weird glove, shoves it in his pocket, and pulls out a small packet of thick soft cloths, each imprinted with a painting. I've seen them in the ware-house, packed them many times, but they've never been on sale at Black Friday. I wonder if he stole them. "Try this." He hands me one that looks like mushrooms on a decaying tree.

"You've got a rip," I tell him as I dab at the blood.

"Crap." He pokes a finger through the hole at his knee.

"No offense," I say. "But don't you have any other clothes? You've been wearing the same thing all week."

Aimery shakes his legs and tries to brush more dirt away from his pants but there's not much good he can do. "I'd be fine if a certain person wasn't trying to kill me with her bike. Why were you going so fast?"

"Why were you standing in the middle of the path?" I ask. "Hardly anybody but me comes out here anymore." Dorian flashes in my mind. We weren't far from here when we kissed. Everything seems so different in the light.

"You know, just looking at the river." Aimery gestures awkwardly toward the water. "It's very pretty."

I draw in a deep breath, pulling river air into my lungs to calm myself down after the bicycle wreck. "It's the one nice thing Corp X couldn't buy and destroy when they came."

Aimery's eyebrows shoot up.

"It's true," I tell him. "They bought up most of the land and businesses and houses, then plowed them down to build the Community of the Future!" I say in a booming voice. "Now everyone's a corporate drone unless you live in Old Town."

"Old Town?" he asks.

I point back over my shoulder.

"Is that where you were coming from in such a hurry?"

"Sorta," I say. "First I visited my grandmother. She's in a MediPlex."

"She . . . what . . . ?" he says. "In a MediPlex?" His face contorts as if he's trying to do a math problem. "Is that why you needed to leave work today?"

"Yes and thank you," I say, embarrassed by the fracas in the warehouse. "I tried to find you afterward but you were surrounded by all your adoring admirers," I tease him.

"Oh, please!" He waves away my gratitude. "I owed you one. Or twelve. You've stood up for me plenty with Rude Jude when he crawls up my butt about my lousy times. He's a real piece of work, isn't he?"

I lift the cloth to check my elbow. The bleeding has nearly stopped. "Yeah, well, he's the piece of work we all work for, so . . ."

"Actually," says Aimery, "you all work for Corporation

Xian Jai, and they might be very interested to know how a guy like that is running the place."

"Are you a mole?" I blurt out.

"A mole?" he asks, confused. "Is that like a squimonk?" He tucks his bottom lip under top teeth and pretends to nibble on a nut.

"No!" I laugh. "I mean a corporate spy. Sent here by Corp X to check up on the warehouse."

This time, Aimery laughs long and hard. His voice echoes across the riverbank and back. "What would make you think that?"

"That's what Jude thinks," I tell him and kick at rocks on the path.

"That makes sense," he says sarcastically. "Because he's an idiot and that's idiotic."

"Are you a rabble-rouser?"

"A what-the-whatter?"

"You know, one of those people who infiltrates and tries to get warehouse workers to band together? What did they used to call it? Unionizing or something?"

"I didn't know that was a thing."

I fold up the soft cloth he gave me. "Do you want this back?" I ask. "I'm not sure I can get the bloodstains out."

"Gross, no," he says. "It's disposable. Throw it away."

"Something this nice?" I say. "I'll wash it." I put it in my pocket. "So, if you're not a mole or a rabble-rouser, what are you doing here?"

"Working," he says. "Like everybody else."

I scoff. "You're hardly like everybody else."

"Neither are you," he says and I start to protest but he cuts me off. "I mean that as a compliment."

Butterflies stir in my stomach.

"So your grandmother," he asks suddenly. "Is she okay? The other day the security officer came and you seemed worried and then today you were hurrying off and . . ."

"It's not a great situation," I admit.

"I'm sorry," he says and steps closer. The sun is beginning to wane and shadow-trees creep across the path toward us. "I know what it's like to worry about someone you love when they're not well."

"You do?"

"My sister's been in a MediPlex since I was really young."

"At the MediPlex here?" I reach out to comfort him but then I stop because that might seem weird. Like nearly everyone in the warehouse, I feel drawn to Aimery. I've seen what happens when he goes down the aisles. People stop and stare because he's somehow inexplicably fabulous. He doesn't look like us or talk like us or even walk like us. There's something about him that makes everyone want to watch him. But the weird thing is, sometimes I find him watching me.

"No, not here," he says. "MediPlex has facilities all over the place. She's in one where I grew up."

Before I can ask where that is, he says, "So your grandmother, is she going to be okay?"

"Truthfully, I don't know," I tell him, surprised by how easy it is to be honest just then.

He moves in closer. The temperature seems to drop and I get goose bumps on my arms. "How not okay is she?"

I hesitate, unsure whether it's okay to confide in him, but

there's a part of me that's ready to burst from keeping all the worry inside. For three days I've gotten up, gone to work, done my job, rushed to see her, and gotten home in time to shove down some food and fall in bed. And the only good part of those days has been Aimery. Every morning when I see him in the warehouse, I find myself smiling, glad to work near him again, even if he is horrible at his job. And he seems equally happy to see me. For the first time since Brie was switched to nights, my tenners have been fun again because I go outside with Aimery. We joke around and talk about all kinds of silly things like which snacks are better (Krispy Krab and Bakon Crickers or SalsaGhetti Squidoos) and what songs on the Buzz make us want to barf. I can make him belly laugh by imitating Ios's butt-shaking "(Quark) Charmed, I'm Sure" song. The truth is, I feel a strange and intense comfort with Aimery that I don't feel with anyone else but Brie, and before I know it, the words are spilling out as I pace back and forth, kicking up dust around my feet.

"I don't know. It's bad. She's old and her memory is slipping and she wandered away and then someone found her and to make a long story short, they're going to kick her out of the MediPlex tomorrow unless I come up with a boatload of cash that I don't have."

His mouth falls open. He looks horrified. "Where was she? Who found her?" His voice is urgent, like a little kid who needs to know the end of a story.

"We don't know," I tell him. "That's the weird part. As best anyone can figure, some Plute was driving by the river and found her wandering in the road a few miles from here. She's incredibly lucky. She could have been hit, or picked up by a maniac, or attacked by a coyolf, or fallen into the river." I visibly shudder at the thousands of ways the story could have ended badly. I look out over the water to the other side of the river, then back at Aimery. "It's probably the first time in history a Plute has ever done anything nice for a Plebe out here."

He laughs, weird and nervous. "There are plenty of nice Plutes in the world!" he says loudly. "Maybe it wasn't even a Plute that found her!"

I scoff. "He was definitely a Plute. The MediPlex people saw his car."

"They did?" he asks, eyes wide.

"Yeah, but it was dark so they couldn't say what kind it was."

A little dragonfly zooms up between us and Aimery jumps. "Oh, no!" he yells and hides his face behind his arm.

"Take it easy!" I shoo the bug away. "It won't hurt you. Dragonflies don't sting like wasps and bees."

"Oh wow, that was . . . it was . . ." He watches it fly off. "Real, wasn't it?" He looks at me, amazed.

"As opposed to a fake dragonfly?" I raise an eyebrow at him.

"Ha, right, yeah. Forget it. I'm a little weirded out by bugs."

"There are no bugs where you're from?" I tease him.

"Not like that," he says. Then he points to my bike. "Hey look, your handlebars are crooked."

"Dang it!" I pick it up and work to straighten them. "Dorian just gave me this bike."

"Is that the big tall dude with the arms?" He pretends to flex. "If I'd known it was your birthday—"

"My birthday?"

"I just figured since your boyfriend got you a present—"

"My boyfriend?" I squint at him. "Dorian is just a friend, an old friend," I say, but a flush crawls up my chest and into my face. Friend doesn't feel like the right word, but I can't call him a boyfriend after just one quick kiss. "And what's my birthday got to do with it?" I snarl, embarrassed by the conversation. "Are we five years old?"

Aimery blinks at me. "You mean, you haven't gotten a birthday present since you were five?"

"Nobody does," I tell him.

"Nobody?" he says and laughs. "From Nowhere?" Then he starts to hum.

A thrill hits me in the belly and I nearly drop the bike again. "Why are you singing that song? How do you know it?"

"There's this thing." He leans close and touches me on the shoulder, sending a ripple down my back. "Called radio. If you have a receiver, which is like a special box you buy on the black market, you can hear it. And sometimes people set up pirate stations."

"I know what pirate radio is! But when did you hear that song?"

"I've heard it a few times," he tells me. "A couple of days ago late at night. Then last night DJ HiJax played it."

"DJ HiJax!" I blink at him, disbelieving.

"He's been playing it a lot. If you want, I'll show you my receiver." He wiggles his eyebrows, but I just stare at him, speechless. "You okay?" he asks.

"Yeah," I tell him slowly, trying to puzzle through what's going on, but it makes no sense. "It's been a weird day, that's all. I should get going. I have somewhere I need to be. See you tomorrow?"

"Tomorrow?" he asks, confused.

"Work," I say. "Remember? That job you have in the warehouse, just like everybody else?"

"Oh, that," he says, but looks uncertain.

"You're not thinking of ditching, are you? Because Ajax will put you on nights if you miss a shift. And if you think working days sucks . . ."

He looks everywhere but at me. "I . . . um . . . yeah . . . we'll see," he mutters.

I figure that's the best answer I'll get out of him and I shouldn't be surprised. People come and go all the time around here. But I'm glad the light is waning because my face burns bright at the thought of not seeing him. I sling my leg over the seat and say, "See you around."

"Good-bye," he calls after me as I head off toward the PODPlex in search of Brie, wondering what Aimery's not telling me.

ORPHEUS

After Zimri slams into me with her bike, then zooms around the curve in the river, disappearing beneath the trees, I stay in the middle of the path. Stuck. I was all set to get the hell out of here. This afternoon in the warehouse when Rude Jude was harassing Zimri, I knew my experiment in Plebeland needed to be over. It was all fun and games when I first got here, but I can go home if I want an asshole to yell at me and tell me what to do. Plus, my father pays better.

Then she knocked me over, literally, and I'm all confused. Part of my brain thinks, *Might not be so bad to stay.* Which is insane! I can't stay at a Complex for a girl. Especially not a Plebe girl. What am I going to do? Settle down in a POD with Zimri and work on the warehouse floor until I die? As if!

But then she came around the curve and made my heart rev. There's something about her that draws me in and makes it impossible to look away. She has all the raw material every PromoTeam hopes for when a kid wakes up from an ASA: charisma, charm, an interesting kind of beauty, natural confidence, and compassion. Only no one in the City would ever expect that kind of thing from a Plebe like Zim.

And so, there's a dumb little part of my brain that keeps saying, *If things were different . . . if she wasn't a Plebe and I wasn't a Plute.* But no, it's stupid. She's the wrong girl. The wrong kind. A Plebe girl. A beautiful, interesting, funny, fascinating Plebe girl who I can't stop thinking about when the workday's done.

I shake myself to snap out of it. I can't go back to that godforsaken warehouse again. Especially when I have a life back home. "This is just a hiatus," I say aloud. "A chance to make my parents fret."

I force myself to picture Arabella, lovely Arabella. I was so mad at her a few nights ago when she wouldn't leave a dumb party to talk to me when I needed her, but that was silly. She was just doing her job. I can't be mad at her for that. It's what her brain is wired to do now and everything else is secondary. I try to conjure up her face, but her image is cloudy. It's hard to remember who she used to be beneath the bigger eyes and complicated braids and body paint. Then Zimri crowds my mind again. I try to imagine her dressed up like a Plute girl and I laugh. She'd never go for it. Zim's the kind of person who'd tell a PromoTeam to shove it and then do her own thing. Like my mom.

My mouth falls open and I look up into the darkening sky. It's become a deep rich blue I've never seen beneath the light pollution of the City, but I'm more astounded by the realization that Zimri reminds me of my mother. Not the mother who raised me but Libellule the superstar. And not in the skeevy way Ios tried to flirt with me by imitating my mom in her prime, which was gross. Like my mom, Zimri has a fierce confidence and independent streak even though she doesn't come from money or power. There's no good reason for either my mother or Zimri to strut around commandeering so much attention, except for the fact that Zimri, like my mom, is more awesome than everyone around her. But unlike my mother, Zimri has no idea of her effect on people. Which is partly what makes her so charming.

I walk quickly along the path with thoughts fluttering in my head like all the little chickadees and bluebirds feasting on bright red bushberries. I think of Arabella again. I stop and close my eyes to relive our last kiss in Nahmad Gallery. So quick and fleeting. Every time we fooled around before her surgery, we never got it right. We were always interrupted or one of us just stopped. Then there was that split second in my kitchen when we both slumped over the counter, laughing. I thought that would be our moment but she jumped away. What would have happened if our lips had found one another? Our tongues entangled? In my mind, the kiss is wonderful. We find a rhythm with our mouths and it's perfect and amazing and when I pull away to look into her face, my eyes pop open because the person I'm picturing in my mind's eye isn't Arabella.

"Oh, hell!" I say out loud, then I'm striding up the path again.

I can't deny that I feel something for Zimri. And sometimes, I think she might feel the same way about me. If she had an ExoScreen, I'm certain our carapaces would be a perfect match. But the whole thing is impractical. I start muttering out loud to the birds and bugs buzzing all around.

I only planned to be gone until my money ran out. Just long

enough to make my parents sweat. Then I'd go home. They'd feel guilty and let me have a say in what to do with my life.

I come to the giant willow tree along the shore and duck beneath the low ropy branches into the cool underbelly where my car is hidden. In the dusky light I can barely make out how messed up it is, but I know the whole passenger side door is scraped and dented where I ran into the rail that stopped me from plunging into the river. The back right tire has gone flat. I have a RoboJack but I don't know how to use it and I'm not sure it would do much good anyway. The last time I drove it, from the MediPlex to here, it hissed and banged like something inside the engine was messed up, too. Finally, I pulled over and pushed it beneath this tree, sure I'd never make it back to the City.

Now I don't know if I want to go back and I'm not even sure why. Guilt, maybe? Guilt that I can leave and Zimri can't even though she's smart and hardworking and just as deserving of a good life as I am.

"The truth is," I declare aloud to the peepers and crickets who've begun to sing their evening song, "if she'd been born in the City, into a different family, or at a different time, she would never stay a Plebe. She's the kind of person who would rise above the system like my mother did when that was still possible."

Maybe that's the reason I have this strange compunction to help her. I want to do something grand and sweeping to make up for the crappy cards Zimri has been dealt. But what can I do? Take her home with me? That'd go over well. *Hey, Dad, look what I got at the Corp X warehouse. A Plebe girl. Can I keep her?*

Then I think about her grandmother in the MediPlex. She

must be the woman I almost hit the other night. She didn't know her name. Didn't know where she was from. So I looked up the nearest MediPlex and dropped her off, hoping someone there could help. Since the MediPlex is run by the same corporation as Alouette's, I was able to establish a link with the RoboNurse who did the old woman's intake but I haven't been back to see her. I've thought about it, but I'm so tired after my shift each night that I can barely make it to the Strip to scrounge up some food, then crawl back to my banged-up Cicada to sleep. Now, though, finding out she's most likely Zimri's grandmother feels like a sign. As if everything that's happened over the past few days is part of a strange confluence of events meant to bring me here to meet Zimri.

I climb on top of my car then hoist myself onto a sturdy branch and clamber up the tree, scraping shins and palms on rough bark, to get a better look at the sky, as if the answer will be written in the stars. When I come to a fork in the willow, I rest and wonder if this is the kind of place Zimri and her friends played when they were kids. Climbing real trees seems infinitely more fun than the precisely manicured and preplanned Plute playgrounds where everything is designed to maximize childhood development, but none of it is half as interesting as this one tree with its bugs and worms and birds and moss.

I stare up through the leaves and branches at the stars beginning to peek out beneath the flashing lights of delivery drones. In the City, I always feel big and weighty, as if my existence is the center of everything important. Like when I was little and took for granted that the universe must spin around me. Out here, on the periphery, I see how easy it is to feel small and insignificant. Like I am nothing more than a speck on someone else's screen. Which is why I like that song so much. *Nobody from Nowhere, I'm here, I'm here, I'm here. I'm Nobody from Nowhere, listen to me scream.*

For the first time in my life I realize how convenient it is for Plutes like me to assume we deserve everything we have. My parents both worked hard, right? I did well in SCEWL. We all played the game. As if that entitles us to be rich snots. No way! Over the past few days I've seen how hard the warehouse pickers work on their road to nowhere. Then again, my choices are limited, too. Either I stay away, hiding from my parents while working a crappy PONI job, or I go home to have my brain zapped into genius mode and live a Plute life I won't enjoy because I'll be too obsessed with making music. Seems like I'd be trading one trapped existence for another.

For the past few days, I've purposefully not checked the Buzz. For one thing the reception is blocked in the warehouse, and at night after work, I've kept my ExoScreen glove off in case anyone has been trying to reach me. Instead, I've relied on my receiver to catch waves of pirate radio. DJ HiJax has become my solace, playing stolen tunes and talking up Project Calliope, which is still all over the news. I feel a little bad for HiJax if he believes Calliope can beat my father. It's nice to hear someone dreaming big but they have no idea what they're up against.

Tonight, before Zim came along, I'd put my ExoScreen glove on to find out what was happening in the City. I figured if I was heading back, I should be up to speed. Now, I pull it out of my pocket again and slide it over my pale left hand, then click my thumb and forefinger together to activate the digital connection. The carapace slowly warms to a purple glow and the screen on my palm lights up. I slip my EarBug in place (no nasty wires needed) and click together my middle finger and my thumb to access the Buzz.

DJ Lazy Eye's rap opera premieres in Shanghai.

The last great diva of pop stardom, Taylor Swift, died today at a MediPlex outside of Nashville, Tennessee. She was 100 years old.

Quinby Masterson record sales broken by 14-year-old whiz kid Olivia Ganza's reproductions of celebrity death masks.

Elston Tunick exhibition opens at Niarchos Gallery in Athens to lukewarm sales response.

"Jeez!" I say aloud. I've only been gone three days and already so much has happened, but oddly none of it seems important. Because what I really want to know is the story of my disappearance. My heart climbs in my throat. For the first time, I feel guilty for running away. My mother has probably been sick with worry. My dad has probably screamed and pitched a fit at Esther, telling her that she'd better find me. I'm sure Rajesh and Arabella have pinged me a million times and must think I'm mad at them since I haven't answered, which is true, but I should at least let them know I'm okay. I take a deep breath and ask the Buzz for all the headlines about Orpheus Chanson over the past three days, then brace myself for the onslaught of sound bites about my disappearance.

Only, there are none.

Sure that I've made a mistake, I search again. And again. I search my name, my father's name, and my mother's, but the only stories that come up are about Calliope's lawsuit against my dad, and my mother yammering about a new line of clothing.

I pull up my ping history. I see the usual batch of group pings from the past few days. My friends all announcing where they'll be and making plans to meet up for maximum Buzz, but there is nothing out of the ordinary. Nobody asks me directly where I am or if anyone has seen me. Then again, maybe it shouldn't surprise me. If I'm not helping their Buzz ratings, then I barely warrant any attention. Not even from Arabella.

Then I see the pings from my parents buried in the history from the first day I was gone:

From: Libellule
To: Orpheus
Where are you? Can't reach you. Has your
father taken you for surgery? I'm FRANTIC!

From: Harold
To: Orpheus
Where the hell are you? If you think you can
hide behind your mother, you're mistaken. I
WILL find you!

From: Libellule
To: Harold
CC: Orpheus
Where is Orpheus?!?!?! You can't force him
to have surgery against his will! I'll call every

facility, every surgeon, until I find him. I have connections too, you know!

From: Harold
To: Libellule
CC: Orpheus
I don't have him and you know it! Stop playing your stupid games. I'll drop the story of you standing in his way straight into the Buzz, Li. You know I will.

From: Libellule
To: Harold
CC: Orpheus
Go right ahead and drop your little lies. They'll get buried under the avalanche of your other disasters. And I'll drop my own: Tyrant Patron Forces Only Son to have ASA That Left Daughter Incapacitated. How will that look for Chanson Industries?

From: Libellule
To: Orpheus
I don't think Chanson has him. Harold's threatening me, but I can tell he's worried. We might be able to use this to our advantage. Plant a story to advance the cause and gain some public sympathy for the project.

From: Libellule
To: Orpheus
Oops! Ignore that last ping. Not meant for
you. But Orphie, baby, PLEASE reach out to
me. I'm so worried. Let me know you're okay
and that Daddy doesn't have you locked
away somewhere. I'm going out of my
mind!!!!!!

From: Harold
To: Orpheus
Enough of this nonsense! Come home
immediately or you risk losing everything. I
WILL find you and when I do . . .

I stop reading and sit in the tree, dumbstruck. Even when I'm missing, my parents snipe at one another rather than work together to find me, which couldn't be too hard now that I think of it. Surely my car has some kind of tracking device. They could release pix of me over the Buzz and offer a reward for information. They could trace my spending and send out private security to track me down. That's what usually happens when Plute kids disappear. But none of that is going on. Instead, once again, I'm caught in the middle of their protracted battle.

But the weird thing is, their whole exchange took place several days ago and there's been nothing since then. Nothing in the Buzz. No planted stories as threatened by both sides. No one trying to reach me again. And what's with Mom's ping about using my disappearance to gain traction and sympathy? For what? Her new clothing company?

As I listen to the soothing night sounds of the river, it slowly dawns on me that no one is looking for me because if they were, they would have found me by now. It makes no sense, though! I'm a Chanson, after all. Something's not quite right. It's as if I've disappeared off the face of the planet and nobody seems to care. Or maybe the truth is it's more convenient for me to be gone.

Then I really get nervous. If I've disappeared, does that mean all my money's gone, too? Quickly, I pull up my spending account on my ExoScreen to check my balance, then fall back against the branch, relieved. I still have quite a bit of money from my last monthly automated entertainment deposit. I guess working all the time while living in my car doesn't cost much. At this rate, I could stay here at the Complex until autumn living large. Hell, I could go up to the Strip and buy drinks for everybody. Noodles on me! Or shower Zimri with presents to make up for every birthday she's never celebrated. Assuage my guilt with gifts the way my parents did when I was little and complained they were never around. I shake my head, disgusted with myself. Just another Plute jerk with no regard for money. The kind of cash I have on hand could do some good out here. Change someone's life. I could easily pay off Zimri's grandmother's MediPlex bill.

I smack myself on the forehead so hard I nearly topple out of the tree. What an idiot I am. "Of course!" I say aloud and begin to climb down. I could pay Zimri's grandmother's bill. I don't know why I didn't think of it before. "Probably," I tell the tree, "because I'm a self-centered Plute brat." I hit the ground and realize that for once in my life, the choice to do something for someone else feels easy. But first I have to make sure the woman I took to the MediPlex is who I think she is.

It doesn't take me long to find her. Since this facility is run by the same corporation that runs Alouette's and I have twenty-four-hour access in the City, I walk in no problem, even though visiting hours are long over. I still have my link to her RoboN-urse, so my ExoScreen leads me straight upstairs to a circular room filled with sleeping patients behind flimsy curtains.

"Hello," I call gently as I tiptoe to bed number seven.

The old woman pushes herself up and peers at me. "You my doctor?"

"I'm a little young to be a doctor, don't you think?" I tease.

"Least you're human," she says dryly and I laugh.

"You don't remember me?"

She knits her brow.

"The other night. I was in my car. You were on the road. I almost hit you then I brought you here." I'm not sure how I coaxed her into my Cicada that night. She'd probably been so exhausted and disoriented that she would have accepted help from an alien who'd just landed on earth, which is probably what I looked like to her.

She narrows her eyes and shakes her head. "You must be mistaken," she says. "My daughter brought me here and she'll be back any time now. I'm going home."

"Your daughter?" I ask. I've never heard Zimri mention her

mom. "Do you have a granddaughter named Zimri who calls you Nonda?"

"Yes," she says and smiles big. "Do you know her? Is she okay?"

"She's fine. I was with her almost all day. We work together."

"Work?" she says. "You must be thinking of someone else. My Zimri is only eleven. And she's all alone. Her father died. Her mother's gone. I'm all she has. Oh, now, wait a minute." She stops and looks perplexed. "Let me think. That's not right, is it?" Nonda looks at me, a bit frightened and unsure.

I step up closer and offer her my hand.

"I'm not sure," I tell her. "But the Zimri I know is about sixteen and works in the warehouse and sings all the time."

"Yes!" She gives my fingers a squeeze. "That's her. She's not little anymore. Sometimes I get lost in the past."

"That's okay," I assure her. "The past is a good place to go, sometimes."

"Depends on what you're remembering," she tells me.

I settle into a chair beside her. At that moment, I miss Alouette and wonder if she'll know when I'm not there for our usual weekly visit. Right now, she's the only reason I'd go back.

"So you work at the warehouse, too?" Nonda asks me.

"Yes," I tell her. "Interesting place."

"Hellhole," she says and I chuckle. Then she spends the next half an hour telling me stories about growing up out here, all the changes that took place when the centralized government imploded and Corp X came in.

". . . and all these anarcho-capitalists had the nerve to tell us folks that things would be better this way. That the free market would solve all our problems. Hmph, like to see those fat cats in the City walk a mile in my shoes!"

"You're right," I tell her, leaning forward, enraptured by her take on a world I've never even considered. "It'd be good for every Plute kid to come out here and work in a warehouse for a week. They'd appreciate their lives so much more if they did."

"Warehouse work can be tough," she says. "Wears some folks down. Like my son-in-law, Linus, Zimri's daddy. He couldn't take it."

"What happened to him?" I ask.

"He was always . . . um . . ." she searches for the word, then settles on, "fragile. And after my daughter left, he got depressed. And the work. It got to him. Not everyone is cut out to be a picker."

"Tell me about it," I mutter.

"He took the plunge. That's what we call it when workers throw themselves in the river."

I rear back. "Does that happen a lot?"

"Sure," she says with a cold shrug, sending a chill down my spine.

"Poor Zimri," I say. My chest aches at the thought of her as a little kid losing her dad like that after her mother left.

"Don't you worry about my Zimri. She's one tough cookie. Just like me."

"I don't doubt that," I tell her.

A RoboNurse wheels into the room, blinks at me with green LED eyes, and says, "Visiting hours are over. Please proceed to the exit."

Instead of leaving, I pull out my ExoScreen glove and link to Nonda's account. The Robo's head swivels to me and the face screen lights up with her info. It takes less than two minutes for me to transfer half of what's left in my spending account— a paltry sum to my family meant to keep me entertained for a few weeks. But paying off Nonda's MediPlex bill makes me happier than anything I've ever bought.

"So," I say to her when the bill is settled. "I guess I should let you get some rest now."

"Wait," she says and grips my hand. "I don't know your name."

"Orpheus," I tell her, knowing full well she'll never remember, but still it feels good to say my name out loud. "I'm Orpheus Chanson."

ZIMRI

Brie's POD is always a wreck, which is one of the reasons I love to come here. The retractable furniture is usually out: table and benches and kitchen counters covered with dishes; sleeping unit and couch both rolled out from the walls so there's only a narrow space to walk. And since she and her mother, Elena, have been on opposite shifts for the past week, the place is messier than usual. Laundry, shoes, shopping bags, and empty food containers cover nearly every surface.

I stand in the gap between the kitchen area and main living area, acting out today's warehouse drama for Brie who lies in the nest of covers on the bed. "Then he's all like, 'You're staying and working late!'" I pretend Jude is hustling me to the side against the flow of bodies.

"He's such an enema!" she squeals.

"I know, right?" I'm so relieved to see her and tell her everything that I nearly throw myself in her lap. "Just a few days ago he was asking me to do him a favor, then he acts like that!"

"What favor?" she asks.

"Oh my god, he picked me up in his stupid little cart and he was like . . ." I flop down on the bed beside her and grab her thigh, just like he did to me, then I get my face way too close to hers and say in a deep grumbly voice like his, "You know we make a great team."

"Ew, gross! What kind of *team*?" Brie asks. "Beach volley-ball? Tennis doubles? Two-man bobsled?" she jokes and we laugh. "For real, though." She rolls to her side and props her head up on her elbow. Her brown curls are especially wild today and her freckles are out since she got some sun. "What did he mean about being a team?"

"He thinks there's a mole from Corp X and wants me to keep an eye on him," I explain.

"Who is it?" she asks, leaning forward, eager for more details. She has the same eyes as Elena, dark brown with flecks of gold that match her warm skin.

"A guy named Aimery," I say, trying to sound nonchalant, which is hard when his face flashes in my mind, grinning at me with those perfectly straight white teeth while running his hand through his mat of dark hair that has grown unruly over the past few days, as if he hasn't showered.

"Do you think he has a thing for you?" Brie asks.

"Who, the new guy?" My palms get sweaty and blood rushes into my cheeks as I think of him by the river tonight. What was he doing there? And that strange glove on his hand, like the one Tati described seeing in the City . . .

"No," says Brie. "Jude. Because of the way he grabbed you and what he said. Hey, wait a sec." She sits up and examines my face. "You're blushing. Are you . . . do you . . . ?" She flings herself away from me then whispers, "Do you have a thing for *him*?"

"For Jude?" I squeal. "God, no! Ugh, ew gross, yuck!" I pop off the bed and shake and shimmy to get the very idea off my body.

Brie cackles with delight at my response. "Calm down. I'm just messing with you." She settles back into the pillows. "What about this Aimery guy. Is he really a mole?"

"No!" I laugh. "But there is something odd about him that I can't quite put my finger on. It's hard to explain but he doesn't act like a Plebe."

"What's he act like then?" she asks.

"Like this." I move across the floor, slow and languid but full of confidence with my chin held high. "And he says hello to everyone!" I pretend to be Aimery walking down the warehouse aisles, greeting people. "Hey, Peggy Sue. How's it going, Ana Ng? Jennifer! Juniper! Look at all my friends!" I point and grin and pretend to shake everybody's hands. "I swear, after two days in the warehouse, he knows more people than I do." I drop down beside her again. "And everybody *loves* him!"

"Including you?" asks Brie, her sly grin returning.

"No," I say defensively. "Don't be ridiculous."

"But then why . . ." She points at me and rubs her cheeks. "Why are you are so flushed?"

I wasn't going to talk about Aimery. Or at least about the weird thoughts that flutter through my mind about him. How kind he was after Billingsley came to tell me Nonda had been found. The way he raises both eyebrows at me whenever something absurd happens in the warehouse, then we both have to look away so we don't laugh. How he said my name is fitting and asks me every night after work if I'll show him a good place to get some food, but I haven't yet because I've been in a rush to visit Nonda. Not to mention how he stood up to Jude on my behalf and sang my song to me on the river path tonight.

Brie grins like she knows something.

"What?"

She keeps grinning.

"What!" I demand.

"Dorian?" she says slowly, slyly, crawling toward the edge of the bed while keeping her eyes on me. "Is this about Dor?"

"Is what about him?"

"All this blushy, hand-wringing stuff you're doing. Are you holding out on me?"

"No! Not at all!" I protest way too much. My stomach does an inside out whamma-jamma rollover when I think about kissing Dorian by the river and how he came to security with me and stood up to Medgers then hugged me tight and offered to stay with me if I didn't want to stay alone. How he found me during a tenner after word spread that Nonda was in the MediPlex then gave me the bike and told me that he missed me. I bury my face in my hands. After all that, how can I have these feelings for Aimery!

"Oh, god," I say, "this is all way too complicated and I don't have time for any of it!"

"Why?" asks Brie, clearly excited. She gets off the bed and grabs my shoulders. "I think it's fantastic. You and Dor have known each other since you were little. You have a ton in common. You like all the same things. He's gorgeous. What's complicated about that?"

I stand there, trying to find the words to tell her everything, like how sometimes when that kiss by the river floats through my mind, I watch myself pull away but when I look up, I see Aimery instead of Dorian.

"So complicated. So complicated," I mutter. Then to make matters worse, my HandHeld beeps. I look down and see that Dorian has arrived.

"I don't know about this." Dorian paces as Brie shoves clothes and shoes into the closet and retracts the sleeping unit into the wall so there's more room in the main space for the three of us.

I sit on the couch with my head in my hands. I didn't expect Dorian to try to talk me out of doing the concert tomorrow night and the argument is giving me a headache.

"Don't you think it's weird, though?" he asks. "First the doctor and then that guy from the warehouse, what's his name, Avery?"

"Aimery," I mumble, trying to seem indifferent.

"They both heard your song on the waves."

I feel my body buzz and soar at the thought of DJ HiJax playing my song.

"If they heard it, then Medgers could have heard it and if she heard it, she'll have her ear to the ground, listening for any hint that you're putting on a show," Dorian says.

"But Tati has my back," I tell him again. "She'll cause a distraction at the PODPlex so security will be busy."

"Still," Dorian argues. "If Medgers gets the slightest hint, you know she'll come after you even if the entire PODPlex is on fire. She's had it in for your family for years!"

"Even if you do get caught, what's the worst-case scenario?" Brie asks as she shoves laundry into the MicrobeZapper.

I look away. I still haven't told either of them about Smythe and Beauregarde snooping around the other day.

"Best-case scenario, a justice broker shows up at your door and demands the money you made for playing music," Dorian says. "And if you can't pay, you go to jail to work off your debt. Worst-case scenario," he presses his fingers into the sides of his head, "bzzt!"

"Oh, come on!" I say. "That's just a myth. Has anyone ever really gotten their brain zapped for playing illegal music?"

"I don't know, but I don't want to be the one who finds out. You know full well that big City corporate justice brokers are way better than the ones we get assigned by Corp X, and Arbiters always side with the bigwigs, so I wouldn't test those waters," Dorian says.

That shuts me up. He is right, of course. Anytime a Plebe goes up against a Plute company, the Plebe loses big-time, like my mom or Levon or my father's friend Captain Jack.

"And this concert is different than the others you've done," Dorian goes on. "Because people will be paying you directly for the music. Maybe there's some gray area when you put on a show to benefit someone else and you never touch a dime, but there's no doubt that what you're planning to do is one hundred percent, totally illegal."

I slump back against the sofa. "If I don't show up at the MediPlex tomorrow with a wad of cash, Nonda goes home and that can't happen yet."

"If you get caught then she could be worse off," Dorian argues. "But I think there's another way."

Brie and I both blink at him. "What?" we ask at the same time.

"Just don't sing," he says. "When people show up, ask them to donate some money to Nonda's care. You've done enough for other people. No one will begrudge you that."

"That's not a bad idea," Brie says, but I stand there flabbergasted.

My stomach curdles. My fingers and toes clench. "Don't sing?" I say through gritted teeth.

"I'm suggesting that you don't sing for money tomorrow night," he clarifies.

Every ounce of anger I've ever felt over being told to be quiet all my life comes rushing through my body. Nonda shushing me in the bath. My father smacking me on the mouth for singing on the tram. RoboNannies taking apart the instruments I created out of our meager supply of toys.

"All my life, everyone has warned me that music would ruin everything, like it did for my mother," I say as I stomp around Brie's POD, tidy now that all the furniture's put away. When we were little, Brie and I took turns lying in the bed as it retracted into the wall to see who could stay inside the longest. Brie couldn't last for more than a few minutes and needed me to talk to her the whole time to prove I hadn't left. I, on the other hand, could have stayed inside that dark and cozy space for hours singing to myself. But hearing Dr. Garcia and Aimery sing my song today made me realize I don't want to keep my music hidden any longer.

I turn to Dorian. "You know that music is the one thing

that makes my life worth living, so if I want to make music then I'm going to make music," I tell him. "And if a concert is the only way I have of taking care of my grandmother, then I'm going to do it. And I won't let some a-hole in the City who thinks he owns everything, or a weasel like Medgers—or you—stop me. I decide what to do with my life!"

"But you're putting yourself at risk!" Dorian yells.

"You sound like your dad," I yell back.

"It's better than being your mom," he says. "She wouldn't stop either and look what it got her!"

"OUT!" I yell at him as I stomp toward Brie's door. "It got her out of this hellhole life."

"If you get caught, you could lose everything," Dorian calls after me. "Just like your mom did."

I spin around and stare at him, seething. "What did she lose? A crap job in a warehouse?"

"She lost a lot more than that!" When I stare at him blankly, he steps toward me with his hands out and he says, "She lost you."

VERSE FIVE

ORPHEUS

Since I've decided to stay at the Complex for a while longer, I have a few things to take care of the next day after work. First, I have to find a shower and some new clothes. Five days in the same pants has killed the self-cleaning microbes in the fabric, and washing in the river isn't doing much to get me clean. Second, I have to find a place to live because if I sleep in my car much longer, I'll permanently become a hunchback. When I come out of the warehouse after the seven o'clock buzzer, I look for Zimri. Jude moved me to a new sector today, no doubt as payback for standing up to him, so I haven't seen her all day, which sucks.

While I'm searching the crowd for her unmistakable puff of hair, a girl called Veronica, who worked in the same sector as me today, saunters up. "Hey there, Aimery! You heading up to the Strip for some fun?" she asks in a singsong voice.

"Um, well, sort of . . ." I say.

"We're going that way, too," her friend Jolene says. "Come with us."

"The thing is," I tell them while scanning the thinning streams of people, "I need to do some shopping."

"You sure do," the third girl, called Rhiannon, says. "Those pants have seen better days."

"I know, right?" I pat the dusty fabric covering me. "I'm a mess."

"Get you out of those clothes and you'd look just like a boy in the Buzz," Jolene says and laughs.

"What?" I step away, my heart bumping.

"Mm-hm, with that hair and those teeth." She fakes a big smile, which cracks the other two up. "Too bad you're just a Plebe boy!"

"Yeah," I say with a nervous twitter. "Too bad."

"You'll have to hit Black Friday tomorrow," Veronica tells me.

"Black Friday?" I ask.

"To buy some pants," says Jolene.

"Isn't there anyplace open now?" I ask.

Rhiannon screws up her face. "You could buy stuff from the warehouse, but . . ." She shakes her head.

"That would be dumb?" I ask and they all nod. "Because . . . ?"

"You'd pay Plute prices, duh," says Rhiannon.

"Good to know," I say.

"So get them tomorrow because right now we all gotta eat," says Veronica, then she grabs my arm and drags me toward the AutoTrams.

Resigned that I'll never find Zimri tonight, I follow the girls.

As the tram pulls away from the warehouse, I look up at the fleets of drones continually taking off and landing on the roof.

I cringe at the thought of myself in the City mindlessly pressing order buttons, then huffing and moaning when my packages didn't arrive within an hour, as if no one was on the other side of that order picking out what I wanted, packing it in a box, and attaching it to a drone that had to fly all the way to find me.

"Don't you hate the Plutes?" I blurt to Veronica who's in the seat next to me. "They're so entitled and demanding. They think they need—no, not just need, but *deserve*—everything they want, the minute they think of it."

Veronica looks at me perplexed. "But if they didn't act like three-year-olds about everything then we wouldn't have jobs, would we?"

"Oh," I say quietly. "I never thought of that."

"Doesn't mean we like them," says Jolene who sits with Rhiannon, facing us.

"Or that we're not jealous. I mean, dang, nice life, right? All they do is flit from party to party taking pix of themselves." Veronica scooches into the seat with Jolene and Rhiannon and slings her arms around their shoulders, then they all hold up their hands and pretend to shoot pix with FingerCams. They switch poses every second, exaggerating goonish smiles, and I realize what jerks we must seem like to them.

"Their lives are one big, endless party," Veronica says. "Until they get their brains zapped and wake up famous."

"That's not exactly how it works," I say. They all look at me skeptically. "They go to SCEWL, you know."

Jolene snorts. "I can tell you one thing for sure, their school ain't nothing like the one we went to."

As we get out of range of the warehouse signal, all the Hand-Helds wake up and begin to ping with headlines and messages from friends. Except for mine because I never set up the feed so my HandHeld is as useless as a brick on my wrist once I leave the warehouse. While everybody else is connecting digitally to the world, I look out the tram window. We pass rows and rows of PODPlexes, rising like boxy white mushrooms from the land. Somewhere in there is where Zimri sleeps at night and where she starts her day.

"Ios LiveStream starts at 7:00," Jolene says.

"New song from Minerva VaVoom drops today," Rhiannon says.

"Merle and Loretta are heading to the Strip, too," Veronica adds. "They want to meet us there."

"Ew, did you see this about some Plute kid who died?" Jolene asks.

"What?" I ask. "Who?" They all three look at me.

"Poor baby," Veronica says, pointing to my dead HandHeld. "Technology not your thing?"

"Something like that," I tell her. "But who died?"

Jolene sighs and skims the story on her palm. "Some patron's kid was missing. Now they think he wrecked his fancy flying car into a river somewhere." She shrugs. "They say he was on drugs. Nothing new."

The tram makes a sharp left, sending me across the seat, scrambling to get near Jolene's screen. "Who was he?" I ask.

"Who cares," Veronica says as we pull up alongside the Strip. "I'm starving!"

"But wait!" I grab Jolene before she can get up. "What was his name?"

Jolene takes one last glance at her screen as everyone pours out of the tram. "Orpheus Chanson."

After scarfing down a big bowl of slightly slimy grubworm-meal noodles with reconstituted microshrimp and spinocoli sprouts, I slip out of the Strip, leaving Veronica and her friends scream-singing along with Ios's latest LiveStream. I take the shortcut I found yesterday through the middle of the PODPlexes toward the river path. I need to get back to my Cicada, still safely hidden beneath the tree, where I can find out more about my supposed death. Do my parents really think I crashed or did one of them plant the story to up their Buzz? Either way, the shower, new clothes, and place to live will have to wait until tomorrow, my first day off since I arrived.

As I hurry past the SQEWL where RoboNannies patrol the perimeter of a big dirt patch, I hear sirens. All the kids inside the Y.A.R.D. run to the fence to watch five black-and-white security cars scream around the corner and I panic. Have I been located? Are they after me? Did someone realize I'm alive and well? I look around for a placc to hide but there's nowhcre to go; the buildings are all locked. Guards spill out of the cars, hands on Taser holsters as they run for the SQEWL. Their HandHelds crackle and I hear one say, "Bomb threat! Evacuate the children." RoboNannies quickly corral the kids into straight lines and usher them out of the Y.A.R.D., away from the buildings. In the chaos, I bolt, not stopping until I hit the river path.

Usually by now everyone is either at the Strip or in the warehouse working second shift, but tonight there are people all along the path. They walk in small groups, twos and threes, everyone heading in the same direction, toward the willow tree where I'm going, which makes me nervous. Has someone found my Cicada? Is there a reward for my safe return?

I follow along far enough behind that no one notices me, but when we get to the bend in the river where Zimri ran me down on her bike yesterday, the others scramble over the side of the embankment. I stand back in the shadow of the trees, trying to imagine where they could all be going. A secret party? Bonfire by the river? Down for a swim? Or does this have something to do with the emergency at the SQEWL? Whatever it is, it's drawing a lot of people because more and more come along the path and climb over the edge. After several minutes of watching, I decide to find out for myself what's going on.

It's getting dark and the moon is behind some clouds, so I can't see where I'm going once I get over the crest of the hill. I'm afraid I'll fall into the river, but when I come to the bottom, I find flat smooth ground and another smaller path looping back toward a dim light. I follow the voices and as my eyes adjust, I can make out a door that seems to be carved in the side of the riverbank. As I get closer, I see a sign that says, "WELCOME TO NOWHERE."

Another person comes up behind me. "What is this place?" I ask. The girl, whom I've never seen before, ignores my question as she pulls a black mask over her face and pushes past me. I stand aside as more people slip silently through the door with masks in place. I debate about what to do. The whole thing is creepy. Could it be some sort of secret society that planted a bomb in the SQEWL? Have I stumbled on the nefarious part of Complex life? I think about running away, but then I realize that whatever's going on can't be all that secretive or someone would have asked me what I'm doing here. Plus, everyone who comes over the embankment looks excited as they hurry toward the door.

I peek inside. The space is small and cramped, just a dugout really, but it's packed from wall to wall with people holding cups and chatting as if it's nothing out of the ordinary to stand around wearing black masks. The whole thing is pretty freaky but I'm intrigued and, since nobody tries to stop me, I walk right in.

At the makeshift bar, a masked person says, "Cash only," and points to a wooden box sitting on a counter made from two wobbly boards propped up on old sawhorses.

"Cash?" I say. "What for?"

He points to a handwritten sign that says *For Layla Robinson*.

"Layla Robinson!" I blink back my disbelief.

"She needs it more than you do right now, bub," the guy says.

Other people, also in masks, push me aside and shove wads of bills into the box, then grab cups from the rickety counter and join the crowd forming by a stage at the back of the room. Several of them look at me like they know me but since their faces are hidden, I have no idea who they are. Finally, I tap a girl on the shoulder and ask, "What's with the masks?"

"Just a precaution," she says with a shrug. "And it's kind of cool, right? I mean the whole anonymity thing. We are all Nobody from Nowhere when we're here."

"Like the song?" I ask, more confused.

"Duh," she says and moves away.

Then someone yells, "Here they come!"

I get pushed aside by everyone jostling forward, trying to

get a better view. I stand on tiptoe and crane my neck, but I still can't see over all the bodies in front of me. Then I hear someone smacking sticks together. The crowd erupts as a drummer breaks into a driving beat with bass drum, snare, hi-hat, and ride cymbal. Whoever's up there can really play. Then some backing tracks come in. I hear a fuzzy electric guitar, probably vintage, dirtied up with age and probably worth thousands of dollars. An electric bass with a fat, warm sound, strings boinging beneath nimble fingers. Even an analog keyboard! People yell and clap along. Everyone starts dancing. I push and worm my way forward, looking for any path so I can see what's happening on stage, but I can't get close enough because the crowd is packed in too tight. Finally, I turn around and head back toward the bar.

Slowly and carefully, I climb up on the bar, afraid the whole thing will collapse, but it holds my weight and as soon as I stand, I catch a glimpse of a singer strutting onto stage. She is tall and sinewy, all muscle and tendon beneath her pitch-black clothes. Her face is covered with a black mask like everyone else, but her unmistakable hair gives her away. When she breaks into song, I stumble and almost fall because I know that voice. It has tunneled inside of me and echoed through my mind. I've heard her on the radio waves. I've heard her by the river. At that moment it comes together and I understand.

"Zimri!" I shout but my voice gets lost in the roar of the crowd. "Zimri! Zimri!" I keep shouting as I hop down.

It takes me three songs to push my way to the front, but I'm determined to get closer. Her voice is amazing. Better than the muddy recording I've heard on the waves. On every song, she hits the notes in a two-octave range. By the time I fight my way to the front, Zimri is in the center of the stage.

"Should we really stick it to them?" she yells at the audience. "Show everyone what real music sounds like?" The crowd roars. She lifts up her left hand and I see what looks like a crude ExoScreen glove with a strange camera eye on her palm.

"Do you know who's on the LiveStream tonight?" she taunts as the guy behind her keeps the beat. "Ios," she says, then breaks into a parody of "(Quark) Charmed, I'm Sure," strutting around and shaking her booty just like Ios does. Zimri's done this impression for me before, during our breaks by the river, and every time it makes me laugh.

The crowd around me hisses and boos for fun. I can't believe how much they dislike Ios. What if I told them what she did at summer camp in Malta?

Then Zimri says, "Should we give her the Geoff Joffrey treatment?" Everybody screams. The drummer crashes the cymbals. "Should my eyes shoot right through her Live-Stream . . . *like a laser beam*?" she sings, mocking Geoff's song. The crowd stomps and claps and eggs her on as the drums continue. "Do you dare me to do it?" she demands, working the crowd into a frenzy. She laughs, haughty and full of mischief, and my chest swells.

I hear myself yelling, too. Cheering her on like everyone else around me. At this moment I want more than anything for every person on the planet to see and hear Zimri sing because this show in the jam-packed dugout is better than any concert I've ever seen in a Chanson Industries Arena.

"Here we go!" Zimri yells and the drummer smacks out a beat, the backing tracks swell up, and the crowd joins in, clapping overhead as Zimri turns the palm camera on herself and counts, "One, two, a one-two-three-and!" Then breaks into, *"I am Nobody from Nowhere, a speck upon your screen,"* with everyone singing along.

I nearly lose my mind. I can't believe I'm right there in front of her and she's singing the song that has become my anthem and everyone else's. People jump and scream and punch their fists into the air while she stomps past us onstage. I reach out. I shout her name. I want her to know that I am here and that she's amazing. More than that, I want the world to know. I want everyone to hear what a true musical genius sounds like.

"Zimri!" I shout over and over until finally she looks my way. We lock eyes. Hers through the mask, mine exposed. "It's me!" I shout.

Her voice falters. She backs away and stumbles, her hands held out in front of her body as if to stop me, the camera eye pointing straight at me. "Oh, no! Oh, no!" she says into the mic and then I realize what I've done. *Zimri* is the hijacker. Not Calliope. Zimri is the one my father's after.

"No!" I shout. "No, no, no!"

But the drummer is off his stool in a flash yelling, "Raid! Raid!"

The crowd moves backward as if an undertow is pulling them from the room. Then an older guy with long dreadlocks jumps up on stage just as Zimri and the drummer scramble behind the canvas curtain. "That's it!" the older guy shouts, waving his arms. "Show's over. Everybody out!"

I'm pulled along with the deluge of black-masked people pushing through the door. I try to push back through the tide to reach Zimri and tell her how sorry I am. Confess everything.

Tell her I'll do anything to help her. But by the time I make it back to Nowhere, the door is closed and locked tight. I bang and bang, but no one answers. All around me, people scramble up the hill and run away. I search for another entrance, but the place is like a fortress. Finally after ten minutes, I give up, assuming Zimri made it out. I slink back to my Cicada, sick over what I've done.

ZIMRI

Dorian sits beside me on the edge of the stage with his arm around my shoulders. I can't stop shaking.

"What was that guy from the warehouse doing here?" He spits the words. "He's the one who said he heard us on the waves, right? No mask on his dumb face. Yelling your name. Was he trying to get us all arrested?"

"I don't know." I bury my face in my hands. When I saw Aimery at the edge of the stage, I was sure he was there to bust us. That I'd been duped and he'd been a spy all along, only not for Corp X but for Smythe and Beauregarde and whoever hired them. But then, after Marley pulled the plug and everybody left, nothing happened. We hid in back behind the secret panels for fifteen minutes, but no security ever came.

"I can't believe you would put yourself at risk like this!" Marley shouts as he paces in front of us. "And not just you! Everybody who was here tonight could have been arrested. Is this a camera?" He holds Tati's latest invention in his clenched fist. "Are you kidding me? Did you record it? Are you planning to distribute it? Do you have any idea how much trouble you could get in? How could you be so reckless?"

"Please don't be mad at Dorian," I say. "He tried to stop me but I insisted on playing tonight. I told him I would do it alone, but he wouldn't let me. He was trying to be a good friend."

"You lied," Marley shouts, uninterested in my explanation. "Both of you. To our faces. Nonda asked you and you said—"

"But we were doing it for Nonda," Dorian argues.

"Doesn't matter why you think you're doing it!" Marley yells.

"It's all my fault," I say. "I needed money to keep Nonda at the MediPlex so they could run more tests."

Marley stops, hands on hips and looks sharply at me. "Is that true?"

I nod.

He looks up at the ceiling. "Why didn't you come to me if you needed money?"

"No offense," I say, "but why would you have that much money? Why would any of us have that much? And then I'd owe you money that I'd never be able to repay. That's the whole problem. No one person has more than enough to just get by. That's why we do these shows, so that everybody can pitch in what little extra they have to truly help one another."

Marley's face screws up. "Who else have you raised money for?" he asks, clearly skeptical.

"Levon when his son Luka got hit by a Plute car and the justice brokers claimed it was the kid's fault for riding on a private road. Captain Jack when he lost his arm in the box smasher at the warehouse and the justice brokers decided he had to pay for the broken machinery. Billie Jean when her newborn, that sweet baby James, was in the MediPlex for two months because the RoboNurse went haywire and nearly suffocated him, which Corp X called an act of god—as if Robots answer to a higher power than their CPUs. There's more if you want to know."

Marley sighs and comes to sit beside us. "I didn't know that's what you'd been doing."

I lean away from him. "What else would we be doing?"

"I don't know. Sticking it to the man? Making money off of music? Showing the world that art isn't a commodity to be controlled by the rich?"

"All that sounds nice, but mostly it's just because the justice brokers and Arbiters always screw the Plebes, so somebody has to help."

"And what about this?" He shakes the camera glove at me.

I grimace. "Yeah, that . . . Well, that was a terrible idea."

"Did it go out?" Dorian asks. He looks a little sick to his stomach.

"Go out?" Marley asks.

I cringe and shrink back. "Last time, we accidentally hijacked a LiveStream," I tell him meekly and Marley groans. "We didn't mean to. And the video feed might not have gone out at all tonight. We'll just have to wait and see."

"But if it did go out . . ." Dorian says.

The image of Aimery shouting my name floats up in my mind and my stomach turns over. How long will I be able to deny that it was me? Could I claim a case of mistaken identity? I turn to Dorian and put my hand on his leg. "Even if it got out and they come for me, you know I'd never, ever, not in a million years tell them it was you on stage." I cut my eyes toward

Marley, but he won't meet my gaze. "I'll take the blame and the full brunt of whatever they want to do—"

"Stop." Dorian lays his hand on top of mine. "Nothing bad is going to happen." He doesn't sound half as confident as he's trying to look. "It probably didn't even go out. Or if it did the room was so loud and . . ." He trails off. I can tell that he's nervous by the way he keeps glancing at the door, as if he's expecting Medgers and ten private security guards to bust in at any minute.

Marley lies back on the stage with one arm slung over his eyes; he can't bear to look at us anymore. "God, the world's gotten messed up, hasn't it?" he moans. "All these years I kept thinking things would go back to normal. I thought someday, someone would come along and take that guy Chanson down a few pegs." He laughs but it sounds sad. "Calliope's trying, but she won't get very far. She underestimates the greed in the world. How much money feeds the beast. And the bigger it gets, the more money it takes to keep it going. It's vicious. Every year the whole situation gets worse and worse." Then he laughs. Then he groans again. "Ah, well, you can't relive your past."

Dorian and I look at each other, wondering whether his dad is losing it, until Marley sits up and says, "Look, it's great that you've been using these shows to help other people, but it's also dumb and risky and in the end, you'll be the ones to get hurt. So . . ." He gets to his feet. "I should have done this a long time ago. I'm shutting this place down. Getting rid of the gear. Boarding up the door." He levels his gaze at me. "Like I should have done five years ago."

"This place isn't *yours* to shut down," I tell him.

He stands up taller so he's looking down on me. "I'm the one who built it!"

I get to my feet and stand nearly eye to eye with him. "With my mother."

"Fat lot of good it did her, too! This place ruined her and ruined your childhood. Someone has to be the grown-up here and stop you from ruining the rest of your life, too!"

"Nowhere didn't ruin my life," I say.

"This is the reason your mother got caught and then your father . . ." Marley trails off.

I've had so many questions about my mother all these years but as I get older, one thing seems more and more clear to me. "Come on, Marley," I say. "The trouble she got in was just an excuse for her to leave, but we both know it wasn't the real reason she took off."

Marley looks stunned.

"It couldn't have been easy with my father. He was sick. Unstable. And they both had to work jobs they hated. And then to be told, on top of that, you can't do the one thing in life that makes you the happiest. Making music? She said it herself. If she'd accepted the ruling after you guys got caught, she would have been trading one prison for another. Of course I wish she'd never left, but at least I hope she's somewhere she can make music when she wants."

Marley puts his hands on his hips and looks at the floor as if he's trying to gather himself. "She loved you, Zim." He peers up at me. "She loved you very much."

"Not more than she loved making music," I say.

Marley looks defeated. "Rainey was flawed. We all are."

"Stop," I tell him. "I don't blame her. I might have done the same thing in her shoes."

"No," Marley says. "Rainey was selfish about her art. She did it for herself no matter what the cost. But you . . ." He looks around Nowhere as if he's sad to let it go. "You're different, Zimri. You did this for other people. You used your art for good. I'm just sorry that we live in a world where that's not valued anymore."

My HandHeld beeps. 8:45. "Oh crap, I have to go!" I say. "If I'm not at the MediPlex by nine . . ."

"Want me to go with you?" Dorian asks.

"We shouldn't be seen together. It's too dangerous right now," I tell him. "You should go home. Both of you. Make up an alibi. Say you were together all night at home. I'll go to the MediPlex and then back to my POD. I'll ping you if anything goes down."

Marley nods and puts his hand on Dorian's shoulder. "She's right."

I gather the money from the box.

"Is there enough?" Dorian asks.

"Plenty," I say, teary with gratitude.

I ride my red bike as fast as I can and arrive at the MediPlex with five minutes to spare. At the elevator bank, I push all the buttons, then decide there's no time to wait. I'm worried the Robos have already gotten Nonda out of bed and are shuffling her out the door. What if they put her in the elevator and she's on her way down while I'm going up? So I take the stairs two at a time, clicking off floors, hoping that they'll wait a few more minutes. When I get to the third floor, I zoom around the corner and sprint to her room, yelling, "I'm here! I'm here," while waving the stack of cash over my head. I see Robo wheels beneath the edge of curtain seven.

"Wait!" I yell and rip the curtain aside then hang on to it, panting, "I. Can. Pay." My eyes go straight to the empty bed where the Robo is changing sheets. "No!" I yell. "Where's my Nonda?"

The RoboNurse's head unit spins toward me. "Visiting hours are over in . . . three minutes."

I grab for the Robo but it quickly wheels away from me. I chase after it. "Stop. Where's my grandmother?" My voice cracks. "It's not nine o'clock yet! I can pay her bill. She can stay." I shove the money toward the robot but of course it doesn't care. "Where is Layla Robinson?" I demand.

"Mrs. Layla Robinson . . ." it says and pauses. "Has been moved to . . . the geriatric memory unit on floor five, room six, bed number . . . two. Her discharge date is . . . one week from today."

"What?" I gasp as if the wind has been knocked out of me. "You must be wrong. I didn't pay yet."

The Robo's digital eyes blink at me.

"Oh my god, I need to speak to a human!"

"Would you like to speak with a human?" it asks.

"Yes, please!" I whine. "Dr. Garcia? Is she available?"

"One moment." Its face screen blanks out for a few seconds. I try to catch my breath, calm down, and not cry. The money is sweaty in my grip.

Then Dr. Garcia's face is on the screen. "Can I help you?" she says.

"I can't find my grandmother," I blurt out.

"Oh, it's you!" she says happily. "Your grandmother is doing great."

"But she's not here."

Dr. Garcia cocks her head to the side. "Yes, she is. I moved her to the geriatric unit after her mammogram and set up a consult with the gerontologist for tomorrow."

"But how? I haven't paid her bill yet."

Dr. Garcia looks at her screen, perplexed, but then she smiles again. "Yes, you did," she says with a little laugh. "Yesterday. Or someone did." She splits the screen on the Robo's face so I can see the info, too.

"But wait . . . I didn't . . . Who?" I step closer. "What's this?" I jabbed my finger on the Payment Received link from yesterday, which opened up the transaction. Sure enough, someone's transferred funds into her account.

"There's been a mistake," I tell Dr. Garcia. "This payment wasn't from me. It must be for another patient."

Dr. Garcia shrugs. "Consider it a grace period, then. Billing will work it out. In the meantime, your grandmother is okay, Zimri. She'll be here at least another week while we run more tests and try out some new meds. I'm hoping to enroll her in a trial for a drug that I think will help tremendously."

"Can I see her?" I ask.

"Visiting hours are now over," the RoboNurse says. "Please proceed to the exit."

"Tomorrow," Dr. Garcia tells me. "Come back tomorrow."

"Okay," I say, confused, but I turn to go. Then I stop and

look over my shoulder again. "Thank you," I call to Dr. Garcia. "Thank you for taking care of my grandmother."

"Of course!" she says. "Us Nobodies have to stick together."

I leave the MediPlex and ride along the river path, trying to puzzle through how someone else has paid my grandmother's bill. All I can figure is, the bills must have gotten crossed and soon enough the system will figure out the error. I hope some other old woman isn't out on her ear tonight. In the meantime, I'll put the cash from Nowhere someplace safe until I have to pay up.

When I approach the bend in the river where Nowhere is nestled under the embankment, I speed up. Stomach acid creeps up into my mouth because I suspect Medgers is on patrol, ready to nab anyone stupid enough to still be nearby, but everything is as calm and quiet as when I left half an hour ago. I let out a long sigh and look up into the night sky. The clouds from earlier have begun to move off and the stars are peeking out. It's been the strangest night of my life. Both good and bad, happy and sad. But mostly, utterly exhausting. Somewhere up the river, a whippoorwill cries its name over and over into the night. I join in its sad song, making up lyrics as I go.

"Oh whippoorwill, whippoorwill, I know just how you feel, singing for a broken heart that may never heal."

ORPHEUS

For the next half hour, after I leave Nowhere, I sit inside my Cicada scanning the Buzz, trying to find information about whether Zimri managed to hijack another LiveStream, but there's been nothing. Not that I should be surprised. My father has probably done everything possible to ensure a hijacking never happens again.

There is, however, almost nonstop coverage of my supposed disappearance and potential death. My father, who's off in Europe, claims I ran away after he threatened me with rehab for my Juse addiction. "His mother never let him have a pump so he self-medicates with black-market Juse," he claims, then says they can trace my path that night via my Cicada's GPS. "We know he crashed into a river," he says but refuses to release the exact location for fear of a media frenzy.

"If anyone has any information regarding my son's whereabouts," he pleads, as if weary with worry and fatigue, "ping the Chanson Industries hotline. Otherwise, I beg you to allow us to conduct our search in peace so we can bring him home."

Then they flash pix of me from over a year ago, when I was two inches shorter, ten pounds lighter, and my hair was completely different.

"What a load of crap!" I say aloud. My father's message is coming through loud and clear. He knows exactly where my car is sitting and wants me to stay gone. As I suspected, I'm worth more to him when I'm missing. That way he gets pity points while he battles Calliope in court.

Not to be outdone, my mother has launched her own PR campaign contradicting my father. She insists I don't have a drug problem (thanks, Mom!) and that my father has me locked inside a surgical facility where I'm being forced to have an ASA against my will. My father, of course, denies this and calls my mother unstable. As usual, the media is all over their public skirmish like maggots on rotting meat.

I turn off the Buzz—let them conduct their battle without me for once! Instead, I scan the waves on the receiver until I catch a hint of a familiar voice. The song starts out far away and moves closer as I spin the dials, trying to tune her in. Then I realize: the song is coming from outside, not from the receiver speakers. I open the car door and jump out. Her voice is loud and clear.

"Whippoorwill, oh whippoorwill, I know just how you feel," Zimri sings. "Singing for a broken heart that may never heal."

"Zimri!" I yell as I run from under the willow tree up to the path. "Zimri!"

"Look out!"

Brakes squeal. I spin around, but it's too late. The bike is already on top of me.

"Ooooph." I go down hard on the path. Feel the tires roll over my arm. Hear a clatter and a thud.

"Seriously!" she yells as she slides past me tangled in her bike. "Do you wait in the middle of the path for me?"

"Why are you always riding like a bat out of hell?" I peel myself off the ground and crawl toward the dark lump I assume is Zim. "Are you hurt?"

She kicks the bike away and hops to her feet. "I'm fine."

"No blood?"

"I said *I'm fine*!" she growls.

I pick up the bike and say, "Zimri, darling, we really have to stop running into each other like this!"

Rather than laugh, Zimri runs at me with her arms straight out and shoves me hard on the chest. I drop her bike and stumble backward.

"Hey!" I say. "What was that for? You're the one who ran me over. Again!"

"You could have gotten me arrested!"

"I know! My god." I rush toward her, my hands reaching out. "I'm so so so sorry. But I think it's okay. I've been checking the waves. I didn't hear anything about a hijacking."

"Are you some kind of spy?" she asks, her breath in ragged pants as she keeps her distance from me.

I stop. "I thought we already established that I would make a terrible spy."

"Are you working for Smythe and Beauregarde?"

"Who?"

She stamps her foot in frustration. "Why were you at the show?" she demands from between clenched teeth. "Why were you calling my name?"

"Because I was excited!" I throw my hands up in the air. "Because it was you!" I grab her shoulders. "Because you were amazing!" I give her a little shake. "I just got carried away. I didn't think about what was happening with that camera thingie and the LiveStream. I didn't know you did it the first time. Everybody thinks it was Calliope Bontempi!"

She smacks my hands away but seems to calm down a bit.

"And I don't think you managed to do it again," I tell her. "My da . . . I mean, those people in the City, the patron, they know how to disrupt signals pretty well."

She takes a deep breath. "Are you sure?"

"I think it would be all over the Buzz or at least the waves by now, but I haven't heard a thing."

She bends over and puts her hands on her knees to take a few deep breaths. "Yeah," she says. "You must be right, because if I had broken in, someone would have busted me by now." Then she stands up and stares at me with angry eyes again. "But you outted me. Nobody, not even the people in the audience, is supposed to know that was me. Hello? Black masks? Hidden identity?"

I chuckle. "Are you joking? You're pretty unmistakable on stage. Who else but you can sing like that? Who else but you moves that way? And who else but you has that hair?" I hold my hands out around my head to mimic her wild curls. "It's not exactly hidden under the weird black mask. And why would you want to hide? You're one of the most talented, incredible people I've ever—"

She turns away. "Stop saying things like that about me!"

"But . . . why?" I ask and go after her.

"Because! It's embarrassing."

I shake my head. "Not if it's true."

"That was an illegal concert!" she hisses.

"The hijacking, sure . . ."

She looks over one shoulder then the other. "No, the whole thing. Making music. It's not legal."

"That's not true," I say.

"Yes, it is," she insists. "Hello! Harold Chanson, the big music patron in the City, owns the part of the brain that makes music. How can you not know that?"

I can't help but laugh. "He might like to think he does, but—"

"Good god!" She waves away my words and sighs. "This has been the strangest night of my life."

I inch toward her now that she's calmer and no longer trying to kick my butt.

"What were you doing out here, anyway?" Zimri asks. "And how did you know about the show? Did somebody tell you?" She looks at me and bites her lip as she waits for my answer. I know that look of anticipation. It's the same one any Plute gets when we're wondering if we made the Buzz.

I hate to disappoint her, but I want to be honest. "I just stumbled onto it. I was going to my . . ." I point toward the willow tree then stop myself but Zimri's eyes dart that way.

"Whoa, what's that light?" She heads toward the glowing canopy.

"It's nothing. Don't go under there!" I say but it's too late. She's already pulled back the low-hanging branches to reveal my banged-up Cicada.

"Holy mother of . . ." She turns to look at me with her mouth hanging open. "Is this yours?"

"No, well, yes. I mean sort of, but please don't . . ." I jog over as she disappears beneath the curtain of leaves.

"Whew!" she yells. "It smells like a dirty sock!" She climbs in the driver's seat and pushes all the buttons on the dash like a little kid who's never seen a flying car. "This is fancy!"

"Please don't. You shouldn't . . . Hey, stop it!" I reach in and grab her wrist.

Zimri looks up at me. "Wait a sec." We lock eyes and I think I might be busted. I brace myself for her to put all the pieces together but then she says, "Are you living in here?"

For a moment, I consider denying it. Making up some crazy story, but why? I'm so sick of how I'm living. Sick of pretending everything is fine. So in that moment, I lean against the door and I say, "Yes and if I don't get a shower and a decent night's sleep soon, I'm going to join a pack of coyolves and run off into the wild."

"But why?" she says. "Why don't you just go home?"

"Well, for one thing, home is complicated right now and for another, my car would never make it." I conveniently leave out the part about staying because of her.

"I can't do anything about your home life." She looks up at me and smiles. "But I know someone who can fix your car."

After twenty tries, the Cicada finally fires up and with Zimri in the passenger seat, we clunk and clang down the deserted river path until we get to a fork.

"That way," says Zimri, pointing. "That will take us into Old Town."

"Old Town?" I ask, wary. "I heard it was dangerous."

"Nah," says Zim as we bump down a hill, past scraggly lots of abandoned buildings. "People who say that aren't really from here," she explains. She points down a deserted, pockmarked road. "They moved here to work for Corp X and think everything past the Strip is a wasteland." Around the next corner, we come to a street that looks as if it were once the main drag of a quaint small town with wide sidewalks in front of rows of old limestone and brick buildings. Overhead, old-fashioned stoplights swing in the breeze. "Sure it's a little rough down here. But as Tati says, what do you expect if you come in and take away every ounce of ownership and pride from a town. People find ways to scrape by."

"You mean black market stuff?" I ask.

"Why is it, when Plutes sell us stuff, they call it an economy but when Plebes sell stuff to one another, it's called the black market?" Zimri asks.

"Touché," I say.

"There." She points to an old shop. The windows are blacked out and there's no sign above the door. "That's the place," she says. "Pull up in back."

Inside, the shelves are full of every old device I've ever seen and many that I haven't. Ancient laptops and tablets as thick as my hand. Funny old smartphones people carried in their pockets decades ago. Optical head-mount displays they once wore like glasses. 3-D game systems from when my dad was a kid. All kinds of receivers and radios and lots of stuff I can't begin to name. Then a woman who looks vaguely familiar, short and stout with thick dark hair blunt-cut around her ears, comes out from behind a curtain.

"Zimri!" she says happily. "How'd it go?" When she sees me, she stops. "Who's this?"

"Hello, I'm Aimery." I step up and stick out my hand. "I work with Zimri. Haven't we met before? At the warehouse or the Strip?"

"Not places I tend to frequent." Tati lets go of my hand but keeps her eyes on me for a moment as she turns back to Zimri. "So, my camera didn't work, did it? I watched the LiveStream but nothing happened."

"And good thing, too," Zimri says while shooting me a look that makes me cringe.

"Did you like the little distraction that I caused?" Tati asks. "Had all of security at the SQEWL."

"That was you?" I ask and Tati nods as if we should be impressed.

"Some of us have a gift," she jokes. "If you bring the camera back, I'll see what I can do."

"That's okay," says Zimri. "I'm laying low for a while. Things have gotten . . ." She trails off then says, "Weird. But that's not why we're here. Aimery has a repair job for you."

"Does he now?" Tati asks, eyeing me again.

"It's out back," Zim tells her. "Can I use your bathroom?"

"Of course," says Tati. "You know the way."

After Zimri's gone, I follow Tati through the curtain and out the back door to where my Cicada is parked.

"Nice wheels," she says as she walks around my car.

"They used to be," I admit. "Can you fix it?"

"Probably." She stops and leans against the driver's side door. "How's your friend Rajesh?"

I freeze. A bead of sweat runs down my side. "Rajesh? We have met, haven't we? In the City, right?"

She nods.

"I bought a receiver from you once?"

"Among other things."

My face grows warm at the thought of the empty flasks in my glove compartment.

"I wouldn't think a kid like you would need a Corp X job," she says.

I try to laugh but it comes out more like a cough. "My situation changed since the last time I saw you."

"Just like your name?" she asks, which makes my stomach clench.

I stand up tall so that I tower over her. "I'll pay you what it costs to fix my car, but if you're trying to extort money from me, you won't get very much. I ran away. I left that life."

"Ha!" Tati barks.

"Listen," I say and step closer. "You should know, I think . . . Zimri is . . . what I mean is . . . I've never met anyone like her and—"

"Who has?" Tati asks. "She's one in a million. Which is why you should remember: I know who you are and where you're from and who your father is, so if you so much as—"

"So much as what?" Zimri asks as she jogs down the back steps.

"So much as . . ." Tati hesitates, "think I'm going to give you a special deal just because Zimri brought you here, you'd be mistaken!"

"I wouldn't expect you to," I tell her.

"Then it will be good doing business with you, *Aimery,*"
Tati says as smooth as any business tycoon from the City as
she shakes my hand.

Zimri and I walk back toward the PODPlexes with only the
moon and delivery drones to keep us company.

"I don't think Tati liked me," I admit.

"She can come across as gruff," Zimri says. "But she's a
genius. Truly. She'll have your car fixed in no time."

"Most of what she does in that shop is illegal, right?" I ask.

"I guess so," Zimri says. "But who am I to judge. Putting
on concerts and hijacking LiveStreams isn't exactly following
the law!"

"About that," I say. "I've been thinking. All the songs you
played tonight were originals, right? You wrote them?"

"Yeah, so?"

"So, the music copyrights and brain patents you're worried
about don't extend to original music."

Zimri shoves her hands in her pockets and kicks a rock.
"Doesn't matter anyway."

"Of course it matters!"

"I'm done for a while. Tonight scared the pee out of me. I'm
taking a break. Concentrating on caring for my Nonda."

"No, no, no." I stop in the middle of the street beneath the
yellow glow of the moon. "You can't quit! It would be criminal
for you to stop."

"Criminal—ha! Very funny," she says.

"I'm serious, Zimri." I put my hands on her shoulders. Her eyes open wide. "You were put on this earth to make music and nobody can take that away from you."

Zimri's face blooms into a smile, revealing the little gap between her teeth that makes me want to press my lips against hers, but I hold back. "You're telling me that I *should* make music?"

"That is exactly what I'm saying."

"No one but Tati has ever said that to me. Everybody else just tells me all the reasons I should stop."

"They're wrong, Zimri," I tell her. "You have a gift. You have what every Plute musician in the City wants! What they go through brain surgery and months of training to get. You are the real thing, Zimri Robinson. You are a genius and you should never stop making music."

In one quick motion, Zimri jumps and wraps her arms around my shoulders. She pulls me close and holds on tight. It's one of the best moments of my life. "Thank you, Aimery," she says into my ear. "Thank you for saying that." Then just as quickly she lets go, grabs my wrists, and pulls me forward. "Come on. You can stay at my place tonight."

"So, this is it? This is the whole entire thing?" I stand in the center of Zimri's tiny POD and turn a circle. Sofa, window, wall, kitchenette, and lots of dark and broody paintings lining the short hall to another closed door. I could fit two entire PODs in my bedroom at home.

"It's bigger than your car," Zimri says as she digs inside a slender closet by the front vestibule.

"True. But . . . where do you sleep? Where's all your stuff? Do you have a bathroom?"

Zimri laughs, a musical giggle up and down the scale that makes my heart soar. "First, let's get you clean, then I'll give you the grand tour." She hands me a stack of neatly folded clothes.

"Ahhh," I inhale the herbal scent of the fabric. Lavender or rosemary, maybe? "I never thought I'd be so happy to see clean pants."

"We have a MicrobeZapper." She points to a small circular window embedded in the hallway just past the kitchenette. "Then again, maybe you should burn those pants you've been wearing."

"Well, if somebody learned to ride a bike . . ." I tease as I follow her down the small hall. She grins at me over her shoulder and I have to resist the urge to grab her around the waist and pull her toward me.

At the end of the hall, she passes her hand over an electronic eye in the center of a closed door. It whooshes open. "You can shower in here."

I peer inside the tiny room. It's more like a capsule, with a small sink and mirror on one side and a toilet on the other. The back wall is taken up with a floor-to-ceiling cabinet. "Um, not to be demanding or anything, but when you say *shower* . . . ?"

"What? The sink's not good enough for you?"

"Oh, sure, sorry. Of course." I step inside, feeling like a jerk and also appalled that Plebe PODs don't have showers.

Zim grabs my arm and pulls me out. "I'm kidding," she says while cracking up. "We're not animals." She takes a fresh towel out of the cabinet then presses a button on the wall that makes the cabinet spin. I expect a secret passageway to open but instead, a shower stall appears. "Ta-da!" she says.

"Wow!"

"I'm sure you're exceedingly impressed. There's soap and shampoo inside. Now, I'm going to make some food for myself. Are you hungry?"

"I don't want to be a pain. . . ."

"Too late!" She pushes past me but she's smiling. "We have plenty."

"That'd be great. As long as . . ." I stop. "Never mind."

"As long as what?"

"Just . . . no more grubworm-meal noodles, please?" I grab my gut. "I can't eat another grubworm-meal noodle."

"Don't worry," she says and pats me on the shoulder. "I'll make you something good."

When I come out of the bathroom, freshly clean and feeling like a new man, Zimri's busy at the stove.

"That was quick!" she says.

"I didn't want to use too much water."

"We have more." She turns back to the pots and dishes out two plates full of steaming food. "Do you like morels over corn porridge and watercress?"

"I don't know," I tell her honestly. "I don't think I've ever eaten any of those things, but it smells good."

She carries the plates out of the kitchenette and with her elbow pushes a button on the wall so that a waist-high platform slides out from a slot then two legs fold down, followed by a bench on either side.

"No way," I say.

"What?"

"I didn't expect a table to appear!"

"Maximum efficient use of space," she says and hands me a plate.

I climb in beside her and take a big bite of food. "This is amazing!" I shovel more into my mouth. "You have to show me the packages so I can order some. Do you get it at the warehouse?"

She lays her fork on the side of her plate and turns to face me. "Aimery, I don't mean to be rude, but if you're trying to seem like you're from around here, you're doing a really bad job."

I think about whether to be offended by what she said, but then I realize she's right and I crack up. "That obvious, huh?"

"Painfully," she says.

"OK, fine. I'm not from around here but I am trying hard to do well at the warehouse and I'm grateful for the job and for all your help and for letting me take a shower and giving me clean clothes and feeding me, and . . ." I shake my head. "It's incredibly generous of you."

"It's not a big deal." She pokes at her food with her fork. "It's just what people do."

"Not where I'm from," I tell her. "If some stranger showed up in dirty pants no one would hand him anything."

"First off, you're not some stranger. I've been working with you for a week. And second, the place you're from sounds pretty crappy."

A surprised laugh pops out of my mouth. "I never thought of it that way, but you might be right."

"Is that why you left?"

"Well, that's a longer and more complicated story."

She holds up her hand. "You don't need to explain."

"Thanks," I say and look down at my lap. "For the pants." I glance up at her, hoping that I've lightened the mood. "They your boyfriend's?" I tease.

She pushes her eyebrows into a furrowed *V*. "Actually, they were my father's."

"Oh!" Regret rolls over me like a rain cloud when I think of the story Nonda told me. "I'm so sorry about what happened to him." I put my hand on hers. "That must have been devastating. You were so young."

Zimri pulls away. "Yeah, well, you know, life's rough." She stands up and gathers our empty plates.

I pop up, too. "Let me help."

"It's OK. I've got it. You can put the table away." As she carries the plates to the sink, she stops and looks at me. "Wait. I never told you about my dad."

I freeze.

"Someone else did," I say slowly, then add quickly, "at the warehouse."

"I guess that shouldn't surprise me. You can never keep a secret around here. Everybody's always in everybody else's business."

I push the button to retract the table, then step around the corner into the kitchenette. "Zimri," I say. "I'm sorry if I ruined things for you at the show. I didn't know it was supposed to be a secret."

"Yeah, about that." She chews on the inside of her mouth as she loads the dishes into a zapper. "That could be a problem."

"Why?" I ask. "The music you make . . ." I stop and try to wrap my head around how to tell her that she's incredible without sounding like a sycophant.

"It's illegal. I'm breaking the law."

"I think you're wrong," I tell her.

She laughs and shakes her head. "No, I'm afraid I'm not. And just to warn you, there could be a knock on the door any minute."

"Don't worry," I say, stepping closer. "I'll protect you."

She snorts like she thinks I'm kidding, but really, I'm dead serious.

ZIMRI

"You can sleep in here," I tell Aimery, pointing to the main living area.

He runs for the sofa and plops down. "Ah!" He lies back and kicks up his feet. "This is so comfortable." Then he rolls to his stomach and buries his face in a pillow. "I never knew how grateful I'd be to lie down flat!"

"Um, Aimery?"

He flips to his side and props his head up on his hand. "What?" Then he looks embarrassed. "Oh, sorry. Oh, god. Was that a total dick move? Is this where you sleep? Did I take your bed?" He rolls off the sofa onto the floor. "I can totally sleep here." He pats the rug.

"Seriously, Aimery?"

He tucks his hands behind this head. "This is great! Just as long as it's flat and not inside a car."

"We have beds!"

"You do?" He sits up and looks all around. "Where?"

I lift my index finger in the air then circle it around my head dramatically before I push the button on the wall to release Nonda's sleeping unit.

Aimery's mouth drops open. "No way!" He scurries over to watch the bed roll out. Then he presses his palm against the wall as if it might be magic. "A table! A bed! What else is inside here?"

"Just the screen," I say with a shrug and a laugh. "Oh, and a portal to another dimension."

"Ha!" he says when he realizes that I am joking, then he grins, which sends a tingle down my spine. I quickly look away.

"That's where Nonda usually sleeps and I sleep up there." I point to my loft over the kitchenette.

He runs to the footholds built into the wall and climbs up to get a better look. "Wow!"

I grab clean linens from the closet and laugh at his amazement. "Either you grew up in a cave and this all seems very high tech or you're slumming it and can't believe how real Plebes live."

"That would make a great reality show." He jumps down from the ladder.

"Lifestyles of Poor Losers?" I strip Nonda's bed.

"The Prince and the Plebe," he jokes back.

"How about some help?" I toss him a clean sheet then carry the dirty ones and his clothes to the MicrobeZapper. When I return he's still staring at the bed with the sheet limp in his hands. "What's wrong?"

"Nothing, it's just that . . ." He holds up the sheet. Turns it one way, then the other.

"You've never made a bed, have you?"

"I wouldn't exactly say *never*."

"Then what would you say?"

"I'd say . . ." He pauses. "That I haven't made a bed *yet*."

"Good god!" I grab the sheet from him and stretch it over the mattress. Then I spread out the flat sheet and tuck the corners in just like Nonda taught me. Finally, I throw him a pillow and a fresh pillowcase. "See if you can puzzle through this one."

He tries to wrestle the pillowcase over the pillow from the top but it slips from his hands. He tries to stuff it inside but it gets bunched up. He tucks the pillow under his chin and tries to pull the case up like it's a pair of pants but it won't budge so he jumps up and down with the pillow bouncing off his knees. I double over, laughing at his ineptitude.

"How have you existed this long in the world?" I ask, wiping tears away.

He gets the pillow inside the case, then swings it over his head and bashes me with it.

"Hey!" I yell, still laughing. "That's not fair." I run around the bed and he chases me, bonking me with the pillow.

"Take that! And that!"

I jump up on the bed but he comes after me. "Stop it! Stop!" I yell but I'm laughing so hard that I can barely get the words out. I trip and fall off the bed onto the floor with a thud.

"Attack!" He jumps after me, making the entire POD shake.

I roll into a ball, unable to breathe because I'm laughing as he pummels me with the pillow. Then I get up on my knees and grab hold of it. We tug back and forth as I stand. He yanks it hard and I ricochet toward him. We bump together, the pillow in between us, and we freeze, our eyes locked, our faces inches from one another. Then I hear loud knocking.

"Oh, no!" I whisper. "This is bad." I let go of the pillow and scramble, sure it's Medgers at the door, ready to haul me off. We hear it again but this time I feel vibrations beneath our feet. We each look down. I exhale loudly. "It's coming from downstairs."

"Quiet down up there," a muffled voice yells.

I drop to my knees and cup my hands around my mouth. "Sorry, Mrs. Jones!" I yell at the floor. "Sorry about the noise!"

"Yeah, sorry about that, Mrs. J!" Aimery hollers.

"Shhhh!" I hiss at him and swat his legs. "What are you doing?"

"Apologizing," he says and laughs.

"You're not supposed to be here!"

"I'm not?" he asks. "Is it against the Corp X rules?"

I sit back on my heels. "No, of course not. I just mean . . . You know . . . It might look . . . weird. You. Me. Nonda in the MediPlex."

"Oh, right." He cringes and sits on the side of the bed with the pillow between his knees. "I didn't think of that."

"Me either," I say, blushing. "Until now." I get up and shuffle toward the ladder to my loft. As I'm climbing up, I stop and look at him fluffing the pillows on the bed and turning back the covers. I have no idea where he's from. Who his family might be. What he did before he got here. But I'm not as afraid of him as I am of me. I don't entirely trust myself with him because there's an image that hovers in my mind. What if the knock hadn't come? What if when our bodies were so close with the pillow pressed between us, instead of turning away, afraid of who was at the door, we had moved closer? And what if we had kissed? What would have happened next?

"You okay?" He looks up from straightening the covers and smiles. I see the tiredness around his eyes and the gratitude of relief across his face.

"Um." My cheeks grow warm. I force the image of kissing him from my mind. "Do you have everything you need?"

"Yes," he says and slides into bed with a long, delicious sigh. "I haven't been this comfortable for a long time."

I climb up into my loft bed and command the lights off. Then I lie there, silently. Uncomfortable at first. Wondering what he's thinking. Wondering what it will be like in the morning when we both wake up. Will it be awkward? Both of us have the day off, which could be fun. Or weird. I could take him to Black Friday so he can get new clothes. And I need to visit Nonda.

Night sounds fill the room. The whoosh and whirl of the MicrobeZappers cleaning the dishes and laundry. The low-level buzz of delivery drones overhead. The faint and faraway rushing of the river. Aimery's rhythmic breathing. Then the forlorn cry of a whippoorwill, too far from its riverbank home, drifts in through the open window.

"Whip-poor-will, whip-poor-will." Aimery mimicks the cry perfectly, starting high on the "whip," then down a few notes, trilling the r on the "poor," and ending on a shrill little cry of the "will." He repeats the loop over and over like the bird crying for its lost mate.

"You're good at that," I say.

"I know lots of bird calls," he tells me. "Want me to do another?"

"Sure." Hearing his voice in the dark calms down my spinning mind.

"Jee-eeb! Jee-eeb! Jeeb, jeeb, jeeb!" he sings. "Do you know what that is?"

"Sounds familiar, but I don't know its name."

"Wood duck. How about this one: chit-here-here-here, chit-here! Chit-here-here-here, chit-here!"

"What's that?"

"Eastern bluebird."

"Never heard of it."

"They may have gone extinct. Check this one out. Yank-yank-yank," he sings through his nose.

"Sounds like a frozard."

"Nope, a nuthatch."

"You're a nuthatch."

"No, I'm not, you are," he says, which makes me snicker. "How about this one: Frawnk! Frawnk!"

"I know that! Great blue heron."

"That's right. The old man of the river."

"Do you have those where you're from, too?"

"I doubt it. I'd never seen one before I came here, much less heard its call in the wild."

"How do you know so much about birds?" I ask. Somehow the darkness makes my question feel less intrusive than if we were facing one another in the light.

"My sister," he says quietly. "She has a clock. Every fifteen minutes a different bird sings."

"So she likes birds?"

"She likes . . ." He sighs. "Singing."

"Me, too," I say through an enormous yawn. I burrow into my covers, feeling sleep begin to shroud me. "Are you a lot alike, you and your sister?"

"I don't know," he says, which seems strange but then he adds, "She'd like you."

"I'd like to meet her," I tell him, my voice going warbly with exhaustion.

Aimery is quiet for a moment. I think that he's probably fallen asleep, but then he says, "I'd like that, too."

"Zimri! Zim!" I wake up to Aimery shaking me. The POD is filled with light, so it must be morning, but I can't figure out why he's waking me up.

"What's the matter? What are you doing? It's my day off!" I pull the covers over my head.

Aimery grabs my shoulder. "Someone's at the door!" he whispers.

I hear the knock, light but persistent. "Oh, no," I hiss and kick off the covers. "What should we do?"

"I don't know. Do you want to hide? Want me to answer? I could say you're not here."

The knocking comes again. "That won't work. They'll just come in and look for me."

"You could get inside the bed. I could put it inside the wall. Or the shower. I could spin it around."

"That's the first place they always look."

"Right," he says and looks stymied.

"Zimri?" someone calls my name quietly from the hall. "Zim, you there?"

"That doesn't sound like security," I say, relieved. I follow Aimery down the ladder then we tiptoe toward the door.

"Hello?" I call softly with Aimery close behind. "Who's there?"

"It's Dorian."

My stomach drops.

"Let me in? Are you okay? I was worried about you all night."

"Uh, um, just a sec." I look at Aimery, who points to himself and then to the closet.

I nod, then shake my head and grab his arm. "This is silly," I whisper. "It's okay. We didn't do anything wrong."

But Aimery doesn't look convinced. He scoots away from me and stands with his back against the fridge as I unlock the door.

Dorian charges in and wraps his arms around me. "I hardly slept. I was so worried all night. I was afraid . . ." Then he stops. His body stiffens and he steps away from me. "What? Why is he here?"

I move aside. "You remember Aimery, right?" I say and realize just how idiotic that must sound. "He needed a place to stay, so since Nonda's gone, I—"

Dorian shakes his head. He isn't listening to me. "You let this guy stay with you?"

"Hey, man!" Aimery steps forward and holds out his hand like I've seen him do a hundred times at the warehouse when he's trying to make a good impression. "I was in a bind. Zimri let me crash."

Dorian looks down at Aimery's hand like it's filthy. Then he cuts his eyes to me. "What the hell, Zim?"

"What?" I say stupidly because I know what the whole thing must look like. "He's been sleeping in his car and—"

"Down by the riverside," Aimery adds with a halfhearted laugh. "It's been rough. Zimri took pity on me."

Dorian looks at me and shakes his head, then he says, "No way. I won't do this, Zimri. I won't be that guy for you."

"What guy?" I ask, but he doesn't answer because he's bolted into the hallway.

"Dor!" I call after him. "Dorian, wait. Come on!" I chase him down the stairs. "Slow down!" He slams through the exit door into the bright morning light. I run to catch up and grab his arm before he crosses the Y.A.R.D. "Hey! What's going on? You're acting like a lunatic."

He yanks away from me. "That guy?" he yells. "That's the guy you bring home? Nonda's in the MediPlex. I'm up all night worried that you're going to get nabbed. And you bring home the idiot who could have gotten both of us arrested?" He shakes his head again in disbelief. "Then you call *me* the lunatic?"

I cross my arms and look straight at him. "He just needed a place to shower and sleep. I was being nice. You would've done the same."

"No," says Dorian with conviction. "Not for a guy like that."

"A guy like what?" I ask, genuinely bewildered.

"Who is he?" Dorian shouts. "Breezes in one day, acting like Mr. Charming, but not giving anyone any information. Where's he from? What's he doing here? He's not like us."

"That doesn't make him a bad person."

"I don't trust him, Zim." Dorian steps closer and wraps his fingers around my upper arm. "And neither should you."

"I make my own decisions about people."

He leans over me. "I've seen you on breaks at the warehouse with him. Sharing drinks out back by the river."

"Oh, big deal," I say and jerk my arm away from him. "You could have come and hung out with us."

"You never invited me!"

"Do you need an engraved invitation to hang out with me?"

"I'm not doing this," he yells.

"Doing what?"

He walks in circles, ranting. "It's our parents all over again. My dad loved your mother for years. Did everything for her. Followed her around like a damn dog since they were kids, waiting for her to feel the same about him. She's the whole reason he learned to play drums. She's the reason he built Nowhere. He was trying to impress her!"

"No . . ."

"It's true. He told me. And then she went off and chose your father—some crazy, dark and brooding painter! *He's so talented,* she'd always say to my dad as if his music wasn't enough. So he got on with his life and married my mom, but he always loved Rainey."

"You're exaggerating," I say, but there's something inside of me that thinks he could be right. Why else would Marley have been so devoted to my mother? Why else would he and my father never have become good friends?

"I won't be that person for you, Zimri! I won't follow you around, pining away like my dad did for your mom."

"I never asked you to," I tell him, then watch his face

crumble. He drops his hands to his sides. They hang heavy like dead branches. "Dor!" I reach out. "I didn't mean . . ."

He steps away and shakes his head, then he turns and runs. I stand there, watching helplessly, as he hops the low wall with *Nobody from Nowhere* scrawled across the stone, and disappears among the PODs.

ORPHEUS

By the time Zimri gets back upstairs, I've put the bed away and changed into my clean clothes. I figure my time with her is up and I don't want to be more of a nuisance.

"So . . ." I say when she comes in the door. I rock back and forth on my heels. "That was awkward."

At first she looks like she's going to punch me but then she lets loose a loud and almost painful laugh as she yells, "Understatement! Jeez. I don't know what got into him." She drops down on one end of the sofa.

"Come on, now. He adores you," I say. "Anyone could see that."

"Doesn't matter." Zim hugs a pillow to her chest and looks away from me. "It would never work anyway. We've known each other since we were little."

"Where I'm from," I say and slowly walk toward the couch, "we have this thing called a carapace that we wear on the back of our hand. You enter a bunch of information, all your likes and dislikes, and you rank stuff like whether you prefer dark hair or light or which celebs you think are attractive and what music and movies and books you like, and it tracks all of your purchases. Then it takes all of that info and turns it into a color. You compare your carapace to other people's to see how compatible you are."

"Why? That sounds stupid."

"It's like a shortcut." I sit at the opposite end of the sofa. "A time-saver. You know right away if you have a chance with someone. So, things like your predicament with Dorian don't happen as much because maybe his carapace would be green and yours would be another color, like, I don't know . . ." My stomach clenches. "Purple."

"Yeah, well, there might be such a thing as too compatible," Zimri says. "Like with Dorian, everything's the same for us. We both grew up here. Our parents were friends . . . or something. We work the same job. We both love music."

"I never thought of that."

"And what about all the things that carapace-thing can't measure? Like whether you want more out of life than you have? Or how much of a risk-taker you are? Don't you think that's more important than whether you both like the same dumb songs or bought the same kind of socks?"

I sit back and think of Ara's matching carapace, and how our kisses were always wrong.

Abruptly, Zimri turns to face me. "Why are you here?"

"I can leave." I start to stand, but she reaches out and pulls me back down.

"That's not what I meant. I want to know why you left the City and came here. Mr. Fancy bashed-up car. Mr. Fancy torn-up pants. Mr. Fancy glove thingamabob I've seen on your hand. There's more to your story than you're letting on."

My mouth goes dry and I start to sweat. "Yes, you're right." I debate about how much I can safely tell her. How much she might already know. I start slow. "I had a fight with my family. Mostly with my dad. Although my mom didn't help things."

"And you ran away?"

I nod.

Zimri bites her bottom lip. "Do they know where you are?"

"Let's put it this way: if they want to find me, they can, but they aren't trying."

"I know how that feels," she says quietly.

"You do?"

"My mom," she says but doesn't elaborate. Then she says, "Do you like it here?" and cocks her head to one side like she's contemplating the same question for herself.

"Do *you* like it here?" I ask her.

She shrugs and picks at lint on the pillow between us. "Doesn't matter because I have no place else to go."

"There's always another place."

"Yeah, yeah, another crap job in another crap warehouse or factory in some other corporate complex. But I can't leave my Nonda."

"I know what you mean." I sigh. "My sister is the reason I'll go back, eventually." I reach out and put my hand on top of hers. She doesn't pull away.

We sit there for a moment, hands pressed together, then she says, "I might not know much about you, Aimery, but I don't need a carapace or anything else to tell me that you have a good heart." She weaves her fingers into mine.

I feel her energy surge into my body like I've been plugged into a power source. At that moment I want to tell her everything. Come clean about who I really am. I inhale deeply and lean forward, ready to spill it all, but she lets go of my hand and hops up from the couch.

"Let's get out of here!" she says, charging across the floor.

"Where are we going?" I ask, confused by the sudden shift.

"You need new pants," she says. "And Black Friday opens in fifteen minutes."

"What is this place?" I ask Zimri when we join the crowd gathered in front of dark double doors in a nondescript cement block building. The whole place would take up a city block at home and is surrounded by a cracked blacktop parking lot with straggly weeds and busted out streetlights.

"There are two ways to buy things out here," she tells me. "You can use the COYN from your Corp X account and buy new stuff directly from the warehouse."

"But that's dumb, because then you pay Plute prices," I explain, very proud of my Plebe knowledge.

"The other way to get what you need is this place."

I follow as she shoulders her way toward the front of the crowd until we hit a wall of bodies intent on staying put. Zimri stands tall and strong with her legs wide and arms crossed.

"This is where Corp X sends all the returns, damaged goods, and stuff that doesn't sell off the shelves."

"Must be popular," I say, uneasy with how the mass around us is growing. There must be at least two hundred people in the lot with more coming from all directions.

"It's only open once a week, on Fridays, which is when they restock. You never know what will be inside, but there's almost always something you can use."

"Pants?" I ask and gulp, uneasy with the bodies beginning to push up against me.

"Definitely pants," says Zimri with a funny side grin. "When the doors open, things are going to happen fast. Stick close to me and don't stop until we get to the clothing area and then start grabbing. It takes less than half an hour for the whole store to get cleaned out. And you don't want to be stuck in line to pay or we'll be here all day. It's in and out, as quick as we can."

"Sounds like a secret-ops mission."

"Pretty much."

The crowd shifts closer to the building like one giant blob as a digital countdown clock lights up above our heads. I see cameras everywhere. Mounted over the doors and on the corners of the building.

"Alright, get ready." Zimri hunches lower.

Everyone around us starts the countdown in unison. "10 . . . 9 . . . 8 . . . 7 . . ."

She grabs my wrist. "Stay close!"

On one, the front doors swing open and all the bodies rush forward like water through a broken dam. Zimri holds me tight as we are carried forward in the swell. I'm terrified I'll trip and get trampled to death. Just ahead of us, to the right, a guy falls. The crowd parts around him but not everybody sees and others go down on top of him. They pile up, rolling off each other, covering their heads and tucking their knees up into their chests to protect their bodies from the mob.

"Wait!" I yell, pointing at the people on the ground. I try to drag Zimri back to help them.

"Don't stop! Don't stop!" she shouts in my ear and pulls me forward. I'm afraid I'll get separated from her so I willingly follow, although I feel terrible for leaving those people behind.

Just like in the warehouse, Zimri is quick and nimble. She finds every break in the wall of bodies and weasels through the cracks so that we quickly get to the front of the pack. Up ahead, I see that the flow is parting, people going in many directions, down dozens of aisles with signs overhead that read: Electronics, Furniture, Shoes, Jewelry, Health & Beauty, Party Supplies, Grocery.

"This way!" she yells and pulls me hard to the left. The mass of bodies has dispersed enough that we can run full speed and outpace the pack heading for the aisles.

"In the back!" Zimri yells and takes a right. We zip through an aisle of prepackaged noodles, cookies, cereal, baby food, and power bars. We turn left and right again through an aisle of dolls, toy trucks, puzzles, and games. "Come on! Keep up!" She tugs me forward. My lungs burn. "Here!" she shouts.

We duck into another aisle, this one with stacks and stacks of clothes. "Pants! Pants! Pants!" she yells as she flies along, scanning every shelf. "Here!" She stops and jumps up and down with excitement. Behind us I hear a stampede of feet. "They're coming!" she yells. "Find your size! Find your size!"

"My size?" I freeze. "I don't know my size!"

"How can you not know your size?" She grabs me by the

back of the waistband, pulls it away from my butt then shoves her hand down the back of my pants.

"Hey, whoa!" I yell and she cackles with laughter.

"Thirty-two, thirty-six! Go, go, go!"

We both run down the aisle, which has been flooded with more people. They elbow each other. A woman trips an old guy and yanks a pair of jeans from his hands. A fight breaks out as two men tug on opposite ends of a red-checked button-down shirt. On top of the shelves, cameras zip back and forth, recording every action.

Zimri shouts, "Found it!"

I run to her. Luckily no one else is competing for my size.

"Just grab some!" She pulls an armful of pants and several shirts off the shelves. I do the same. "Now run!" she screams and we take off, weaving around the other people still pillaging the clothing.

As we dart toward the front of the building, Zimri tosses pants over her shoulder. "These are ugly. Terrible pockets. What color do you want?"

"I don't know. Brown. Or blue." I'm wheezing. I can't think about pants and run for my life at the same time.

Zimri doesn't stop. "Just find some that you like. We have to get to the registers."

I do what she says, jettisoning pants as we jog until I'm down to two pairs that might work. "What do you think of these?" I hold up one pair in each hand while I run.

"Those are lame." She knocks the gray ones out of my hand. "But those are good!" She points to the soft brown ones with pockets on the side. "Do you want two pairs?" She holds up identical ones.

"Okay."

"Do you have some shirts?"

"Yes!" I hold up wads of fabric.

"Hold on to them," she warns. "We're going back into the fray."

We turn a corner and I see another wall of people, jostling and fighting for positions in long lines forming to get through the gates at the automated registers. Once again, Zimri grabs my wrist and pulls me forward. "This way," she says and we zip past all the people.

"Endurance! Survival of the fittest!" she hollers and laughs with delight like a complete lunatic. Then she shoves the other pants at me. "Take these," she says. "And meet me there." She points to the very last register where the masses haven't spread yet because it's so damn far away, then she peels off from me.

"Wait!" I yell. But she is lightning quick and has already disappeared down another aisle under a Grocery sign. I hear her, though. She shouts, "Keep going! Don't stop." I look over my shoulder and see a scrum of people heading my way so I take a deep breath and run faster. By the time I get to the gates for the last register, Zimri is speeding out of an aisle perpendicular to me with two small boxes in her arms. "Go! Go!" she yells.

She pushes me through the gate ahead of the rush of people. We jog up to the automated register. "Scan it! Scan it!" Zimri says but I stand paralyzed, no clue what to do. The people surge through the gates and push toward us. Zimri grabs the pants and shirts from me and runs them across the scanner. The total comes up on the screen. "Money!" she demands.

"What?"

"Money! Cash!"

"Cash?" Frantically, I pat my pockets. "I left everything at your POD."

"Seriously?" she yells but then she scans her boxes and two drinks and quickly feeds bills into the machine to pay for everything. She shoves the clothes back at me. "Now, we get the hell out!"

ZIMRI

When we come out of Black Friday, Aimery looks like he's ready to drop.

"You okay?" I pat him on the back.

He puts his hands on his knees, still huffing and puffing. "I feel like I just ran for my life from a pack of wild animals."

"But you got some nice pants, so it was totally worth it, right?" I say, only half joking.

He looks up at me skeptically. "Is that how you shop for everything?"

"Pretty much," I say. "Come on. We'll rest and eat something." I take him by the hand and lead him across the street from the Black Friday parking lot and sit beneath a sprawling oak tree. "This used to be a school when my grandmother was little." I point at the old redbrick building. Aimery falls like a rag doll beside me. "Brie and I used to sneak in there. There are still old paper books they used to teach kids to read and write and do math. Nonda says they even had art classes and music. And it was free. Can you imagine?"

"For free?" he says. "Why? How'd they make any money?"

"That was when the government paid for things," I say. "But I guess it didn't work because eventually Corp X came in with their SQEWL and it closed like almost everything else."

"What's that building?" Aimery asks, pointing at the Paramount Theater next to a dilapidated playground.

"It was a cinema," I tell him. "And a theater for live plays and music concerts. One of my grandfathers played in a band. My mother told me the ceiling was painted to look like a starry sky."

"It's beautiful," Aimery says. "Or it could be, at least. If someone cleaned it up."

"Yeah," I tell him. "The whole town is like that, really."

"Except Black Friday?" He turns and looks over his shoulder at the hulking building behind us and scowls, as if he'd been traumatized by what just happened. "I've never been inside a brick-and-mortar store before," he admits. "I've never had to think about my size or fight for clothes that other people want. That was awful in there!"

I laugh. "Poor baby! Used to everything at the push of a button, huh? This is how the Plebes do it. Now we eat! Here, this is for you." I hand him one of the lunch boxes I grabbed from the refrigerated section of the grocery aisle. "These are pretty good if you can snag one but they go fast." I open mine. A mycoprotein chixen patty on a bun with reconstituted veggie strips and dip on the side. "What'd you get?"

He pulls out a smoked tofurky and facon sandwich with yogurt-covered freeze-dried berries and bananas.

"Yum!" I hand him a power drink from my pocket and open

another for myself. He pops his open, chugs the whole thing, then digs into the food like he hasn't eaten in days.

"You know, it's funny," he says between bites, "but when I was back at home, I never thought for a second about who was packing up my boxes of demands. I wanted socks. I ordered socks. I got socks. Everybody thinks that the old-time stores were so inefficient. Who has time to walk in someplace if you don't know whether or not they have exactly what you want or need? The right color? The right size? What would be the odds of everything lining up in your favor? But, man, after a week of picking for people who know nothing but how to consume, I think, nobody needs eighty-five percent of the stuff they order! And we assume the whole system is automated. I never imagined actual people were running around a warehouse, getting things for me."

"You won't have to worry about that for long," I tell him. "Ours is one of the last warehouses to use humans. They'll automate it someday and we'll be replaced by A.N.T.s."

"But what will the workers do when that happens?"

"Same thing they've always done when jobs dry up," I say with a shrug. "Nonda talks about how her parents and grandparents made cars in factories out here before that industry died. Some of those people had to move away, some found other jobs, and some of them never recovered."

Aimery puts his sandwich down and says, "Sometimes when I'm picking in the warehouse, I wish I could see the names on the orders. I imagine that I might see one of my friend's names. Wouldn't it be strange if you actually knew the people you were picking for? Or if they knew us? Or what if we knew the people who built the stuff we used? What if I could meet the person who made these pants I just bought? Would it make a difference? Would people order less? Or more? Would they be less demanding and more forgiving if they knew it wasn't just an algorithm and robot working for them but an actual person?"

I giggle and lean in close. "Sometimes," I tell him, "when no one's looking, I take out a marker I keep inside my pocket and I write *Nobody from Nowhere* on the packages."

Aimery gasps.

"Oh, come on," I say and shove his shoulder. "It's not that bad."

"No, Zimri." He grabs my knee. "I've gotten one of your packages!"

"Shut up!" I say.

"I'm serious. I knew I'd heard or seen *Nobody from Nowhere* before, but I just couldn't place it. Now I remember." He throws his head back and laughs. "It was on some disposable umbrellas."

"It's like we were destined to meet!" I tease.

But Aimery's face is serious. "I think so, too."

"You're a Plute, aren't you?" I ask.

He looks down at the ground and nods. "Does that make you think less of me?"

I consider this for a moment. "If I didn't know you, I might think less of you, but the way you describe life in the City, it sounds awful."

He shrugs. "Like anything, there's an upside and a downside."

"And an upside down?" I say and do a backward roll to crack the somber mood because I don't want to spend my only day off talking about everything that's wrong in the world.

"How'd you do that?" Aimery says with an astonished laugh. "I want to do it!" He flings himself backward and tries to get his legs over his head, but he gets stuck midroll with his butt up in the air. "Help! Help!" he yells, legs waggling like an upturned bug.

"You're caught now!" I smack his rear.

"Hey, stop. Come on." He laughs and writhes around until I grab his ankles and flip him over so that he lands on his knees. He sits up with dried leaves and little twigs in his hair. I pull two handfuls of grass from the ground and toss them on his head.

"Aw, man!" he says, brushing them away. "Now I'm going to need another shower."

"Payback!" I yell, and throw more grass at him.

"Payback?" he says, laughing and swatting at the storm I'm making. "For what?"

"For beating me with that pillow!"

"Oh, yeah?" He flings grass at me. "Two can play that game."

I duck and roll then scurry behind the tree. "You have to be quicker than that!" I tease, popping out long enough to toss dried leaves at him, then hiding again before he can mount his defense. He hops up and chases me around and around the tree. We both run, hollering and laughing at each other like we're little kids again, until on the fifth time around he stops, spins on his heel to go the other way and I slam right into him.

"Ha!" He grabs me tight around the waist. "I got you."

"No way, sucker!" I turn away and dig my feet in the ground and he steps forward, trying to stop me, but we get tangled up and fall, face first, him on top of me. He keeps hold of my body and we roll, my legs kicking up in the air, both of us laughing and out of breath. I like the way my body fits snugly against his, like we're two parts of one machine. Then we both stop and lie there on our sides, each with a shoulder pressed into the ground. His knees are tucked up against the backs of mine as if we've just woken from a long nap in the sun. We both breathe, his exhale hot on my neck.

"Do you surrender?" he says into my ear.

"Zimri Robinson never gives up!" I proclaim, but I don't try to get away.

"Then you have met your match," he says like a movie voice-over. "Because Orpheus always wins."

"Orpheus?" I wriggle and he lets go. "Who's Orpheus?"

He flops onto his back, tosses one arm over his face, and groans. "Oh, hell."

"Wait a minute," I say, trying to puzzle through what's going on. "Is that your name?"

"I was going to tell you in your POD this morning!" he says. "But then you jumped up and said we were going to Black Friday and . . . and . . . now I've ruined everything."

"No, you haven't." I reach out to touch his knee. "I understand. You ran away. You needed to hide. We all hide a part of ourselves sometimes."

"Says the girl in the black mask?" he asks and peeks out at me.

"Says the boy who outed her and almost got her arrested," I say back.

"Sorry," he says, grimacing.

"So. Orpheus, huh?" I ask, trying to get used to his real

name. "Wasn't he the guy in Greek myths who went to the underworld to save his wife?"

He nods. "He was the father of songs."

"Quite a name to live up to!" I tease.

"You have no idea," he says. "And, there's something else I want to tell you." He looks at me from the corner of his eye then takes a deep breath and blurts out, "I'm the one who paid your grandmother's MediPlex bill."

"What? Why?" I sit up on my knees, my heart beating in my ears.

He exhales, sharply. "Because I'm the one who found her that night on the road and when you said you didn't have the money to keep her in the MediPlex I realized that I did."

"But I put on the concert. I took everybody's cash."

"I didn't know about the concert until after I'd already paid the bill." He shrinks back like he's afraid I'm going to punch him.

"That's so Plutey of you," I say, arms crossed. "Thinking you have to come in here and help us poor dumb Plebes."

"I don't think you're dumb. I never have," he says.

"The only reason someone like me would need the help of someone like you is because people like you took everything away from people like me." I pause and let that sink into his dumb Plute brain. "And I'm paying you back. You know that, right?"

"I don't want your money," he says.

"It's not *my* money. It's the money from the concert."

"No," he says seriously. "I won't take it. I would have put the same amount in the box at the concert."

"What?" I ask.

"I mean it. What I paid for your grandmother is what your concert is worth to me."

I sit there, speechless, my heart fluttering like a bird in flight.

"In fact, you deserve more than that!" he adds. "Do you know how much tickets cost to see a live show at an arena in the City? Your show was a bargain and better than any Plute performance."

My whole body feels liquid and warm. Slowly a smile spreads over my face. I crawl toward him as he yammers on but I'm not really listening to his words, only to the sound of his voice, which is a melody I want to sing. I am overwhelmed by his kindness and by his belief in me. Despite feeling badly that I've hurt Dorian, my feelings for him don't compare to how drawn I feel to this other boy, whoever he might be. It's as if Aimery/Orpheus and I have tiny magnets in our bellies pulling us together. He stops talking, mid-sentence, something about confessing more. Then he blinks at me with eyes wide and uncertain as I loom up into his face. I find the notes. I sing his song then press my lips against his and we both hum, our voices in perfect harmony.

ORPHEUS

I don't know how long we sing-kiss beneath the tree. Our voices blend and balance note after note as we climb up and down the scale. It could have been for one second or forever. Like any good song, it's timeless and stays stuck in my head long after it's over.

"Whoa." I blink when she pulls away.

"Was that okay?" she asks and bites her lip.

"Uh, yeah. More than okay." I lean forward for another round but she shies away and moves beside me so we're sitting shoulder to shoulder in the grass. Two dragonflies zoom by in tandem. This time I don't freak out. Instead, I watch them soar up and get lost among the leaves.

"I think I've wanted to do that for a while," she says.

"Me, too," I admit, then I lean close to her. "Want to do it some more?"

She bumps me playfully. "Yes, but not here." She points to Black Friday where people are still streaming out of the doors with their arms full of purchases. "Too many eyes."

"Are you worried that Dorian will find out?"

She thinks this over then says, "Yes, I guess I am. I don't want to hurt his feelings any more than I already have, but that doesn't change this." She points from herself to me and back at herself again.

"And what exactly is this?" I make the same gesture back and forth between us.

"I have no idea. I don't even know what I should call you now. Orpheus? Aimery? Which is it?"

I reorient myself so we're facing each other then I reach out and put my hands on Zimri's knees. I feel light-headed but I know if I want this to last, I need to come clean right now. "There's something else you need to know."

"Okay," she says and leans forward, ready to listen.

"My full name," I tell her, then I stop to take a breath, "is Orpheus Chanson."

"Chanson?" Zimri says and scoots backward. "Orpheus Chanson? As in Chanson Industries? That kind of Chanson?"

I nod and wait. Zimri sits there, stunned. My entire body feels as if it will melt into the ground, seep into the roots of the tree, and disappear if she rejects me. "I know I should have told you sooner. . . ."

"Good thing you didn't," Zimri whispers.

"Why?" I ask, my stomach dropping. "Do you like me less now?"

"I don't know," she says. "I'm trying to decide."

"Listen, Zimri." My hands hover in front of her because I'm not sure I'm allowed to touch her anymore. "I know this is a lot to take in and I haven't been completely honest but you should know there's one thing that's one hundred percent true."

"Which is . . . ?"

"This." I point from her to me like she did only moments before. "Whatever this is, it's the most honest feeling I've ever had for anyone. That's the truth. And nothing will change that."

Zimri laughs, surprising herself as much as me, then she shakes her head and I can see her fighting not to smile.

"Do you forgive me?" I ask.

"That depends," she says.

"On what?" I plead.

"On how this kiss feels," she says and leans in.

I dive forward, nearly knocking her down. When my mouth touches hers, when my hands find her shoulders, when I breathe her in, it's the way I've imagined every kiss should ever feel—but didn't.

When we pull apart, she sighs deeply and nods. "Okay," she says simply. "I forgive you, Orpheus Chanson." Then she stands up and holds out her hands to me. "Now let's get out of here."

"And go where?" I ask as she pulls me to my feet.

"Well," she says, taking a deep breath. "You should go to the housing office to find a POD. You're paying rent already, you know. It comes right out of your COYN. And I need to visit Nonda. And after that we'll figure out the rest."

ZIMRI

I don't stop smiling for the next hour. Not on my way to visit Nonda. Not as I sit beside her bed and listen to her berate me for keeping her in the MediPlex. "You're getting stronger and better every day," I remind her, but she just sniffs as if insulted. I pat her hand and grin and keep on grinning until I walk outside again and see Orpheus waiting for me on the portico. I run to him and let him catch me in a hug. "What are you doing here?"

"I have a surprise for you!" he says. He reaches in his pocket and pulls out the weird glove I saw him wearing on the river path once before. "Tati fixed my car."

I clap my hands. "I knew she could!"

Orpheus lifts his gloved hand to his mouth and commands, "Pick up." From the AutoTram lot, his car, still banged up but purring instead of clunking, glides toward us. "Open," he commands, and the topside doors lift up like wings. "After you." He bows like some old-fashioned gentleman.

Laughing, I climb inside and ogle the WindScreens all

around that are lit up with maps, scrolling headlines from the Buzz, and video feeds from the City.

"Where to?" the car asks.

Orpheus looks at me.

"Joy ride?" I ask, but he shakes his head.

"Chanson Industry headquarters," he tells the car and we begin to move.

"Are you crazy!" I yell and grip the armrest by my seat.

"Crazy about you," he says and flashes his cheesiest grin.

"You're kidding, right?" I ask.

"About what?" he says, being coy.

"Going to Chanson."

"I'm entirely serious, Zimri."

"Oh, no," I tell him. "No, no, no, no. I can't go there with you!"

"I know I just sprung this on you, but I think it's a good idea. We don't have another day off for two weeks and—"

"You've lost your mind," I tell him. "Your parents are not going to be happy if you show up with some Plute warehouse girl after you ran away."

"I'm not taking you to meet my parents," he says. "I want you to meet Piper McLeo."

"Piper McLeo!" I shout. "She's one of the most powerful producers in the music industry! I can't meet her looking like this!" I motion to my baggy cotton pants, comfy shirt, and my funky orange trainers.

"First off," Orpheus says, "she's an old family friend. And secondly, you look great! You always do. You have your own style. That's the whole charm of you. It's what sets you apart and makes you interesting and amazing."

242

"You need to stop the car," I tell him. "I'm not going with you."

"Look, I get it." He squeezes my hand. "You're nervous. You've never been that far from home and the City seems like a giant overwhelming place, right?"

"No!" I drop his hand. "That's not it at all. Once you get back to the City and see everything you gave up, you'll never come back here. Then what happens to me? I'll be stranded, far from Nonda without enough money to get back." My breath comes in gulps and my head spins.

"That's not going to happen, Zimri," he says.

"Why wouldn't it?" I demand.

"Because what I want most is right here, right now. Not back in the City. This is the only place I want to be."

"Then why go at all?" I ask.

"My father's in Europe and everyone else thinks I'm missing or dead, so we can slip in unnoticed. Otherwise, the 'razzi will be all over me." He slows the car to a crawl.

"What are you doing?" I ask. "Why are you stopping?"

"This is where we decide. Windows," he commands and the screens all disappear so the world outside becomes visible.

He points to an old bridge with elegant arches trussed up by crisscrossing steel beams. The whole structure is propped up on concrete pilings from the days when shipping was meant literally. The river is calm and the sky is bright so the bridge appears to belong in two worlds, one up here with us and one down below the surface of the water.

"Have you ever been this far before?" he asks me.

I swallow hard. "I come here once a year." He blinks at me. "This is the place where people take the plunge."

Orpheus is quiet. Without taking his eyes off the bridge, he reaches for my hand again and this time I let him take it. "Your father?" he asks and I nod. "I'm sorry, Zimri. I'm sorry that happened to you."

"Yeah," I say. "Me, too."

"Have you ever wanted to cross it?" he asks after a moment.

I nod. "But I never had a reason to go." Then I squeeze his hand and whisper, "Until now."

Orpheus tells me a hundred times on our way into the City not to be nervous. At first I say I'm not. After all, I have nothing riding on this crazy plan of his, but the second we walk into Piper McLeo's studios, I think that I might barf directly on my shoes.

The receptionist looks like he's about to toss his cookies, too, when he sees Orpheus in the doorway. He half stands up then sits down like he's seeing someone rise from the dead. "Your father . . ." he says.

"Is in Europe. I know," says Orpheus. "I'm not here to see him. Could you please get Piper for me?"

The guy hops out of his chair and rushes off, then Piper appears within a few seconds.

"Orpheus? My god!" she shouts as she blusters into the reception area. "We've been so worried about you!" She wraps him in a long hug while I stand by awkwardly, trying not to pee myself because everything in the room costs more than I'll ever make in my life. There is artwork on the walls, carpet as thick as river grass, deep soft sofas swathed in beautiful heavy fabric, and quiet calming music piped in through speakers hidden somewhere in the room.

Piper looks nothing like I pictured. She is small and wiry with tired, sad eyes. Not beautiful, but somehow captivating. She's dressed plainly, all in dark blue from head to toe, but I can tell by the way the material shimmers and moves with her body that the clothes are expensive and made to fit her precisely. I look down at myself and feel like one of the shabby, worn-out toys I'd find at the dump when I was little. If I could, I would slink away.

Finally, Orpheus pulls away from Piper. "I'm okay," he says with a laugh. "Really. Look at me! Never better." He holds out his arms and flashes his super smile.

"Your father must be so relieved! He didn't tell us that he'd located you," Piper says. "Probably wants to keep it out of the Buzz for now."

Orpheus lets that slide. Instead, he steps back and puts his arm around my waist. "Actually, I'm here because I have some-one I'd like you to meet." I shrink in on myself, like a frozard burrowing into the mud. "This is Zimri Robinson."

Piper can't hide her shock as she looks me up and down. She clears her throat and holds out a hand to me. "Well, well, well," she says, her voice rising up an octave. "What a pleasure to meet you."

I stand there, like an idiot, while Piper pumps my hand but I can't make any words come out of my mouth.

"Is this your first time in the City?" she asks slowly, like I might be stupid.

I nod but still can't speak, so unfortunately I'm proving her right.

"So . . ." She drops my hand and steps away. "What's it all about, Orphie?"

"I brought Zimri here because I want you to hear her sing."

Piper opens her eyes wide and is as speechless as I am. Finally she manages to say, "Yeah, sure. Anything for you. Just send me a recording and . . ." She tiptoes backward toward to the door.

"No," Orpheus says. "I want you to listen to her today. Here. In a studio. Now."

Piper stops and shakes her head. "Orpheus, I'm not sure where you've been or what you've been up to but you can't just walk in here and—"

"Yes, I can," he says and I see the entitled, take-charge Plute in him and, weirdly, I like it. "It won't take long," he tells Piper. "Just one song."

She draws in a deep breath. Clearly she's used to doing the young Mr. Chanson's bidding. "We were just recording some demo tracks for your friend Arabella."

"Arabella's here?" Orpheus says. I feel him stiffen at my side.

"Yes. I forgot. You two know each other quite well, don't you?" says Piper, a sly smile spreading across her face. "Let's go to her studio. I'm sure she could use a break."

I grab Orpheus's wrist and pull him back. "I can't do this," I plead quietly. "What if I'm horrible? What if I embarrass you?"

"You won't," he says simply.

"Coming?" Piper calls over her shoulder from the doorway. She levels her gaze at me and raises an eyebrow as if it were a challenge she knows I won't have the guts to take.

Orpheus leans in close. "This is your chance," he whispers. "She thinks you're a nobody. From nowhere."

When he says those words, I think of all the people who've ever come to my shows and screamed and stomped for more. I think about DJ HiJax playing my song on the waves. I think about my mother and my father—they never had a chance like this. I force myself to stand up straight. I know that I have to walk through that door for all those people and for Orpheus.

"Yes," I say to Piper, my voice strong and clear even though my heart is thumping wildly. "We're right behind you."

When we walk into the studio, the first thing I see is a beautiful girl at the piano inside a glass booth. Her music comes out through the speakers in the ceiling and is as lovely as she is. There's not a hair out of place on her head. Her clothes are perfect. She has big, soulful brown eyes and sharp cheekbones. And she's singing a sweet, soft melody in a high and pretty voice, nothing like my gravelly, raw songs.

"So it worked?" Orpheus asks Piper, nodding at Arabella. "Her ASA kicked in?"

"Oh yes," says Piper, her voice bolstered with certainty. "It kicked in big time. Piano. Marimba! She's amazing on percussion. I'm thinking of going Brazilian with her. Maybe bringing back the samba, but with a dance beat. You know, sultry but we could remix it for dance trax. And she's gorgeous, isn't she?" Piper cuts her eyes to me and I flinch as if I've been smacked.

When Arabella looks up, her fingers fumble and she hits an off-key chord. I watch her gasp as she rips off her headphones and runs out of the booth. "Oh my god! Orpheus!" she yells. "Orpheus!" She bolts across the room and throws herself at him.

Again, I stand aside, this time feeling like I'm the wrong note that's hanging in the air. Arabella has a stranglehold on Orpheus, who stiffly pats her back. Piper watches them, tapping one finger against her lips as if she's plotting her next move.

"I've been so worried about you," Arabella says. "Why didn't you ping me? Why didn't you tell someone where you were?"

Orpheus disentangles himself from her and steps firmly away. "Pinging works two ways," he says and Arabella winces. He comes to my side. "This is Zimri. She's here to audition for Piper."

Awkwardly, I stick out my hand. "Nice to meet you," I squeak then swallow and lower my voice down to normal. "How long have you been playing piano?"

"How long?" Arabella shakes her head as if she doesn't understand my question. "You mean, when did I have my ASA?"

I look to Orpheus to translate but he says, "Zimri plays every instrument, some of which she builds on her own."

"Oh. How . . . um . . . interesting," Arabella says. "Out of what?"

"Mostly things I find at the dump," I say and enjoy the look of revulsion that passes quickly over her face. "You can get all kinds of great stuff there. Electronics, furniture, bikes . . ."

"And clothing, I see," says Arabella.

I grit my teeth. Something in the way that girl looks at me just then, like I'm from the dump, makes my determination kick in. I drape my arm across Orpheus's shoulder and say, "Oh no, Orpheus and I shop exclusively at Black Friday."

Orpheus cracks up.

"I have another meeting soon," Piper says. "So . . ." She winds her hand around as if the clock is ticking.

The engineer who'd been working with Arabella sets up a microphone in the center of the room for me.

"Is it okay if I use that?" I point to one of the electric guitars hanging on the wall.

"Of course," says Piper. "Do you know how to play?"

"I think I can manage," I tell her as the engineer hands it to me and makes sure the wireless pick-up connects to the amps built into the wall. Unlike the cheap, plasticky guitar my mother left at Nowhere, this one is heavy but perfectly balanced. The strings respond instantly to my fingers, each note glorious and clear.

"Okay," I say, but something doesn't feel right. Then I realize what it is. I've never played my songs for anyone while my face was showing. For a second, I'm not sure I can do it.

Orpheus steps forward and gives me a quick peck on the cheek then he says into my ear, "You'll be brilliant. I know it."

Seeing Arabella blanch over that kiss gives me one more shot of confidence. I take a deep breath and say, "I'm ready."

"Are you recording this?" Orpheus asks.

Piper shrugs. "Sure, why not?" She gives the engineer a wave.

A little thrill goes through me. The only recordings I've ever made have been illicit and dangerous but now here I am, in an actual recording studio, about to sing for one of the top producers in the world. I raise my hand and strum the first notes of my song, then I begin to sing, "I'm Nobody from Nowhere. . . ." The song overtakes me. I get lost. I'm no longer in this room in front of these people. I love that feeling of suspended time when I'm everywhere at once and nowhere in particular. And when I finish and the last notes fade into the walls and floor and ceiling, Orpheus stands up, beaming, as he claps.

The engineer pops out from her booth and gives me a thumbs-up. "That was great," she says. "You're an amazing guitar player, and your voice—"

"Yes," says Piper, cutting her off. She rises from the sofa where she was sitting between Orpheus and Arabella. "That was very interesting, Zora."

"Zimri," I say.

"Sorry, Zimri," she repeats. "You've been singing a long time, I suppose?"

"All my life," I tell her, although she's already turned away.

"Arabella," Piper says. "Zimri must be parched after that. Could you please take her down to the artists' café and get her a bevvie?"

Arabella stays seated, clearly stunned by Piper's request.

"I'd like to speak with Orpheus for a moment," Piper says. "Alone," she clarifies.

"Yes, of course," says Arabella as she walks stiffly toward the door.

I look at Orpheus. He smiles and nods for me to go, so reluctantly, I follow Arabella.

ORPHEUS

Piper leads me to her office where the wall screen rotates through pix and vids of her many successes. Gold records. Grammys. Pixs of her with nearly every major artist over the past twenty-five years, all the way back to a photo of her beside my mom when they were not much older than I am now.

"God, we were young," she says, tapping her finger against the screen. "I was just a production assistant. Running errands. Making sure everyone had enough water, the right lip gloss, a favorite microphone." The picture switches and she turns away. "But even then I had a knack for knowing which musicians would make it and which ones wouldn't."

She loops her arm through mine and draws me over to the plush couch. "Your mom was a no-brainer. Anyone could see she was meant to be a superstar. She was like a vortex, drawing everyone around her in. Want something to drink?"

"Sure." Piper's RoboMestic wheels over and presents me with a tray of choices. I take a fresh fruit drink, something I haven't had in weeks, then I sink down into the softness of the sofa and hear myself sigh. I didn't realize until that moment how much I've missed the little luxuries of Plute life, like comfy couches and cold sweet drinks on demand.

"Other people come to me rough. Like a block of stone," Piper says as she arranges herself beside me. "I think of myself as a sculptor whose job it is to chip away to find what's beautiful inside."

"Like Zimri," I say. "I know she's not polished, but she's brilliant and she has that quality everybody in the industry is trying to manufacture."

Piper cozies up to me so we're knee to knee. She leans in close and peers at me. "I'm worried about you."

"Why?"

"You seem lost. You brought me this girl, but what about you? It's like you've forgotten that all of this"—she motions around the office at the awards and gold records—"is meant to be yours."

"It's funny," I tell her with a sigh. "Ever since I was little, running around these studios, sitting on superstars' laps, everyone assumed I'd be in the recording booth someday, but that's not what I want."

"How can you say that?" Piper asks. "You were made for this and, more importantly, this was made for you. You're Libellule and Harold's son and making music is in your blood." She traces a finger down the blue vein of my inner arm. "It's in your heart." She presses her hand against my chest. "All we need is to wire up your brain." She taps the side of my head. "And we'll all be set."

"You sound like my father," I tell her.

"Good," she says. "He knows what he's talking about."

"He's knows what's best for his business, but not what's best for me." I lean in close, ready to confide in Piper, who's known me all my life. "The thing is, I want to bring music out of other people like you do, like my father used to do before he got so greedy and wanted to take over the entire industry. I want to find that spark in real people, people like Zimri."

Piper jerks away from me. "Oh, god. Don't tell me you've aligned yourself with that horrid Project Calliope?"

"No!" I say. "Of course not."

"They got to your mother, you know."

I roll my eyes. "Come on, Piper. Mom would align herself with anything that makes Dad look bad. Next week she'll lose interest and be on to something else. Like her clothing line? What's up with that?"

Piper sighs. "You're probably right about your mom, but come on, Orpheus! What's your fascination with this Plebe girl?"

"You heard her," I say. "You watched her. She's the *real* thing. She could be another Libellule."

Piper shakes her head. "I'm not sure what you've been through in the past week or so, but it looks to me like you think you're in love. The problem is, it's blind love. Stone-blind love. The kind that makes you do stupid things."

"I can't deny my feelings for Zimri, but I see very clearly what she can do. I've watched her perform onstage. I've seen the way people react. I've heard her on the waves. You can't tell me that you, of all people, don't see it, too. There's something else going on here if you're trying to convince me otherwise."

Piper stands up to move away from me. "Even if I wanted to, I can't. If I took in some random person off the street, no matter how talented and engaging, it would upset the entire structure of the industry."

"Zimri's not a random person," I argue. "I brought her in."

Piper leans back against her desk. She crosses her arms over her chest and her legs at the ankles. "What about people like your friend Arabella, who've paid their dues, waited their turn, and played by the rules? What message would that send to them if a girl like Zimri can waltz in from a warehouse job, no ASA, and I make her a celeb?"

"It would say that anyone, not just the rich, should be able to profit from their own art and that talent is more than the wiring inside your brain!"

"A hell of a lot more!" Piper says loudly. "It takes a Promo-Team and distribution and funding. You think this girl you plucked from a Complex is the only natural-born genius? There are tons of people out there who could make music, but the industry is dedicated to promoting a different kind of artist. She can go make music for the Plebes. But making money, making *art* is the providence of the plutocracy. Of which you're a part. So don't throw your life away on some Plebe girl with a good voice and a nice ass. Think about your future and the future of this entire company. It's time you were on your way back home to get your ASA. You and Arabella are naturally compatible. We can get a duet for the two of you, plus capitalize on this whole Plebe adventure of yours. The public will eat it up."

"I could never do that to Zimri," I say.

"Sure you could," says Piper. "She'd go back to her old life and do just fine without you. In fact, she'd probably be better off. You know how hard the spotlight is. A Plebe like her could never handle this life. You'd be doing her a favor to let her go."

"Piper," I tell her as I stand. "The only person I'd be doing a favor for in that scenario is you. Because together, Zimri and I are going to kick some Plute ass. So watch your backside."

ZIMRI

As we zip through a corridor of flashing 3-D billboards lining the Distract SkyPath, Orpheus is sullen and quiet.

"Hey." I touch his forearm. "You're not upset about what happened back there, are you?"

"Of course I am," he says. "Aren't you?"

"Not really," I admit. "What did you expect? We'd waltz in unannounced and Piper McLeo would hand me a record deal?" Before he can answer, I add, "Heck, I didn't even expect her to let me in the building, much less listen to me play."

"You should expect more."

"Hmph!" I snort. "Spoken like a true Plute."

Orpheus slumps in his seat and sighs. "It would be one thing if I was wrong about you, but I'm not and Piper knows it. You're more talented than . . . than . . . any of those idiots!" He points out the window at bigger-than-life holograms singing and dancing across the rooftops eye-level with his car. "In fact, you're more talented than anyone who's walked into her office since my mother!"

"First off, I doubt that's true," I say, blushing. "And secondly, that's not the way the world works."

"Yes, it is," he insists. "That's exactly the way *my* world works."

"*Your* world." I point out the window at the chaos of lights and noise. "Where you're never told no. At least not by the people who work for your father."

"Piper's not the only gatekeeper," Orpheus says bitterly. "There are plenty of other producers in the world."

"But there's only one patron that matters," I remind him, which makes him slump again. "The thing is, Orpheus, I don't need your father to sell my music in order for me to be happy."

He looks at me, horrified. "So you want to work in the warehouse for the rest of your life?"

"I didn't say that."

"You deserve to make a living off of your genius, Zimri! The same as any Plute."

"Maybe I do," I shrug. "But your father and Piper McLeo don't deserve to make money off of me."

Orpheus stares at me for a moment. Then he blinks. And blinks again.

"What?" I ask.

"Oh my god!" he shouts and bangs the steering wheel. "I never thought of it that way!" Then he leans over to plant a kiss on my cheek. "You're absolutely right. They don't deserve you!"

When we arrive at Alouette's MediPlex outside of the Distract, I can't believe the same company owns this and the crap hole

Nonda is stuck in back home. I stop outside the opulent entrance lined with potted palm trees and marble statues surrounding a three-tiered fountain.

"I know it shouldn't surprise me that everything for Plutes is bigger, better, and nicer, but come on!" I say.

Orpheus looks at the grandeur as if seeing it for the first time. Then he takes my hand. "I'm sorry. It's not fair."

"Yeah, well as Nonda always says, fair and real are two different things."

As soon as we pass through the entrance, Orpheus's entire demeanor shifts. He visibly relaxes as we walk the pristine hall with artwork and plants and beautiful music pumped in through the ceiling. When we reach Alouette's room, he shoves his ExoScreen and EarBug in his pocket, then sighs deeply, as if he's stripped away all the frustration of the last hour.

"Do you want me to stay out here?" I know how important she is to him. She's the main reason he'd come back to the City for good.

"Of course not!" He tugs me toward the door. "I want her to meet you."

Alouette's sanctuary is lovely and I can see why he likes to visit. The room is cozy and pretty. In here the rest of the world seems far away. Alouette lies in the bed, a beautiful ruin. Like Orpheus, she has dark olive skin but hers is ashy, not glowing. Her hair is the same deep brown as his, but thin and brittle against the bright white pillowcase where her head rests. She has his features: deep-set eyes, strong nose and jaw, but they're sunken into her emaciated face. She doesn't seem to register our arrival until Orpheus touches her on the forehead. She draws in a breath and lets it go as if she, too, is relieved.

"Sorry I haven't seen you in a while," he tells her quietly. "I was away, but I brought someone to meet you. This is my friend, Zimri."

I step up beside the bed and touch her withered hand. "Hello," I say. "Orpheus has told me so much about you."

"Zimri is a singer," Orpheus says. "Like you."

"Would you like to sing a song with me?" I ask.

Orpheus looks at me. "She doesn't really . . ."

I ignore him and sit on the edge of Alouette's bed. "What do you like to sing?" I listen to the rhythm of the room. The ticking of the songbird clock becomes my metronome. I tap a rhythm on my thigh as I hum a few notes over the whoosh and swoosh of the machinery. Orpheus walks around the bed and settles into an easy chair. He slips off his shoes and props his feet up on the bed. I continue to hum, not expecting anything except to let the music take me where it wants to go. Then the clock strikes the quarter hour and the call of a whippoorwill fills the room.

Orpheus and I smile at one another and we both join in. "Whippoorwill, whippoorwill," we call back and forth. When the clock is done chiming, I continue the song I made up by the river.

> *Whippoorwill, whippoorwill, I know just how you feel,*
> *Singing for a broken heart that may never heal.*
> *Singing for your lover, singing for your mate,*
> *If you find each other, then it's truly fate.*

When I get back to the chorus again, Orpheus joins in.

Whip-poor-will-you, whip-poor-won't-you, sing throughout the night.

Then Alouette sings with us.

Until you find another one that will hold you tight.

I find the harmony as we repeat our chorus over and over. Our voices meld like three notes on the same instrument. Singing with Alouette and Orpheus is the purest form of music for me. Not meant to entertain or titillate, no money generated. Our song is just for us. It doesn't need to be captured or repeated or remixed and sold. It's the thing unto itself and it is perfect. When our song fades, we sit in a comfortable silence.

After a while I get up and look around the room at all the family photographs. Orpheus and Alouette as little kids sitting in a tree. A fresh-faced and gorgeous Alouette blowing out the candles on an elaborate birthday cake. The two of them in fancy clothes beside their mother who was stunning in a long silver gown, holding a silver statuette.

"Who's this?" I pick up a picture of a woman at a grand piano.

"My grandmother," Orpheus says.

"Your mom's mom?" I ask. "Was she a musician, too?"

"No, actually, that's my father's mother." He gazes at the photo over my shoulder. "I never knew her but my father said she was a brilliant pianist. A child prodigy. She studied with famous teachers, went to some place called Juilliard, and even had a record deal, but the way my dad tells the story, she never figured out how to play the game. She couldn't bend and mold herself into a groove that fit a marketing category so the one record she made was a flop and her label dropped her. She got depressed. Wrote sad and moody songs nobody wanted and eventually washed down a handful of sleeping pills with a bottle of bourbon. My dad was six years old."

I quietly digest this story. "So your dad and I have something in common."

Orpheus blinks at me, uncertain. "Other than me?"

I set the photo down. "Both our mothers left us when someone tried to take their music away."

Orpheus puts his hands on my shoulders and lays his chin on top of my head. "I never thought of it that way." I lean back against him and he wraps his arms around me. "I liked singing with you," he says.

"Me, too," I tell him. "I think Alouette liked it as well."

"The doctors say the auditory cortex is the only part of her higher functioning brain that works anymore, but that she doesn't derive any real pleasure out of music."

I turn and look at him. "That's a load of crap and you know it."

"You're probably right," he says.

I reach up and put my hands on his shoulders. "Orpheus, I would understand if you needed to come back permanently," I tell him. "For her, I mean."

He kisses my forehead. "Someday I will, but only when you can come with me."

"I—" I'm interrupted when the door flings open and a woman flies into the room. When she sees us she yelps. I jump away from Orpheus, my heart in my throat.

"Mom!" Orpheus says.

"Libellule," I whisper to my childhood idol. I spent hours learning all her songs and singing them to myself in the bathroom mirror when I was little. Now here she is in front of me and even more beautiful in person. Shorter than I imagined, but willowy and strong, like she could withstand a powerful storm.

"Orpheus!" she exclaims and launches herself at him.

"What are you doing here?" He pulls away from her hug.

"I should ask you the same thing!" she exclaims. "And who's this?" She looks me up and down, but unlike Piper or Arabella she doesn't sneer. Instead, she strides over to me and holds out her hand. "I'm Libellule!"

"I know," I say, starstruck and silly, but manage to squeak out, "I'm Zimri."

"What a fitting name!" she exclaims.

Orpheus and I look at each other and burst out laughing.

"What's so funny about that?" she booms, but she smiles, large and effusive, like all the fun in the world belongs to her, which sets me at ease.

"That's exactly what he said when we first met," I tell her.

"Smart boy," she says and winks at him. "But who are you? Where did you come from? Orpheus!" She turns back to him. "My god, where have you been?"

Every ounce of tranquillity drains away from Orpheus. He holds his body rigid again and the muscles in the side of his jaw twitch. "If either you or Dad had bothered to look for me—"

"You're the one who left!" She flits across the room to plant a kiss on Alouette's forehead. Then she smooths the girl's hair back and straightens up her covers. "Didn't you get my pings? I've been frantic!"

Orpheus looks up at the ceiling as if praying for patience.

Libellule ignores him and turns to me. "I ran away from home, too, but I was only fourteen," she tells me like it's a competition and she's winning. "I knew I was meant to be a star. Can you believe it?"

"Actually," I tell her, "that doesn't surprise me at all." I can see how beguiling she can be, but also how she could turn on you like a snake. Instinctively, I move closer to Orpheus as if to protect him. "You seem like the kind of person who goes after what she wants."

She beams at me. "You're a good judge of character."

"Yes," I say and take hold of Orpheus's hand.

"Zimri's a musician," Orpheus says.

Libellule's mouth drops open. "You're joking!"

"A damn fine one, too," he adds. "In fact, she reminds me of you when you were young."

"In what way?" Libellule steps back to appraise me.

"Well," says Orpheus as he thinks this over. "She's a natural-born genius with the kind of talent every patron is trying to engineer." I blush redder than the cardinal on Alouette's clock. "And she commands attention when she's onstage."

"Sounds promising," Libellule says. "But can she sing?"

"Mom," says Orpheus, dead serious now. "There has been no voice like hers since yours."

"Hmmm," says Libellule. "I'm intrigued."

I think that I might die. Libellule, *the* Libellule, is intrigued by *me*.

"Now that I think about it," Orpheus adds, "there's one major difference between the two of you."

"Oh," his mom says, batting her lashes. "What's that?"

"Zimri uses her music for the people but you used people for your music."

For a quick moment, hurt passes over Libellule's face, then she recovers. "I'm trying hard to rectify that, you know."

Orpheus rolls his eyes. "How's that?"

"Project Calliope," she says.

"Oh, right," says Orpheus, unimpressed. "I heard you on the Buzz saying you support their cause."

"Wait, Calliope?" I ask. "Calliope Bontempi?"

"Yes," they both say at the same time.

"My mother knew her," I tell them. "They made music together."

"*Spiritus mundi,*" says Libellule. "We are all connected. Synchronicity! Who was your mother? Do I know her?"

I shake my head. "Just a warehouse worker making music on the side."

"Too bad Chanson Industries made that illegal," Orpheus adds.

"That's exactly what we're trying to combat," Libellule says. Then she looks at Orpheus. "You should really give us a chance, darling. You could be a big help to the Project."

"Wait a minute," Orpheus says as if he's putting something together in his mind. "Are you the one who put Calliope up to all of this?"

Libellule draws in a long breath through her nose. "Let's just say I've been biding my time, waiting for the right person to come along and take your father down a peg. When Calliope showed up in the City a few months ago, I knew I'd found a cause I could get behind."

Orpheus's mouth hangs open. "You sent her to find me, didn't you? The night of Quinby's opening?" he asks. "You're the one who told her I was on the fence about having an ASA."

Libellule blinks at him but refuses to answer.

"And you knew I was here, didn't you?"

She shrugs but glances away. "I happened to look at the security cam from Al's room and when I saw you, I rushed right over."

Orpheus steps toward her. "What do you get out of this?" he asks. "What's in Project Calliope for you?"

"I never liked those nasty surgeries," she says. "Even before Alouette's life was ruined. Now that I'm out from under your father, free and clear, I'll have the satisfaction of watching him go down in flames."

"But why now?" Orpheus asks. "After all these years?"

For the first time I see a genuine sadness pass over her face. She stands up and reaches for Orpheus, caressing his cheek. "When Harold started pressuring you to have an ASA and you were uncertain I realized I had to do something drastic or he would get what he wants. Again."

Orpheus stands, speechless, so Libellule continues.

"Genius is a thing that should happen only once in a very great while. Not every day on an operating table." She looks at me and winks as if all of her concern from a moment ago has now evaporated. Then she grabs his hands in both of hers and pulls him close. "I know I'm not a great mother, but believe me when I say, I'm doing this for you, sweet boy. Project Calliope is all for you and your sister."

Orpheus is unmoved by her drama. He pulls away. "No, Mom. Like with everything Dad does, this is about the two of you, not me and Al." He takes my hand then leans down to kiss Alouette once more. "It was nice to see you, but Zimri and I have to go. We have work tomorrow."

VERSE SIX

ORPHEUS

When the rounded toe of Zimri's funky orange trainer trips the laser sensor at the Strip, no MajorDoormo announces our arrival, no spotlights illuminate, no 'razzi drones swarm us, no headlines flash onto the Buzz, and yet it's just what I need after our disappointing trip into the City.

"Aimery!" a shout goes up from the bar when we step inside. A group of girls, with Veronica at the center, lift their cups. Out of habit, I step slightly behind Zimri and put my hand on the small of her back then flash my widest, most camera-ready smile at the crowd.

"What are you doing?" Zim asks and ducks away, embarrassed.

I laugh. "Oops, sorry. Old habits die hard."

Veronica rushes up and plants one on my cheek. "I haven't seen you since we went out the other night. Where have you been hiding?"

"I've been around," I say and try to sidestep back to Zimri, who's found her best friend in the crowd.

"Let's dance!" Veronica attaches herself to my arm like a barnacle and drags me toward the back.

"Zim! Zimri!" I call, but she's smirking at my predicament. Just to get her back, I twirl Veronica around, dip her a few times, and put on my best moves, all while keeping Zimri in my sight. She lurks on the sidelines, next to Brie, giggling and pointing, but I can tell she doesn't love the way Veronica keeps dancing back to me. Finally, I spin Veronica like a top, sending her whirling across the floor. Then I dance over to Zimri, grab her around the waist, and pull her to me.

"Come on!" I yell in her ear. "Give a guy a break. I know you can dance better than these other girls."

With a half-smile/half-smirk she says, "Oh what the hell!" and finds the rhythm of the techno remix medley of Geoff Joffrey's biggest hits featuring Minerva VaVoom. I love watching Zimri spring and pop on her rubber-band knees, like the best backup dancers on any stage. Nobody in the Strip can take their eyes off her. Even Veronica, who stands to the side, arms crossed and clearly annoyed. I do my best to keep up with Zim while staying out of her way until she grabs me. I hook my arm around her waist and pull her close. We move cheek to cheek under the lights so everyone can see that Zimri Robinson has chosen me.

When the song ends, we head to the front and plop down at a table with Zimri's friend Brie, whom I've heard a lot about but only met this evening. I already like her. She and Zimri finish each other's thoughts and laugh at jokes I don't understand. They're so excited to see each other now that Brie is switched back to days again that they barely notice me. Behind Zimri, I glimpse Dorian's blond dreds. I hold my breath, preparing myself for an ugly scene, but he glances over at us then moves off into the crowd like a shark disappearing behind a reef. I let my breath go, relieved.

"Admit it," I turn to Zim and say. "You're having fun!"

"No way," she teases and downs a fizzy drink. "This sucks. I hate the Strip with all its sanctioned entertainment."

"She always says that," Brie tells me.

Up on the giant screen behind the bar, two announcers, Isolde and Ike, whom I knew at SCEWL, both perfectly proportioned and beautiful in that plasticky Plute way, banter over a steady stream of pix and vid about what movies debuted today, which celebs are dating, and how far up the Stream the latest songs have gone, but for the first time in my life, I'm truly more interested in the conversation in front of me than what's happening in the Buzz.

"So, Brie," I say. "Do you have any embarrassing stories about Zimri when she was young?"

"Oh believe me, I've got stories!" she says, eyes twinkling.

"Don't you dare!" Zimri punches Brie on the shoulder.

"Was she always this violent and bossy?" I tease.

"She was way worse when she was little," Brie tells me.

"Got any pix of Miss Bossypants?"

"Embarrassing ones?" Brie asked.

"Of course," I say.

"All right, that's enough!" Zim says, but she's laughing right along with us.

From the screen behind Brie's head, I hear Ike say, "And now a quick sneak peek at an anticipated new release from Chanson."

"This one's sure to be hot," Isolde adds.

I ignore their drivel until I hear, "It's Arabella Lovelace giving us a taste of her debut song, which will officially drop next week. . . ."

Zimri's head snaps around to stare at a twenty-foot-tall Arabella taking up the screen. She's in a thick denim jumpsuit, cut off just below her butt. Her hair is up, her zipper down to reveal a hint of cleavage, and a name patch, which says *Nobody,* is sewn above her breast. She clings to a metal shelving unit where dancers ride up and down in giant baskets. All around her RoboForklifts drive in formation as the beat comes in and Arabella begins to sing.

> *I am Nobody from Nowhere*
> *A speck upon your screen*
> *An non-automated worker that you've never seen*
> *I've packed your purchased footholds*
> *I'll tie them with a bow*
> *But I live a life that you'll never know*

I stare stupidly as Arabella dances half-naked with guys in skintight jumpsuits gyrating all around. Then Zimri's on her feet, shouting, "What the hell?"

Everyone in the Strip has stopped to stare at what's going on.

"That's not her song!" someone in the crowd yells.

"That's about us!" someone else calls.

A bowl of noodles goes flying and hits screen-Ara square in the ass.

"I . . . I . . . I . . ." I stammer. I cannot wrap my mind around what I'm seeing and hearing.

"We were just there!" Zimri says, horrified. "Like three hours ago. How is this happening?"

As quickly as the snippet started it's replaced again by Ike. "Can't wait to see the whole thing," he says.

My face burns. My hands are in fists and there is a roaring in my ears. "They stole it! They stole your song!"

Then I hear Ike say, "Big news from Elston Tunick," and my attention swerves back to the screen. "The renowned video artist released her newest remix today and sparked controversy when she claimed to have located missing music industry heir Orpheus Chanson."

This time on the screen there is a slow-motion video of shoppers flooding through the doors at Black Friday. Bodies undulate, arms flail as if underwater, and faces become distorted as they grimace slowly in the onslaught of bodies pouring forward. I watch the man I saw this morning trip, again. This time each motion of his fall is caught in agonizing detail. How his head travels back, his eyes widen with the realization that he's going down. He opens his mouth to yell but the sound is guttural, a howl of despair as his chest heaves forward. He slumps to the floor with others landing on top of him like heavy sandbags tossed against a riverbank during the rains. And then there I am, as clear as anything. I pass by, each movement a slo-mo ballet. I reach for the man. Over my shoulder, Zimri comes into the frame, a warped smile on her face as she reaches out to me and pulls me back. The video stops on a close-up of my face, twisted in a strange grimace halfway between excitement and horror.

"Chanson Industry spokesperson Esther Crawley says they are cautiously optimistic that Chanson has been found," Ike says. An image of Esther in front of my father's office flashes on the screen.

"So far this sighting is unconfirmed. It may be a staged event with a look-alike meant to draw attention away from Project Calliope, but we have not yet ruled out foul play," Esther says. "If it is Orpheus Chanson then we believe Project Calliope may have kidnapped and brainwashed him when he was in a most vulnerable, drug-influenced state. Harold Chanson is cutting his trip to Europe short and returning to retrieve his son."

"What the . . . ?" I whisper.

My father, blustering toward his jet, quickly replaces her on screen. The whole thing is so clearly staged. Probably by Piper, who is a master at unfolding these kinds of dramas. "Project Calliope is a terrorist organization," he shouts. "Hellbent on destroying the sanctity of private property. They will stop at nothing to bring me down. First Calliope Bontempi brings a spurious suit against my company and now her group has taken advantage of my family's deepest tragedy." Then he looks straight at the camera and says, "I'm coming, son. Don't worry. Your father is here for you."

"Oh. My. God," I say and fall into my chair.

"Sources close to the family say Orpheus Chanson has battled a Juse addiction and acted erratically the last time he was seen in public," Isolde says.

Then Rajesh is on the screen from the garden at the Deep End restaurant. His thick black hair is pomped up and he's wearing a sleeveless shirt to show off his impossibly buff arms. The words *Best Friends of Orpheus Chanson* scroll below.

"I tried to talk him out of running away," says Rajesh, "but he's a complicated and troubled person with a tragic secret."

"Liar," I say. My stomach roils with anger.

"What sort of secret?" Isolde asks, eyes wide with interest.

"I'll reveal everything in my new book about our friendship," Rajesh says and he lowers his sunglasses. "The first installment is available now," he adds with a twinkle in his eye. A link to the e-book appears on the screen below him.

I shake my head, appalled by how conniving he is.

The camera pans right and there is Elston next to Rajesh at the table. "I couldn't believe when I saw Orphie in the footage I'd found today. I knew I had to make it public. You can view the whole video and others like it at the Niachis Gallery through next Friday." A link appears on screen for Elston's new exhibit.

"Even Chanson's newest star, Arabella Lovecraft, had something to say," Ike adds.

The camera sweeps right again. Arabella, at the table with Rajesh and Elston, pushes up her gem-encrusted sunglasses then dabs at her bright and blinking eyes until a single tear rolls down her perfect cheek. "I just hope he's okay," she says. "My heart goes out to his family, especially his father, Mr. Chanson, who is such a generous and giving patron to be releasing my debut song, 'Nobody from Nowhere,' next week."

Before I can react to my supposed friends' performances, the vid switches and my mother comes on the screen.

"Libellule! Libellule!" voices shout as she scampers down the steps outside of her apartment building in a flowing shirt with wing-like sleeves. At first she appears shocked to find 'razzi on her doorstep, but I can see the calculation in her face.

"What do you think of your son?" Ike asks her through a drone.

She stops and blinks her giant eyes at the camera. "I'm just thrilled that he is safe and alive!"

"Do you think he's been kidnapped and brainwashed?" Isolde asks.

My mother laughs this off as ridiculous. "Orpheus is a young man of the people. He understands the price Plute children pay for sparking false genius with Acquired Savant Ability surgeries. Just as Calliope Bontempi has brought the issue to the surface by suing my ex-husband. Orpheus is working a real job like a real man and I am proud of him! Like every mother, I just hope my son has found his bliss because in the end, that's what each of us deserves."

Zimri turns slowly in her chair to stare at me, but I can't look away from the screen because there's my mother's skeevy boyfriend, Chester, jogging down the steps behind my mother wearing a patchwork blazer that looks as if it's made of ten different drapery fabrics.

"And have you found your bliss?" Ike asks my mother, a preplanned question if ever there was one.

My mother cozies up to Chester who slings his arm around her shoulder as she tosses her hair back and lifts her chin to laugh, an old trick to hide the lines around her eyes from the cameras.

"Yes," she says. "I have. I've started a clothing line." She opens her arms and both she and Chester twirl as if they've been practicing this routine for hours. She stops abruptly mid-spin, whips her head toward the camera, sultry and inviting, then purrs, "Dragonfly Designs."

Ike comes back on screen in front of the freeze-frame image of my twisted face from the Black Friday vid. "Could this really be Orpheus Chanson shopping like a Plebe?" he asks Isolde.

She flips her hair. "Guess some people will do anything for a discount?" she says, then a laugh track kicks in as if her snide remark is the funniest thing ever uttered, and they move on to the next story.

I feel like I'm in a slow-motion Elston Tunick video then. It seems to take hours to get out of my chair. Forever to locate an exit for my escape. All eyes have turned to us. "Quick," I say to Zimri. "We have to get out of here."

Despite the shock she's suffered, Zimri takes my hand and pulls me out the door while Brie puts her body in between us and the crowd. Outside, I look up and down the street, sure that at any moment, 'razzi drones will be on my tail.

"We have to get away."

"In here." Zim hops into a dark alcove between the buildings just as the door to the Strip opens and a deluge of people come outside.

"Where is he?" Veronica shouts above the noise of the crowd. "We have to get pix with him!" Swarms of people hustle by the alleyway but Zimri and I stay pressed against the wall, holding hands until they're gone.

When the street is quiet again, Zimri lets her breath go. "I can't believe it," she says, shaking her head. "I just can't believe it. How'd they do it so fast?"

"I'm so sorry, Zimri. I'm so so so sorry. I knew they were bad, but I didn't know they were this horrible. I would have never let Piper hear you sing if I had known this is what she would do!"

"What about all of those awful people using your situation to get attention for themselves?" Zimri says. "Your friends! Your father! Your mother! After we just saw her."

"Oh please," I say, waving away her disdain. "Doesn't surprise me for a minute. I guarantee, hits are going through the roof for my father's company, Rajesh's book, Elston's exhibit, orders for my mom's clothing line. Even Arabella's stolen song."

Zimri's face goes dark. "My song," she mutters.

"Yes," I say. "Your song."

She shakes her head. "This is terrible."

"You think that's bad? Just wait a few hours until the 'razzi swarms the Complex. Then you'll see how bad it can get. I have to hide before they find me."

As I pull her out of the alleyway, Dorian steps out of the Strip. Zimri stops in her tracks. They lock eyes. Then he stands in front of us, blocking our path, fists clenched and chest heaving.

"You're a Chanson?" he demands.

"Dorian," she says and steps between us.

"No, it's okay," I tell her. "No reason to deny it."

"And you're still with him?" he asks Zim.

People walking by slow down to watch.

"Yes," she says simply and relief floods my body.

Dorian scowls, as if the situation makes no sense. "But Chanson, his father . . . he's the one who prosecuted your mom! He's the one who filed the suit against her for stealing his company's music! He's the one who demanded that she pay back the damages times two and when she couldn't, he was going to force her into jail to work off her restitution, which is why she took off."

"Is that true?" I ask Zimri.

She blinks and blinks as if trying to process what he's saying.

"Yes it's true!" Dorian stomps toward us, pointing at my chest and the small circle of people around us stirs. "This guy's family is the reason your family fell apart!"

"Zimri, I . . ." I start to say.

"Stop it!" she yells at Dorian. "Just stop it!"

"How can you stand beside him after what his father did to your mother?" Dorian yells.

"What about what your father did to my mother?" Zimri screams back at him.

Dorian staggers. "What are you talking about? She's the one who broke his heart."

"He threw her under the bus!" Zimri yells. "She took the blame for everything. She never named him. Or Tati. Or Calliope Bontempi. Or anybody who came to her concerts or paid her for the downloads. She protected them all. I was there. I was at the trial. I remember. When the Arbiter asked her who else made music with her, she said she was the only one. When they asked her who hacked the HandHelds, she said she did it on her own. My father begged her to out Marley and Tati and Calliope so her sentence would be lightened, but she wouldn't do it. It's time everyone knows that!"

The people around us murmur in surprise, but Dorian's face collapses.

"We are not our parents!" Zimri says. "I am not my mother. And he is not his father. And we can't right their wrongs. So please, Dorian, please," she cries. "Stop telling me who I can be with and what I can do with my life because so far you've gotten all of it wrong. The only thing you've gotten right is that I am like my mother. And I'm going to do what I want—just like she did."

Someone in the crowd says, "Right on, girl!" But Dorian refuses to make eye contact with her.

"Then you're on your own, Zimri," he tells her and she nods as if she's known that all along.

The next morning in my new POD, I get up early and ready myself for the 'razzi. I kept my Exo off all night because I didn't want to answer any questions or see any more coverage of my disappearance and Elston's miraculous discovery. I think back over our meeting with Piper, trying to put the pieces together. Zimri made a joke about shopping at Black Friday. I wonder how long it took Piper's minions to find the video and leak it to Elston? I wonder what my father promised her if she released it to look like she'd stumbled across it on her own? And my mother? How much did she know in advance? Most likely producers were calling her for a comment and she jumped on the bandwagon like Rajesh and Ara, hustling and scraping for whatever attention they could get.

By now news-stream producers probably know where I work, where I live, and all my usual routines, but for a second or two on my way down the stairs, part of me worries that the 'razzi won't be waiting. What if I step outside, ready to be swarmed, and there's nothing there? I told Zimri I wouldn't wish that kind of media scrutiny on my worst enemy, but the truth is, for a Plute, being irrelevant is far worse than choosing to remove yourself from the limelight. It was one thing for me to run away, it's another for nobody to follow, ever again.

But the 'razzi do not disappoint. Outside, dragonfly drones have settled like a thick mechanical carpet on the walkway. Other workers skirt around them, peering close, trying to understand what they're seeing. Since my ExoScreen glove is in the POD, they can't locate me via GPS, but surely they've sent scanners to recognize my face in a crowd. I put my head down and join a stream of people walking toward the warehouse trams until one of the drones makes a beeline for me. I don't try to outrun it or pretend I'm someone that I'm not. Instead, I stop and turn to face it.

"Hello," I say when it zooms up and hovers in front of me. "How thoughtful of you to come."

"Oh my god!" a guy yells and ducks as all the other drones lift up, almost in unison.

"What the hell are they?" a woman shouts, swatting and swerving around the automated cloud.

I move off the walkway and cross the Y.A.R.D. I chose this place on purpose last night. I knew the drones would follow me, silver wings whirring in the early morning light as I position myself in front of the wall with the words *Nobody from Nowhere* clearly scrawled behind me.

For ten minutes, I answer questions piped through the drone's audio feeds from producers back in the City. I evade all the questions about why I left. I deny being a Juse addict or having any ties to Project Calliope. Over and over, I reiterate the story the way I want it to be told. If there's anything I learned from watching Piper McLeo all these years it's this: Control Your Narrative.

"Working in the warehouse has given me a greater appreciation for the luxuries I've grown up with," I tell the drones. "It would be good for every Plute to work in a Complex for a week or two. After my time here, I'm more appreciative of what people like me have and I'm more aware of what working folks are up against."

But of course, I know it won't really matter what I say. It only matters how the Buzz will spin my words into the story they want to tell. Plus, I'm only killing time until I spot Zimri emerge from her PODPlex building, then I take off with the 'razzi in pursuit, as I knew they would. She sees what's coming and she freezes by the door. When I reach her on her stoop, I grab her and hold her tight against my side. She stands stiff and frozen in my arms as the 'razzi descend.

"The reason I came here was to discover new talent that's been overlooked by Chanson Industries," I announce. "And I'm pleased to say that my search has been a success! This is Zimri Robinson, the next self-made musical superstar of the century!" I proclaim. Then, after ten seconds of flashing pix, the door behind us opens and someone drags us inside.

ZIMRI

"Come on." Brie hauls us in the POD building by the backs of our shirts then slams the door, making sure it's locked. "Get away from the windows so they can't see you," she tells Orpheus and me. "Let's go up to my POD. We can watch from the screen there."

My heart pounds wildly. I can't believe the army of drones that has descended on this place, or that Orpheus just dragged me into that maelstrom. "What the hell is wrong with you? Why did you do that?" I yell at him as the three of us charge up the stairs.

"I had an epiphany last night," he tells me, huffing and puffing through the flights. "The Buzz is only stupid because people talk about stupid things on it. So, I decided to say something interesting. Stand up for something I believe in. I decided to use the Buzz as a platform for something good!"

I stop on Brie's landing, spin around, and shove him in the chest. "And that's what you chose? You could have talked about something truly important! You could have told the world about the injustices in the warehouse. About how they're always threatening to replace us with A.N.T.s if we don't produce superhuman times."

"Oh, you so do not understand the Buzz," Orpheus says. "The more I talk about something of substance, the quicker the 'razzi will buzz off. People would tune out if one of the richest kids in the world took a stand on Plebe worker rights. Nobody would care. If you want to fight the powers that be, Zimri, *you* have to make everybody see what's going on here. If you step into the limelight and sing about this life, people will listen."

"You totally overestimate people," I say.

"And you underestimate yourself," he says.

"Enough!" Brie shouts. "Get inside." She opens the door to her POD and shoves us both in.

But Orpheus and I don't stop fighting even as Brie runs around commanding all the blinds to close. Her wallscreen silently plays the scene unfolding outside as hundreds of 'razzi drones swarm the building.

"You sound just like a Plute!" I shout at him.

"Of course I do. I am one!"

"Well, I'm not," I say.

"Then think like one for once," he tells me. "You might get farther in life."

My mouth drops open but my eyes get narrow. "What did you say to me?"

"If you sing your song people will understand what it feels like to be a nobody from nowhere. Your music gives voice to people who deserve dignity."

"In case you forgot," I snarl, "your girlfriend stole my song!"

"She's not my girlfriend," he yells back. "You are!"

That stops me. I stand in the center of the floor trying to catch my breath. "What did you say?"

"Shut up, both of you!" Brie turns up the volume on the screen as Calliope Bontempi strolls out of a justice brokerage office in the City.

A voice-over says, "Earlier this morning, after overnight deliberations, Arbiter Venetia Sanders split the judgment on the case between Calliope Bontempi and Chanson Industries. She ruled in favor of Ms. Bontempi on the charges of personal damages, citing Chanson Industries's knowledge that the reversal ASA surgery would result in amusia."

"No way!" Orpheus says, catching himself against the kitchen counter. "My father never loses! This is incredible."

Calliope stops on the sidewalk and allows the drones to surround her. "This is a victory for brain activists the world over!" she proclaims. "And make no mistake, we will continue to fight Chanson. This is just the first step."

The commentator's voice says, "Despite Ms. Bontempi's optimism, the Arbiter dismissed claims of property damages, saying Chanson Industries was within its rights to sell Ms. Bontempi's contract."

Next, Orpheus's father comes out of the building. He is tall and handsome with thick, wavy dark hair and brooding, deep-set eyes that could look soulful on a kinder face, but the lines on his forehead and cheeks have hardened into a perma-scowl that makes him appear angry with the world.

"Calliope Bontempi's claims were clearly spurious," he says. "Any person is free to make and distribute original music through any legal channels. I never stopped her from doing that."

"Whoa, wait," I say. "Play that again." Brie rewinds the clip. I step closer and listen carefully, then I turn to Orpheus, my heart thumping. "He said original music is okay?"

"Yes," says Orpheus. "I've been telling you that since the day I met you, which is why—"

"You mean, this whole time, all the concerts and broadcasts I've been doing in secret have been okay?"

"Yes!" he yells at me. "Except when you hijacked the Geoff Joffrey concert, of course." He laughs. "That might have been illegal. And you should have seen my dad! He was furious."

"But that means . . ." I say, trying to work it out.

"That Piper and Arabella can't steal your original music!" Orpheus finishes the thought for me. "It's your property and they stole it. We'll sue my father's company."

I drop down on the couch. "We'd never win," I tell him.

"Why not?" he says.

"Because we'd have to prove to the world that it was my song in the first place."

"That's easy," he says. "You have recordings!"

"No, I erased them all. I thought they were illegal." My nose begins to itch and my chin quivers.

"But people have heard you sing that song before," Orpheus says.

"They'd be too afraid to admit that," I tell him.

"But why?" Orpheus asks.

"You don't understand how scared people are here," Brie says from her post by the window where she's peeking through the blinds. "Justice brokers are never on our side."

Orpheus stands in the center of the room with hands on his hips, shaking his head in frustration.

"Wait!" says Brie. "Use the 'razzi!"

"What?" we both say.

She points outside. "All those annoying drones buzzing around. Use them to play Zimri's song to the world."

"That's brilliant!" Orpheus says. "We'll put on a legal concert. No masks, no hiding, no money for someone else. All original music. People will come. Then they'll admit they've heard you sing the song before once they realize they're safe. Then there will be no question that the song belongs to you and not Arabella."

I sit there, stunned. "I don't know," I whisper.

Orpheus walks to me, arms out, as he says, "This is your moment, Zimri Robinson, and the next time you're in the 'razzi spotlight the world will finally hear you sing."

CHORUS

In the quiet backwaters of the river, away from the activity along the shore, a dragonfly nymph emerges. After years of feasting on mosquito larvae in the water, it climbs up the sticky stem of a cattail reed ready to shed its childhood skin. A great green heron and frozards lurk nearby, looking for a late lunch, but the soft-bodied creature cannot flee. It's not ready for the world, yet. First it must bask in the sun, waiting for exoskeleton and wings to harden and take shape. And so it waits, while other bugs buzz around, busy as the people bustling back and forth from Complex to Old Town along the river path.

It's taken less than forty-eight hours for Orpheus and Tati to set up the concert. Always the wheeler-dealer, Tati had the keys to the Paramount Theater (a poker game with the owner who headed south years ago). Zimri used the money stashed since Nonda's concert to hire Captain Jack and his Old Town gang, who've descended on the abandoned auditorium to bang the dust from worn red velvet seats and moth-eaten curtains and wash the dirt-caked floors until they gleam. Tati hauls out a generator to run the lights and an old PA.

At night, Orpheus and Zimri spend hours out at Nowhere, discussing the set list, rerecording new backing tracks. He knows just where a string swell will draw out the emotion of a lyric. Where a drum fill will add the most drama. How to best use her weird homemade ZimriDoo for effect.

Every day at the warehouse, Orpheus and Brie spend their tenners selling tickets to the show (which everyone knows is legal after what Harold Chanson admitted on the Buzz). And, as soon as they get home after a full day, they head up to the Strip to sell more tix.

The 'razzi drones love this, of course—Chanson heir turned Plebe promoter—and Orpheus can't resist talking up the event.

"People haven't seen anything like this for generations," he promises the press. "This isn't some whitewashed, focus-grouped, PromoTeam surgical creation. Zimri is a natural-born superstar who's going to blow your minds!"

"Will Chanson Industries lure her away from you with a big contract deal?" some commentator asks.

"If my father is smart, he'll try," Orpheus teases. "But she won't go. Zimri and I are a team."

Every day, more drones show up to send pix and vid back to the Buzz where ratings are high. But some of the drones go haywire. Lose their bearings. Roost in trees. No one quite knows why. A few are snatched midair by bewildered wax-wings and warblers who spit them out. They roll down the embankment, bouncing over tufts of grass and knotty roots, to take the plunge. Blip. Blip. Blip. Their last transmissions are air bubbles from curious little frozards' mouths.

And what of our nymph, sitting pretty on the reed as all of this goes on around her? She has learned to breathe the air as she sheds her old skin. It stays stuck to the reed, a perfect replica of her past that will soon decay. Her exoskeleton is hardened now into a protective shell. All she has to do, when the time is right, is spread her wings and fly.

VERSE SEVEN

ZIMRI

I always felt a frenetic energy before the shows at Nowhere, but I would never say I was nervous. For one thing, I didn't know for sure who was in the audience and no one acknowledged me as the singer. It was an anonymous endeavor, as if that masked girl on stage were someone else. When the show was over and the masks came off, I retracted her inside of me like the hidden furniture of our PODs. But standing backstage at the Paramount Theater, stars twinkling from the ceiling just like my mother said, I am jangling with fear. My legs shake, my heart pounds, and I feel like I might barf because the next time I step through the curtain, I, Zimri, will unmistakably be the one on stage, and that's terrifying.

"How's it look out there?" I ask Orpheus.

He flicks the worn velvet curtain and grins. "Full, I think."

"You're lying!" I push him aside and peek out, expecting to see a handful of people milling around the mostly empty space. Brie and her mom, Captain Jack and the Old Town guys, and maybe a few people from the warehouse that Orpheus bribed or charmed. I about fall over when I see every seat of the auditorium filled, plus people in the aisles and spilling out the doors beneath hundreds of 'razzi drones congregated like a heavy storm cloud overhead.

I jump away from the curtain and press my back against the wall. My heart races and my head spins. "I can't do this!" I say, my breath shallow.

Orpheus laughs with pure joy. He puts his hands on my shoulders and gives me a tiny shake. "Of course you can."

He signals to Tati who lowers the lights. The crowd begins to stomp and clap and chant my name.

"All your life, Zimri, you were only waiting for this moment," he tells me. "This is what you were made for. Listen!"

Stomp stomp clap! Stomp stomp clap! Zim-ri. Zim-ri!

This time if I step on stage, I'll be all alone. There will be no drummer smacking sticks above his head because Dorian hasn't forgiven me for what he sees as my betrayal. It's not just that I chose Orpheus over him, which would be bad enough, but he believes Harold Chanson was responsible for my mother's disappearance. Although it breaks my heart to lose Dorian's friendship, I also know he's wrong. Dorian's father, Marley, is equally culpable for my mother leaving. But in the end, I also know that nobody is to blame but my mother herself. She's the one who chose to walk away, just like I'll be the one who decides whether to step on stage tonight or not.

"It's time to give them what they want," Orpheus says.

I let the rhythm of the crowd slow my heart and calm my nerves. They are a song I will sing. I open my eyes and reach for Orpheus, holding his wrist tightly.

"You okay?" he asks.

I swallow, trying to find my voice while fighting back the tears bullying their way into my eyes. I want to tell him many things right then. How grateful I am to have him, someone who believes not just that I *could* but that I *should* make music, and no matter what happens tonight, for that I will be eternally grateful. But the only thing that comes out of my mouth is a very small and shaky, "Thank you," because I'm afraid if I allow myself to say anything else, I will lose it right before I walk on stage.

He pulls me into a hug and says, "Use all that emotion you're feeling as fuel for the show."

I nod, still unable to speak, and promise myself that when this is all over, I'll tell Orpheus everything I feel for him.

He gives me a quick kiss. "See you on the other side." He pushes through the curtain and steps onto the stage to introduce me.

The crowd's roar pulls me like a tide drawing in the ocean. As I step through the curtain, it all comes back to me. I know how to do this. Orpheus is right. I was made for this. I lift one arm and wave. Blow kisses as I squint into the bright lights. I can't make out faces in the crowd or distinguish voices and that calms me. I pick up my mother's old guitar and strum the first note of my first song, and in that moment, like in every moment when I play, I'm immediately lost inside the music.

I sing "The Picker Symphony," I sing "Poor, Poor Whip-poorwill," I sing "Greens and Beans" about my grandmother who's coming home soon, and "Swirling Eddy" about my father who'll never return again. I sing "For the Great Blue Heron" and an old, old song called "Chante Alouette" for Orpheus's sister. We've rearranged the set list many times, but Orpheus and I have agreed on one thing from the start—we saved "Nobody from Nowhere" for last. And so, when I am done with all the other songs, I pause.

At Nowhere, I only spoke to the audience to rile them before I turned on the video camera, but tonight I have something else to say. I shield my eyes from the lights and look out at the crowd for Orpheus. I find him on the floor, off to the side, beaming up at me. When I catch his eye, he does a big exaggerated pointing motion toward the center of the front row and mouths something that I can't understand. I scan the audience, not knowing who to expect. I squint and keep my hand above my eyes. I recognize a lot of faces—people from the warehouse, folks from Old Town, friends of my parents, kids I knew from SQEWL, and plenty of people I've never seen in my life. I even spot Brie and her mom and Tati seated all together. I look back at Orpheus. He jabs his finger toward the center again but the spotlight is in my eyes so I can't figure out who he is pointing to.

Then I step up to the mic. "Like most of you," I say as I tune my ZimriDoo, "I work in the warehouse." The crowd erupts with approval. I noodle with my strings, twisting and turning to find the exact right notes while I speak. "We spend our days packing boxes full of things for people who will never see us or give us a second thought. But I'm proud of the work we do. We do it well. We work hard for our money." I sigh and shake my head. "So hard for it, honey. We may seem like a bunch of nobodies from nowhere . . ."

When those words leave my mouth the crowd screams and stomps and I have to wait for them to quiet down until I can talk again.

"But each of us is somebody. You are a daughter or a son.

A friend, a sibling, a mother, or father. Your job does not define you. So the next time you're made to feel like nobody, remember, you're somebody to me."

As I strum the first few notes, I notice a commotion in the center of the crowd but the lights are too bright for me to make out clearly what's happening. As the first words leave my mouth, bodies jostle off to the side. I continue to play, singing loudly, figuring people want to move to the music like they did out at Nowhere. I try to find Orpheus in the ruckus unfolding on the floor, then I see people rushing up the steps on the side of the stage. I laugh through my music and back away to make room for them. I never thought I'd have a packed house and I certainly never imagined people would rush the stage. Orpheus is probably kicking himself for not hiring Captain Jack and his pals as security.

I turn to welcome the stage rushers to sing with me but then I see Medgers, a cruel smile on her face. Behind her is Billingsley, followed by Smythe and Beauregarde. My fingers tangle in my strings and my voice goes sour, then the roaring of the standing crowd fills my ears as Medgers tackles me. We stumble sideways, my ZimriDoo smashed between us. People clamor toward the stage. Frantically, I look for Orpheus, but Medgers has me pinned. Then Billingsley is on the ground beside me. "Just hold on, Zimri," she shouts over the erupting chaos. "We'll get you out of here."

Medgers wrestles me to my stomach and yanks my arms behind my back.

"Easy there!" Billingsley yells and pushes her away. She kneels down, one knee beside me, her hands on mine. "I have to cuff you," she says, "but it's going to be okay."

Then I hear someone else on the mic. "You must all remain in the auditorium. You have all violated copyright laws by attending this concert."

"No!" I scream and writhe around. Billingsley allows me to turn my body so I can see. In the center of the stage at the mic is the blue-eyed woman who always speaks on behalf of Chanson Industries whenever there is news in the Buzz. The crowd goes berserk. People push one another through the aisles and out the doors into the dark night.

At the side of the stage, I see Orpheus trying to break free from Smythe and Beauregarde who have his arms twisted behind his back as they drag him toward the wings.

"Orpheus! Orpheus!" I scream and kick. Billingsley and Medgers haul me to my feet. From the corner of my eye, I see Harold Chanson. He claps his hand on Orpheus's neck and yanks him away. Then he glances over his shoulder at me and smirks as if I don't even warrant his full attention.

ORPHEUS

With his enormous hand clamped on the back of my neck, my father pulls me out of the theater.

"Let go of me!" I yell. "Let go!" But his goons, Smythe and Beauregarde, have a hold of my arms and keep me in line.

"You want us to go after them?" Smythe asks my dad, pointing at the people escaping through the side doors of the old theater and disappearing into the night like squimonks on the riverbanks making themselves scarce.

"Let them go," he says. "We'll track down the ones we need the most."

"For what?" I ask but they don't answer.

"Call his Cicada," Dad tells Smythe.

"I'm not leaving!" I say.

"Yes, you are," he says. "You're going back to the City, tonight."

"No." I jerk away from him but there is no place for me to go. We're inside a fenced-off area beside the building. In the dim light I can see ramshackle playground structures—a bent slide lying on its side, empty chains of seatless swings stirring in the breeze, the backboards of old basketball hoops standing like sad soldiers at either end of the lot. "I won't go anywhere without Zimri," I tell him.

"I've had enough of you slumming out here with the Plebes," Dad says. "At first it was okay. Our Buzz ratings went up when you went missing and we got another bump when you were *miraculously* found. But now you're beginning to tarnish our image."

Overhead, the lights of my Cicada sweep the playground. People duck and run for cover in the trees, likely afraid a security helicopter is coming to arrest them. The Cicada touches down at the far end of the playground on an empty patch of broken concrete. I back away.

"I won't go. You can't make me. Where's Zimri?"

Dad grabs my arm and shuffles me toward the car. "Your little Plebe slut is going on trial. Piracy, among other charges. I'm tired of people like her, Calliope Bontempi, and that scum DJ HiJax trying to take what's not theirs."

"You stole from *her*!" I yell.

But he just shrugs. "Doesn't matter anyway. I'm making an example out of Zimri Robinson. It'll send a message to brain activists everywhere that if they take me on, they will lose." He commands the doors of my car to open. "Smythe," he calls. "Take him to my office. He can watch the trial from there. I'll come get him when the surgeon's ready."

"Surgeon?" I ask. "What surgeon?

"You're going home for an ASA."

"No!" I bend my knees and drag my feet but he easily pulls me through the dirt. "Leave me alone! Let me go!"

Smythe jogs up beside me. She puts her hand on top of my head and together they shove me in the car. My dad bends down next to the open door while she runs to the driver's side.

"You would have made a decent producer, Orpheus," my father says. "Zimri's very talented. I haven't seen someone like her since your mother."

I gasp as if he's punched me in the stomach. "So use her," I plead. "Let her sign a contract with Chanson. I'll get the ASA. She and I can be a duo. The public will eat it up!"

"You still don't get it, do you?" he says, shaking his head. "Like I always said, you're not a businessperson at heart, Orpheus. Because if you were you'd understand that if I sign someone like Zimri, then the whole system falls apart."

"Dad, please," I beg.

He stares at me for a moment. "Isn't it ironic, don't you think?" he says.

"What is?"

"That tomorrow when you wake, you'll be the musical genius and her brain will be scrubbed."

"No!" I yell, struggling to get free, but my hands are locked tight behind my back and his body fills the doorframe. "You can't do that."

"Maybe, if you want, I can ask the surgeon to scrub a little of your short-term memory so you'll have no recollection of this part of your life. That's all it takes to forget her." He reaches out and presses his fingers into my temples and says, "Bzzzt!" Then he stands up and hits the top of the car twice, calling, "Best be heading out now before traffic in the City gets too thick."

On the flight back to the City, I beg Smythe over and over to let me go. Finally, near tears, I plead, "Please, anywhere. Just land and let me out. Say that I forced you. Say that you stopped for something to eat and I got away. I'll leave and never come back."

But she doesn't budge. Doesn't flinch. Without taking her eyes off of the WindScreen NewsFeed (covering every moment at the Complex with running Celeb commentary) she says, "If I let you go, you'll head straight to that girl. I saw the way you looked at her." She shakes her head and sighs, "I hate to squash young love and see all that talent go to waste, but there's no way I'll cross your father."

ZIMRI

Everything happens so quickly. Billingsley and Medgers take me to the Complex security office and put me in a cyber courtroom with a justice broker named Fernando who's been sent out by the Justice Consortium to handle my case.

"Why was I arrested?" I demand.

"Piracy," Fernando says. "You performed copyrighted material for profit, right?"

"No!" I say.

"It's okay," Billingsley assures me, her hand stroking circles on my back. "We're going to get this straightened out."

The blond woman from the stage comes in the room. She nods curtly then settles at a table across from us. "We've located an Arbiter who has contracts with both sides," she announces. "She'll be online momentarily."

"What's that mean?" I ask.

"The Justice Consortium, which represents you, and Chanson Industries agreed on an Arbiter to hear the case," Fernando explains.

"I didn't agree on anything!" I snap. "I don't even know you."

He shrugs. "You have the right to hire any broker you like. But I follow the unified legal code and am in good standing with the Justice Protective Association, plus I'm covered by your insurance plan through Corp X. If you choose to go with someone else, you'll have to pay out of pocket."

I look to Billingsley, my only ally in the room. "Best to use him," she says. "They can make me hold you in jail if you delay and it's very expensive to hire someone. You've already paid for this."

Then the Arbiter comes on screen. She's old, with thick stripes of gray through her black hair. Her forehead wrinkles as she looks over her tablet and scowls. "What's the charge?" she barks and settles into her seat. "And why can't it wait until tomorrow?"

"Hello, thank you for agreeing to oversee this matter, ma'am. My name is Esther Crawley and I'll be representing Chanson Industries."

The Arbiter's eyebrows shoot up. "Chanson?" she says, clearly impressed. "Out here?"

"Yes, we have an urgent matter," says Ms. Crawley. "Due to the public nature of the incident and the distance I've come from the City, we'd like to take care of this matter tonight, if possible."

"Do you have your witnesses and materials in order?" the Arbiter asks.

"Officers Medgers and Beauregarde are collecting witnesses now and we're prepared to begin," says Ms. Crawley.

The Arbiter looks at Fernando. "And you?"

He shrugs, noncommittal. "Now is as good a time as any."

"No wait!" I cry. "This isn't fair. I didn't do anything wrong."

The Arbiter scowls at me. "Then you have nothing to worry about, do you?"

"Where's Orpheus?" I ask. "I want Orpheus here with me!"

"Who's Orpheus?" the Arbiter asks.

Fernando shakes his head, as confused as the Arbiter, but Esther Crawley says, "Orpheus Chanson's role in this matter is immaterial to the complaint. He's decided to return home with his father."

"You lie!" I yell. "I saw Smythe haul him off. He didn't want to go."

Ms. Crawley whips her head toward me. "At the request of his father," she says firmly, "he's been removed from the premise and no charges have been filed against him."

My stomach rolls as I realize that they've taken Orpheus away and are blaming everything on me.

"Ma'am." Ms. Crawley turns back to the Arbiter. "We are prepared to prove that Zimri Robinson has willfully and repeatedly promoted and distributed music illegally for the past five years through pirated radio and for-profit concerts and by hijacking a LiveStream. Her actions culminated tonight in a bold and egregious act of piracy at a public, for-profit concert in which she blatantly stole Arabella Lovecraft's copyrighted song 'Nobody from Nowhere.'"

"That's *my* song!" I yell and jump up from the table. "I wrote that song! They stole it from me."

The Arbiter leans forward so her face glowers at us from the screen. "Then this matter should be quite simple and you will get your turn, but you cannot disrupt these proceedings or I will have you removed from the room. Do you understand?"

Billingsley tugs on my wrist for me to sit down. "Yes," I say quietly and return to my seat.

The courtroom door opens and people file in, followed by 'razzi drones. At first I'm relieved to see so many people have come to support me—Brie, Elena, Tati, Jude, Veronica, Marley, and even Dorian, along with many others from the warehouse and Old Town, but as Esther Crawley calls them up one by one, it becomes clear that they've been rounded up and brought in by Medgers and Beauregarde to testify against me.

"To your knowledge, when did Zimri Robinson first sing for the public?" Ms. Crawley asks Brie's mom, Elena.

Elena squirms as she hems and haws until the Arbiter sternly compels her to answer. "Four or five years ago," Elena says. "She was around eleven years old at the time."

"That wasn't a concert," I whisper to Fernando, but he doesn't seem to care.

"And did you pay to see her perform?" Ms. Crawley asks.

"We, um, sort of, but not exactly. I mean after Zimri sang, we donated money to her grandmother to help pay some of her bills," Elena says then turns to the Arbiter. "You have no idea what they were going through."

"That's immaterial," Ms. Crawley says. "Can you recall any of the songs Zimri Robinson sang at that show?"

"It was so long ago," Elena says.

Crawley refers to the notes on her tablet. "Did she perform songs by Sarah Vaughan or Libellule?" How she knows the details of what I sang when I was eleven years old is beyond me, but clearly someone has ratted me out. Probably Medgers.

Elena looks at me. "I'm so sorry, honey," she says, then she turns back to Ms. Crawley, nods, and says quietly, "Yes, I believe she did."

"And after that, you gave money to her grandmother?"

"Yes, I did."

"And would you have given money to her grandmother if Zimri hadn't sung?"

"If she'd asked me to."

"Did she ask?" Ms. Crawley demands.

Elena hangs her head. "No," she says. "She didn't ask."

This goes on and on as Ms. Crawley ruthlessly works her way through nearly everyone who knows me, asking questions that paint me as a self-promoting music thief. No one says that I made my own music because Ms. Crawley never asks them that. And they can't admit to attending one of my concerts for fear they'll be implicated in a crime none of them committed, but they don't know that because Fernando rarely counters or asks a decent question on my behalf.

Then halfway through Ms. Crawley questioning Tati, the door in the back of the room opens. Everyone turns to see who it is. An audible gasp goes up when Calliope Bontempi slips inside. Ms. Crawley stops badgering Tati long enough to do a double take while everyone in the room whispers. But Calliope seems to take no notice. She quietly slides into a seat near the back and speaks to no one. Ms. Crawley continues questioning Tati about how long ago I set up my transmitter, how often I broadcast, and how far my signal can reach. Tati keeps her answers short, vague, and hostile, but she can't deny that I regularly broadcast music.

When Ms. Crawley excuses Tati, she turns back to the Arbiter and says, "Ma'am, I'd like to submit records of radio transmissions by DJ HiJax that correspond to the times Zimri Robinson broadcast from this setup nearby. It is our contention that Zimri Robinson is DJ HiJax."

I burst out laughing along with every other Plebe in the room.

"Our records show that DJ HiJax began broadcasting at roughly the same time Zimri built her antenna. All of our records of HiJax's transmissions come from near here. We believe the link is clear."

"That's absurd!" Tati says.

"Then produce DJ HiJax," Ms. Crawley says, "and disprove my theory."

At that moment, Calliope Bontempi shoots out of her chair and runs from the room, leaving everyone stunned as the door bangs shut behind her.

Finally, Ms. Crawley stands to make her closing argument. "Ma'am," she says to the Aribiter, "I stood here five years ago, a younger and more naive justice broker at the beginning of my career with Chanson Industries, and I brought a very similar case against this girl's mother."

I inhale sharply. Esther Crawley's bright blue eyes have dulled somewhat and her skin has become more mottled, but the picture is clear in my mind. She told me to stop singing then, and now she's back to stop me again.

"Zimri Robinson is a product of her mother's deviance regarding music, but that is no excuse. She is sixteen, an adult under the law who holds a full-time job, and she knows the difference between right and wrong. But like her mother, she has no regard for private property and is a thief. Rainey Robinson never paid her debt to Chanson Industries and she never served her jail time. I implore you not to let this Robinson get away with the same thing."

"Zimri," the Arbiter says, "would you like to make a statement?"

"Yes," I say and stand up. In that moment, I understand why my mother never named names and I know that I won't pass the blame either. I lift my chin the way my mother had at her trial. "I admit it. I have put on concerts many times. I found the places to play, I promoted the shows, and I sold the tickets. I played alone. No one else was involved."

The crowd shifts and murmurs. I hear Brie gasp and say, "No!"

"But," I add and the room gets very quiet, "the music I make and share is mine and mine alone. The only exception was when I was eleven, a child grieving the loss of my parents. Then I sang my mother's favorite songs because I missed her. Money had nothing to do with it. I would have sung those songs whether people gave my grandmother money or not. Since then, all of the music I've made and shared is mine. And Harold Chanson said himself that anyone is free to promote and distribute original music. That's all I do."

"That's not true!" Ms. Crawley says. "This very evening you knowingly sang an Arabella Lovecraft song."

"That's my song!" I shout at Esther. "I wrote it. I sang it. I even recorded it long before Arabella stole it."

"Wait a moment," the Arbiter says. "Can you produce a

recording of this song prior to the release of Arabella Love-craft's version?" she asks me.

I stand, my mind reeling. I think about the digital and video recorders I scrubbed clean, the waves I sent out that dissipated into the night. I was so careful to erase all of the evidence of my music that I can't give her what she wants. My eyes sting and my nose itches like I might cry. I start to shake my head. My knees begin to give out, but then I remember. "Piper McLeo!" I shout. "When I auditioned for Piper McLeo, the engineer recorded me singing 'Nobody from Nowhere.'" The whole crowd lets go a collected breath. "That recording will be time-stamped a few hours before Arabella dropped her sneak peek of the song."

The Arbiter sits back and turns her attention to Esther Crawley. "You'll need to get Piper McLeo on the screen."

ORPHEUS

Smythe keeps her word. She deposits me in my father's office then guards the door as I watch helplessly while Esther tears Zimri apart on the screen. Esther parades witness after witness from the Complex, each more scared than the last. When Calliope Bontempi comes in, I gasp along with the rest of the crowd. I can't imagine what she's doing there. When she runs out again, I hope and pray that she's smart enough to tell my mother what's going on since I can't reach her myself.

Mostly, I sit slumped and helpless. I can't believe I put Zimri in this position, and I need to get her out of it. Then she shouts, "Piper McLeo!"

I jump up from my chair, cheering, "Yes! Zimri, yes! You're brilliant. Why didn't I think of that? Piper has the song!"

Even Smythe hurries over to see what's happening. She looks at me and smiles. "See?" she says. "Justice can prevail."

Now Smythe and I sit together, waiting like everyone in the courtroom with Zimri, for Piper to come on screen. And when she does, she does what Piper McLeo does best—she spins the story in her favor.

"Yes, Orpheus brought Zimri along when he visited me, but I have no recording of her," she says as if the idea is preposterous.

"Liar!" I scream at the screen.

"Did she sing for you?" Esther asks.

Piper pretends to think this over, as if her memory of Zimri is so murky. "She may have," she says. "But it was nothing special. I pulled Orpheus aside and told him I was worried about him. Clearly he'd been beguiled by this girl. It was almost as if he had been brainwashed by her. I can't think of another reason a person like Orpheus Chanson would give everything up to work in a warehouse. What can I say, maybe he was in love, or maybe he'd been coerced. But I told him the truth—Zimri could never be a superstar."

I shake with fury over how she spins her words. None of them are exactly lies, but they are not the truth either.

Then Zimri shouts, "Ask Arabella!" The drones all zoom in on Zimri's face. She stands tall, unflinching, stronger than I could ever be. "Ask her if that song is hers."

The Arbiter sighs and thinks this over. Then she says, "It can't hurt." Esther begins to protest but the Arbiter overrules. "Get Arabella on the screen."

When Arabella comes online, Zimri's disheveled and disorganized justice broker stands up to question her. "Um, hello, Ms. Lovecraft. What a pleasure. I enjoyed your song."

I groan aloud.

"What an idiot!" Smythe says.

"So, um, could you please tell us about the song 'Nobody from Nowhere'?" he asks.

Arabella blinks. Her eyes say it all. There is a blankness in her stare. The ASA has changed her. She's no longer the kind and empathetic person I grew up with. The first girl I thought I could love. She is driven now, and obsessed. Her mind is filled with music and there is no longer room for compassion.

"It's a song about Orpheus Chanson," she says. She's so calm, as if lying is the most comfortable thing in the world. "I was trying to understand what he was going through. How he could leave our life behind and become a warehouse worker. When he came into the City that day with Zimri, we spent some time together and he told me all about his job. The song is my tribute to him."

I want to shout at the screen. I can't believe what a conniving little worm Arabella has become.

"So you didn't steal the song from Zimri Robinson?" Fernando asks.

"Oh, heavens, no," says Arabella with a little laugh as if the accusation is absurd. Then she cocks her head to the right, raises her eyebrows high and does a sweet tiny frown. It was an expression we'd practiced at SCEWL called Condescen-Pathy, the art of talking down while you seem to care. "That's so sad that she thinks it's her song. I guess Plebes have big dreams, too."

Right then I know it's over. Esther closes up her arguments. She accuses Zimri of being DJ HiJax, a willful and repeat offender. She claims she brainwashed me—how else to explain why I'd work as a picker in a warehouse, pay her grandmother's MediPlex bills, embarrass myself in front of Piper McLeo, and attend an illegal concert that would hurt my father's company? She claims Zimri is a dangerous criminal and a mastermind who has no regard for private property— the irony being that's a more apt description of everyone on my father's side.

It only takes a minute for the Arbiter to rule in favor of Chanson Industries. Then she asks Esther to name the punishment for Zimri.

"Ma'am," Esther stands and says, "I cannot put a price on all the music that she's likely stolen through her concerts and illegal radio broadcasts. And I can't quantify a price for the week she stole from Orpheus Chanson's life. All I can say is that Zimri Robinson clearly has no intention of stopping. It's possible that she's not even able to control herself. Like her mother, she seems compelled to steal. Her obsession is detrimental not only to herself and those around her but to the free enterprise of the music industry. Therefore, the only way to rectify this situation is to get to the root of the problem. Chanson Industries respectfully requests that as retribution for her acts of piracy, the auditory cortical regions of Zimri Robinson's brain be scrubbed, which will result in amusia."

Everyone in the courtroom screams when the Arbiter responds, "Punishment is granted."

BRIDGE

Zimri shivers beneath a thin sheet, groggy and disoriented in a cold room where everything is made of clean white tile and smells of antiseptic. She wishes someone would turn off the bright light. She wants desperately to sleep. Her head pounds, like a bass drum keeping an excruciating beat inside her skull that wakes her each time she slips toward unconsciousness. In and out she goes, memories swirling like an eddy in the river, and she thinks, *Maybe I'm a dragonfly.* She remembers darting upriver while looking down with myriad eyes at the dark splotches of electronics graveyards and landfills between the Complex and the City.

Zimri surfaces from this strange delusion. The cold white tile and harsh bright lights clear her mind and she remembers, *This is not where I belong.* She knows that she is far from home, from Nonda and Brie and the warehouse where she works but she can't recall the rest. It's as if she can hear traces of a melody in her mind and the rhythm of words but she can't quite sing the song. *How's it go again,* she keeps asking herself. *How does it go?*

And there's someone else, Zimri thinks. A boy with straight white teeth. She sees his dazzling smile as if his image has been tattooed on the inside of her eyelids. He was beautiful and kind and she thinks he may have loved her once. Or was he a lyric from the song she's trying to sing? Because those kinds of boys don't exist in reality.

Orpheus runs through a labyrinth of low-ceiling halls. His bare feet slap against the tile. It's late. The facility is mostly dark and empty, but he knows that Zimri's here, too, because Smythe didn't turn off the Buzz when the trial was over. They watched the whole thing hand in hand, both fighting back tears as Medgers and Beauregarde pinned Zimri down in the courtroom. She kicked and screamed when the medic came at her with a tranquilizing needle. Then the drones trailed them as commentators provided a play-by-play of her transfer to a surgical facility in the City. The same one where Orpheus has been deposited by his father because only the finest surgeon will do for the Chanson heir's ASA and this wretched girl's induced amusia. The surgeries are scheduled one right after the other.

Orpheus turns corner after corner. Cold air wafts beneath his surgical gown. He shivers while he sweats. At any moment the nurses will realize that he's missing and will come looking for him. Another corner, another empty corridor, but somewhere in this building is the room where they will destroy Zimri. Take away the part of her mind that is fundamental to her soul. The thing that makes her truly and uniquely herself. The part she cannot live without. So he won't stop running, must not stop looking, until he finds her.

Around another corner, and Orpheus sees light spilling from a window. He slams his body against the plexiglass and there she is. On a table, shrouded in a white sheet beneath a bright light. He tries the door but it's locked. He pounds on the window. "Zimri!" he shouts. "Zimri!"

Zimri hears that boy calling her name. It echoes in the auditory recesses of her mind. "Open your eyes!" he calls and she tries, but the drugs are like a heavy blanket over her consciousness and she can't quite remember what to do.

"Open your eyes, Zimri!" She hears it again and savors the cadence of his words and the melody of his voice. She repeats it to herself as she drifts again toward deep sleep and a dream of floating down the river. Or is she flying through the air? A dragonfly? A fish? No matter. Either way, she is leaving behind the world that she's known and the boy who fought for her.

Orpheus collapses against the window, arms overhead, fists balled, head bowed as if in defeat as Zimri cycles out of her dream. The pounding in her head has stopped. It is quiet and cold and for a moment she thinks she is floating in the river under the sun. *How did I get here,* she asks. *Did I take the plunge? Have I become my father, spiraling away?* She thinks of Nonda—who will care for her? When her father went under, did he think of Zimri and try to fight his way back to the surface, or was death such a relief that he let himself be pulled into the abyss? She will not be her father. *Swim,* she tells herself, *swim,* and forces herself to wake up.

The light assaults her eyes. She squints and turns away to find herself inside a room with someone at the window. Her body feels heavy, as if gravity has shifted and weighs her down. She tries to sit up but her arms and legs are tethered to the bed. She tries to remember what came before. Why she's there. Was there an accident, is she sick, did she do something wrong? She calls out to the person on the other side of the window but her voice is a dry little rasp. Nothing more than desiccated willow leaves skittering across the ground on a blustery fall day. The weeping willow by the river. Her solace and her hiding place when she was young. She sat in it for hours, talking to her father after he was gone, and then later she found someone else hiding there but she can't remember who it was.

She swallows and tries her voice again. It's never failed her before. "Hey," she cries in a husky whisper. "Hey, you there!" She wiggles her arms and legs, trying to loosen the straps around her wrists and ankles. She bucks her hips, slams her body against the bed. "Hey! You! Help me! Get me out of here!"

Orpheus looks up but his breath has fogged the window. He can't see inside. Then he hears footsteps and voices in the hall and knows they're coming for him now. Through the foggy window, he sees Zimri's shape struggling to get up. He throws himself against the glass but he does not yell. Footsteps and voices bounce down the corridors, obscuring their location, but they are getting closer. He motions to Zimri—his hands out straight and he lifts. He wills her body off the bed. *Get up! Get up!* he thinks but doesn't dare say it out loud. She fights like a fish in a net desperate to be free. The sheet slips off and he sees that she is strapped down.

Zimri kicks until one foot comes loose. She manipulates her long, dexterous fingers—fingers suited to keyboard keys and guitar strings—to loosen the clasp at her wrist until she can slide her hand through the thick fabric loop. She uses her free hand to undo the other two tethers, then swings her legs over the edge of the bed, which sends her head spinning.

Orpheus knows he needs to move to a safer place. The voices are getting closer. He can't tell how many people are looking for him in this maze. They seem to be coming from all directions. He hears his name echo down the hall, but he can't take his eyes off Zimri. She hoists herself off the bed and loses her balance. Woozy and weaving, she hangs on to a metal bar as if she's fallen overboard and feels the tide dragging her toward the darkness.

From the other side of the window, Orpheus wills her to go faster. To morph back into the fleet-footed, nimble girl he chased through warehouse aisles. The one who stomped around on stage as if indestructible. But he knows how quickly a person can go from invincible to fragile. How fast a life can plummet, like a songbird dead in flight.

He grabs the doorknob and rattles it, pointing to the handle inside, hoping she's lucid enough to understand she must open the door. She squints at him. The light is too bright. The window is too foggy but she sees the door. She doesn't know where it will lead, but it doesn't matter. Any door is a way out and she forces herself in that direction.

On the other side of the room, the sound of an opening lock

reverberates against the tiles like a thousand tiny doors about to open, but none of them big enough for Zimri to go through. Orpheus sees a nurse come in. He's wearing blue operating scrubs. His head is down and he is focused on a tablet in his hands. Then he glances at the bed and does a double take as he zeroes in on Zimri.

"Hey there," he says gently, as if talking to a mischievous child. "You're not supposed to be up."

Somewhere in the muddle of Zimri's mind, she knows she must get away despite the kindness in the man's voice, so she propels herself forward, lurching and stumbling toward the boy in the window, but when she looks again he's not there and she wonders if she's hallucinating and if any of this is real.

In the hallway, Orpheus crouches below the lip of the window so the nurse will not see him, but he keeps the handle in his grip. *Open, open, open,* he silently commands. At the far end of the corridor, three women dash by but do not turn the corner. He presses hard against the door, trying to force it open without being seen.

Zimri fumbles with the handle. Her fingers are thick and useless.

The nurse laughs. "Where are you trying to go?"

After three clumsy tries, Zimri catches hold, pushes down, and the door swings inward. The boy falls at her feet.

"What the . . . !" the nurse yells.

Orpheus scrambles up, clawing at Zimri who reaches down for him. For one quick second he smiles, relieved to be in her arms, and then she knows that he is real.

She takes his hand and they bolt.

The nurse panics. "Security!" he shouts, but a guard is already in the hall. He heard the commotion. Ran down to check. Now there are two kids, hand in hand, in surgical gowns, trying to run.

"You take the girl," the guard shouts to the nurse while he lunges for Orpheus. He gets one arm around the boy's waist as the nurse pulls the girl away.

Zimri grips Orpheus's hand tighter. She won't let go. But the guard is strong and rips them apart.

"No!" Zimri screams as the nurse drags her away.

"Let me go!" Orpheus demands, writhing and kicking, not willing to surrender because from the moment he first met her, he wanted to fall into her hug, singing, *We belong together!*

Orpheus charges backward across the hall, slamming the guard's head into the wall. Then he shouts her name and reaches for her, dragging the guard behind him who won't let go. "Zimri! Zimri!" The notes are urgent and full of despair. A dirge, a funeral song, a death march.

She twists so she can see him, but her body is slow and heavy as if all her muscles are waterlogged.

"No, you don't!" The nurse yanks her away.

"Orpheus!" she screams as it all comes raging back to her mind. His smile, his kisses, his belief in her. Her frantic high-pitched scream bounces off the metal and tiles in the room. There is nothing to absorb the noise and she thinks it will echo on forever. She bends her knees deeply, sinking to the floor, pulling the nurse down with her. They tumble. Zimri smells the biting antiseptic of the nurse's scrubs and gloves. She kicks, trying to catch a soft spot, something vulnerable to make this man leave her alone. Behind them in the hall, the guard loops one arm around Orpheus's neck and heaves him, arching backward.

"No!" Zimri cries. She sees Orpheus's face, red and enraged, as he grapples with the guard's arm. He pulls down to free himself but the guard's grip is too tight. The nurse scrambles away toward the medical supplies across the room. Zimri tries to push herself to a stand but she is slow and off-balance, lurching as if being tossed by relentless waves.

Then she hears other voices. Someone yells, "Down there!" The sound of pounding feet comes toward them. More guards, she thinks and knows she must get to Orpheus, but she is knocked sideways into the wall. The nurse, with gritted teeth, is on her, pressing into her so Zimri cannot move. Then she sees the needle in the nurse's hand. A bead of liquid quivers from the tip. Zimri's arms are pinned. Her body is smashed tight and her feet slip on the tile floor so she can't push away. The nurse jabs the needle into the flesh of Zimri's upper arm. She gasps and winces at the pain as the cold serum quickly spreads through her veins. The room begins to spin. She wobbles and feels her legs go slack. Orpheus has given up the fight, too. He slumps in the guard's arms as if being cradled. Zimri feels herself begin to float away. The edges of her vision become dark and blurry again.

In the hall, she sees three more bodies. Women. Tati, Elena, and Brie? No. Smythe and Beauregarde and Medgers? No, not them either, but somehow they are vaguely familiar. If only she could concentrate.

"Calliope? Mom?" Orpheus yells. "You found us, thank god! Who's that?"

Then, from the other direction, two more people run. A man and a woman.

"Dad! Esther!" Orpheus shouts.

Calliope Bontempi shoves the other woman, the stranger who is somehow familiar, ahead of her. "Tell them!" she cries.

Zimri feels the world slipping away. Her eyes are heavy, her mind spins. Who is that at the door? A woman, hair spiraling out like tendrils reaching for the sun, long legs and arms reaching, too. Zimri wonders if she is seeing herself, years from now, when all of this is over.

"I'm DJ HiJax," the woman says.

"DJ HiJax!" Orpheus, Harold, and Esther say together.

"But I thought you were a man?" says Orpheus.

From the ground, Zimri blinks up. "It's you," she whispers.

HiJax pulls a small digital recorder from her pocket. "I have Zimri Robinson singing 'Nobody from Nowhere' before the release of Arabella Lovecraft's song. It's time-stamped from when she released it on the waves. I recorded it and replayed it many times since then."

Esther grabs Harold's arm and blinks, her mouth agape. "Rainey Robinson?" she says.

DJ HiJax whips her head around. "Yes," she says. "That's me."

"Mom?" says Zimri as she's pulled under. Then she knows that she must be dreaming because everything is warm again and she's in Orpheus's arms.

CODA

ZIMRI

When the meandering lights along the river come into view through the window of Orpheus's Cicada, I squeeze his hand.

"Do Nonda and Rainey know you're coming back today?" he asks.

"No," I say, basking in the golden light of early autumn dusk. The sky is turning pink around us, illuminating the yellow- and orange-tipped leaves on the treetops down below. I sigh happily. Coming home is my favorite part of being on the road. "I want to surprise them," I tell him and he grins. He knows how much it means to my mom to have me in her life again.

"Prepare for self-navigation," the car announces and Orpheus takes the wheel.

I roll down my window to inhale the river air as we land on the road a few miles outside of Old Town. Things are looking nicer around here these days. Ever since Libellule and Calliope moved in, our town has become the newly minted mecca for musicians existing outside the patronage system. Orpheus and I are part of a tribe of touring artists on a small circuit of communities, like ours, scattered around the country, that value authenticity over the slickness of patron production.

Only a few 'razzi bother us anymore, like the stalker drones that just picked up our trail. They still follow us around, always hoping something sensational will happen. But, it's been over a year since my trial so we don't get much Buzz these days, which is fine with us. Sometimes, Tati likes to catch the drones and reprogram them to do subversive things like roost in trees or dive-bomb the river or record audio of birds singing to confuse the algorithms searching for good songs.

In town, we drive past the school, the old brick buiding where Nonda learned to read. We reopened it with some of my settlement money from Chanson. Elena and Brie left their warehouse jobs and abandoned their PODs to live in Old Town and work with the kids along with several other fine folks who were eager to swap the Complex life for our community. So far, the student body is small, but it's growing as word gets out about our radical ways with human teachers and a curriculum that values art and science. Plus music, of course. Always music whenever I'm in town.

In the playground next to the Paramount Theater, we see kids playing.

"Look, there's Xenia," I tell Orpheus as we drive by a little girl with beaded braids and polka-dotted pants. "She's the one I was telling you about. She soaks up everything. Matches pitch, can keep any rhythm that I throw at her. She loves the ZimriDoo. I told her I'd teach her how to make one of her own the next time I was home."

"Can't wait to meet her," he says, then he points out his window. "It's Captain Jack."

We wave as we pass the funny three-wheeled electric car that Tati built so Jack could get back and forth from the school (where he does maintenance) to his bungalow near the river. He's even got a little boat he takes out fishing on calm days.

"Look at that!" I point at yet another little shop that's cropped up on the Strip like mushrooms after the rain. Each time we come back, more people have moved in.

"I heard it's a bakery," Orpheus says. "And there are rumors someone's thinking of opening a restaurant."

We pass by Calliope's big brick house near the Old Town square. The stalker drones leave our trail to dart over and scan the license plates of two nice cars sitting in the driveway. So far no bona fide celebrities have sought Project Calliope's help. Mostly we get young PONI artists wanting to know how to navigate the tricky world of copyrights and distribution for their original music, but you never know who's going to jump ship and come to our side, especially with Libellule on board.

At the corner where Tati's shop still sits, we turn right and head to Nonda's old house, where she and my mother live again.

"Hello!" I call when we walk inside, leaving the drones roosting on the porch.

"Zimri!" my mother yells. "Is that you?" She rushes down the hallway, arms open wide.

At first, I didn't like having her around. I needed answers from her. *How could you have spent five years so close to me but never once reached out? Didn't you hear me calling you over the waves?* She said it was for my protection. She said she was trying to reach me through the music she played on air. She said it's more complicated than I understand. But I don't believe her. As far as I'm concerned, she went on the run as DJ HiJax for herself, and for herself alone. But, as Orpheus and Nonda have pointed out to me, Rainey has suffered for her sins and so I let it go.

The Arbiter was forced to overturn my case when Calliope produced my mother who had a recording of my version of "Nobody from Nowhere," snatched off the waves. It was proof that Arabella and Piper stole the song from me and I was set free. Libellule prevented Orpheus's ASA, but Harold Chanson still got his revenge.

My mother's trial was quick and decisive. She didn't deny a thing. After all, she had been pirating music for years. This time, though, there was no escape for her. The punishment Esther requested for me was conferred to my mother and the auditory cortical region of her brain was scrubbed. The one thing that made Rainey Robinson who she was, the thing that she passed on to me (along with the gap in my teeth and the curl of my hair) was erased from her mind forever. Like Calliope, her best friend, she will never again find pleasure in music. To them, songs are nothing more than a series of dissonant sounds. That fate is cruel enough. And so, slowly, I've let my anger toward my mother recede like the river after a storm. Now I do my best to take care of her and Nonda when I'm home.

Once she's done hugging Orpheus and me, we follow Mom to the newly yellow kitchen where Nonda's enjoying a cup of mint tea.

"Looks good!" I say, nodding at the walls, and planting a big kiss on my grandmother's soft cheek.

"Maybe I'll invite Medgers over," Nonda jokes. The meds

have been working well and she's mostly back to her feisty self, although her short-term memory still slips now and again. But that's okay. She has my mom and Marley (who comes often though Dorian stays away) so they can revisit the past together.

"How's your mother?" Rainey asks Orpheus.

"Fine, I guess," he tells her with a shrug.

"I like that Libellule," Nonda says. "She's the real deal, that one."

"She's something else, that's for sure," he says.

Libellule took the biggest house in town, of course, the one up on the hill. She brought Alouette and a RoboNurse with her but left Chester and her clothing line behind to focus her energy on Dragonfly Recordings, a record label she swears will surpass Chanson Industries some day. Since Alouette is here, Orpheus is happy to live in the big house with his mom, but he spends most of his time at the studio we built in our backyard. This is where we record our music and continue the legacy of DJ HiJax, now a legal radio broadcast and digital podcast that promotes original new music.

I look at him and can tell he wants to get into the studio behind his mixing board again. Being on tour for weeks makes him itchy to record when we get home.

"We have a new idea for a song," I tell my mom and Nonda.

"Go on," my mother says, shooing us out the back door. "Get it down while it's fresh, then come back for dinner."

"Thank you," I say and kiss her on the check.

Orpheus and I head across the yard where Nonda's marigolds are beginning to fade into fall. It's dusky out now and the breeze carries up sounds from the river. I stop for a moment to listen. There's the faint buzz of a bee, the chirp of small birds in the trees, and from far away the cry of a whippoorwill. I call back to him so he knows that he's not alone.

"Hey, look!" Orpheus laughs and points at my shirt. "You've got a little friend."

I turn to see a dragonfly sitting on my shoulder, its myriad eyes taking in the world all around, and I wonder what it sees. How much the world must have changed since its early ancestors buzzed across this landscape with dinosaurs, then wooly mammoths and migrating tribes of humans making the first instruments out of bones. And yet, somehow, through it all, the dragonfly has managed to stick around.

"Hello," I say, then I blow and watch it lift up into the sky, iridescent green wings thrumming as it darts away. I take Orpheus's hand. "Come on. We have music to make."

ACKNOWLEDGMENTS

Many strange things have to collide for a novel to come into the world. This book started with a bump on the head that made me see stars and hear music, then lingered for weeks as I nursed my bruised brain through the mind-numbing recovery from a concussion: No reading, no writing, no watching screens, just plenty of time to think as my husband and children made music in our house. Then the writing began, but that's not all it takes to make a book.

I would like to thank the many fine folks at Feiwel and Friends, including Jean Feiwel, my editor Liz Szabla (for her endless encouragement, patience, and confidence in me), creative director Rich Deas and his team—Heiko Klug (who must have built a time machine to travel to the future of my creating in order to snap a photo of the dragonfly drone that she created for the cover art), Kathleen Breitenfeld, and Elizabeth Dresner. I'm astounded by the beauty of this book!

My deepest gratitude to everyone at LGR Literary, especially Stephanie Kip Rostan (for leading me through the maze of publishing for the past eight years) and Shelby Boyer (who takes care of everything I would otherwise forget).

Special thanks to the Vermont Studio Center for providing me with a two-week residency overlooking the beautiful Gihon River, where the first draft of this book was written. I'd also like to acknowledge the real Carrie Elston Tunick, whose video installation work inspired a key moment in this story.

As always, all of my love and gratitude to Emily (without whom none of this would be nearly as fun), Adam (from whom I stole the idea of dragonfly drones), my parents (who never questioned whether I could make a life as an artist), my children (xoxoxoxoxo), and Dan (who provides all the back tracks for our lives).

Thank you for reading this
Feiwel and Friends book.

THE FRIENDS WHO MADE

GIFTED

POSSIBLE ARE:

Jean Feiwel, Publisher

Liz Szabla, Editor in Chief

Rich Deas, Senior Creative Director

Holly West, Editor

Dave Barrett, Executive Managing Editor

Kim Waymer, Production Manager

Anna Roberto, Editor

Christine Barcellona, Associate Editor

Emily Settle, Administrative Assistant

Anna Poon, Editorial Assistant

Follow us on Facebook or visit
us online at mackids.com.

OUR BOOKS ARE FRIENDS FOR LIFE